COME SEELING NIGHT

PAXTON LOCKE BOOK III

DANIEL HUMPHREYS

Stephenson Memorial Library
761 Forest Road
Greenfield, NH 03047

Newsletter

Want to keep up to date on news, new releases, and convention appearances? Join the Silver Empire Newsletter!

For Rex—
Mentor, friend, and first reader.
You are missed.

Be innocent of the knowledge, dearest chuck,
    Till thou applaud the deed. Come, seeling night,
    Scarf up the tender eye of pitiful day
    And with thy bloody and invisible hand
    Cancel and tear to pieces that great bond
    Which keeps me pale. Light thickens, and the crow
    Makes wing to th' rooky wood.
    Good things of day begin to droop and drowse;
    Whiles night's black agents to their preys do rouse.

William Shakespeare
    MacBeth — Act 3, Scene 2

CHAPTER ONE

ALEISTER—SATURDAY MORNING
  Leesburg, Virginia

It was a cookie-cutter house in the midst of a mass-produced subdivision, but Aleister Knight doubted that any of the houses in the neighborhood had anything close to the scene in the living room of this particular abode.

The woman he'd tied to the chair was attractive, though a bit slimmer than he preferred. She wore the same sports bra, yoga pants, and sneakers that she'd been wearing when she returned from her morning jog.

She lived alone, though the living room seemed arranged for entertaining. A sofa and a pair of love seats squared off the room, facing a fireplace with a gas log. The brightly-colored decorative rug in the center of the room made for a convenient landing point for the chair. The even lines and balance between each piece of furniture appealed to Knight's sense of order.

Resuming consciousness, his prisoner raised her head. She

jerked in surprise as she caught sight of him standing in her house, and she twisted her head wildly, assessing the rest of the room.

All was as she'd left it before her run, save for the few things he'd brought. His carefully-folded topcoat lay across one arm of the sofa, held down by the weight of his walking stick. The polished obsidian ball on top of the cane drank in the light even as it drew her eyes to it. There'd been a spot of blood on it after he tapped her on the back of the head, but he'd polished it clean even before securing her to the chair.

He gave her a moment to look, then snapped his fingers next to her ear. "Over here, love. There's nothing over there to get you out of your predicament."

The woman in the chair narrowed her eyes and adopted a haughty tone. "I'm not your love, friend. My name is Kristin Hughes, and if you had any sense you'd turn around and walk out of this house right now."

Knight had to give her credit—he'd seen more than a few men and women in the same predicament break down into a blubbering mess. This one had some spine.

He almost felt bad for what was to come.

"I need your assistance with something then, Kristin. Rumor is you're just the person I need to get what I want."

"I work for the Bureau of Alcohol, Tobacco, and Firearms," Kristin said, taking her time with each word and emphasizing each syllable. "I'm a mid-level administrator. We process background checks. Do you understand the world of hurt you're going to be in, messing with a government employee?"

Aleister laughed. "Cut the crap, doll. I know that you work for ATF, but you're actually in M Division. You have much a more important job than rubber-stamping background checks."

Her face went a little pale, but she was good. Her voice remained smooth. "There's no M Division. I'm not sure what—"

"Enough." He raised a hand, cupped his fingers, and cradled a ball of roiling, liquid flame. "How about we skip the boring part where you pretend to not know what I'm talking about?"

She kept her eyes on the fire and nodded. "All right."

He snapped his fingers again, banishing the fire. "Lovely. You work in the regional field office not far from here, correct?" He grinned. "The one over the facility known as the Menagerie?"

"How—" She caught herself, took a breath, and continued, "You'll never get inside. Our security's too good."

"No worries, love, I have no use for any of the oddities and critters you keep down in the basement. Leave it to Americans to be sentimental about some of the most vicious beasts to ever walk the Earth. No, I'm more interested in the secure vault in your research laboratory."

"Like I said, our security—"

"Yes, yes," he said, annoyed. "State of the art, layers of hexes, curses unto the nth generation and all that. I'm quivering. But then, I'm not going to be the one opening the vault, am I?"

The third member of the party, silent up to this point, cleared her throat. She rose from her seat behind Kristin, strolled around the living room and stood next to Aleister. "I'll be handling that part. I'm Liliana."

The captive woman frowned. Aleister imagined it was a combination of things—the revelation of a third party, her introductory assertion, and, of course, her appearance.

As was his habit, he dressed well, albeit comfortably, in sensible shoes, black dress slacks, and a bleached button-down shirt. It was the sort of outfit that blended into pretty much any social situation and could dress up or down as needed. His companion's appearance was more extravagant.

Liliana dressed all in black—skintight leather pants, high-heeled boots, and a cable-knit sweater that had probably cost more than his entire ensemble. *She's fussy like that.*

The woman in black wore her blond hair in a tight ponytail,

her lipstick and glittering nail polish a bright crimson. She raised her hand, lifting a laminated ID card attached to a thin lanyard.

"If you think you can use my badge and just walk in there—" Kristin started.

Liliana sighed theatrically and turned to Aleister. With a pout, she said, "Can we get this over, already? I'd like to take some time to settle in before I go in."

"But of course," Aleister said with a nod. He turned and strolled to the sofa. He took a seat and leaned into the plush cushions. "This is more comfortable than it looks, Kristin. Excellent taste."

A confused look on her face, Kristin looked back and forth between Aleister and Liliana. "Both of you are insane. I—" She looked back to the other woman, her jaw dropping.

Writhing, Liliana shucked the leather pants around her ankles and stepped out of them. She'd already slid the boots off and set them to one side. Reaching down, she pulled the sweater over her head, revealing that she wore nothing at all in the way of underwear.

Stunned into silence, Kristin continued to stare at the other woman's naked breasts as she walked a slow circle around the chair. As attractive as they were, Aleister would have been more concerned with Liliana's lack of a belly button than heaving bosoms, had he been in the same situation.

He had an unfair advantage, though—he knew what was about to happen.

Kristin gasped, recoiling back as the surface of the other woman's body *rippled*. It expanded like rising dough in some areas while pulling in, in others. After a few seconds, the glamorous ice queen now bore the appearance of the woman in the chair—identical down to the butterfly tattoo above the swell of her buttocks.

The Division M agent stared at her duplicate and screamed in terror.

CHAPTER 1

"You'd be screaming even more if you saw what she really looked like," Aleister said. "Might as well save your breath. I've warded the living room—no one will hear you."

"There's no need to be so mean, Aleister," Liliana said. She moved to the fireplace and studied her new reflection in the mirror over the mantle. "Her hair's so *plain*," Liliana whined, her voice an exact duplicate of Kristin's.

"It's only until Monday," Aleister reminded her. More sternly, he added, "I'll remind you that I've doubled your usual fee."

"Fine."

"I don't know what you are," Kristin interjected. "But it doesn't matter. You may look and sound like me, but there are passcodes—things you'll need to know." She took a deep breath and threw her shoulders back as far as she could with her arms tied to the chair. "Do your worst. I won't tell you *shit*."

Aleister shrugged. "I believe you. No worries, love. I'm not going to waste my time torturing you. Liliana has a far more effective means of getting the information out of you."

"And I am so, so hungry," the duplicate said. She stared at the woman in the chair and licked her lips.

"How long will this take?" He asked. "I may step out for a bite, myself."

Liliana hung the lanyard around her neck and flipped the badge around, reading the name printed on the card. "No more than an hour. And call me 'Kristin', Aleister."

"Enjoy the silence. I'll be back directly."

She didn't wait long. As soon as he opened the door and exited the house, Knight was chased by screams that escalated from terror to agony in the blink of an eye.

CHAPTER TWO

Paxton
Location unknown

I woke up with a blindfold over my eyes, a foul-tasting rubber block between my teeth, and one hell of a headache.

For a few unnerving seconds, I struggled to recall how I'd gotten into this mess. My memories of the past few hours came back to me through a haze, my thoughts slow and murky.

I've been drugged, I realized. I let out a little bit of a giggle before I realized that sort of thing was nigh-impossible with something wedging your jaw open.

Pushing through the fuzz, I forced myself to remain calm and breathe through my nose. The last thing I needed to do was freak out and choke myself into unconsciousness. Focusing on my other senses, I worked my way down my body starting at the top of my head. My scalp *felt* bare, which didn't make sense considering until I wrinkled my face and realized that something soft and circular circled each eye. *Goggles?* Whatever they were, they

CHAPTER 2

rendered me blind. I'd have to be careful. A hood might obscure any expressions I made, but as I regained more and more of my faculties, it became obvious that most of my face was bare.

I felt a similar pressure to that of my eyes around my mouth and one side of my nose. Cool air tickled my lips, and I detected a faint, medicinal whiff from the breeze. This was a bit more confusing until I put two and two together. I'd come awake from an unnatural sleep, and the source of the cool air seemed concentrated in a small area around my face. *Is that an oxygen mask?* That, or something similar, I reasoned.

There was a strange hum in the air, though everything seemed muffled. A subtle vibration in my hips, transferred through whatever I was sitting on, buzzed in time to the sound. As I puzzled it over, I swallowed, and my ears popped.

Airplane. That can't be good.

With each passing moment, my mind was growing clearer. Memory trickled in, and it became harder not to panic. I remembered coming upon the smoldering ruin of my friend Kent's house and overhearing that my mother had taken Cassie. I remembered losing my cool and revealing myself to the mysterious Federal agent who'd been haunting my steps over the past few weeks. At once, I realized that there was a sore, throbbing ache in my right bicep—if I'd been drugged, it seemed likely that had been the site of the injection. I tried to reach up to rub at the pain, but straps secured both of my arms at wrist and elbow. A quick test of my legs found them strapped at the ankles as well as mid-thigh. Whoever had put me on this plane didn't want me free to cause any trouble.

For your average Joe, that would have been all she wrote. And even though I myself am no master escape artist, Houdini himself would weep in frustration at some of the tricks up my sleeve.

My name is Paxton Locke, and I'm a wizard.

Although come to think of it, I don't remember Gandalf,

Raistlin, or Dumbledore ever getting into this sort of predicament. Perhaps it's best to not put on airs.

I took a deep breath, gathered my focus, and...nothing.

A few days before, I'd picked up a new spell that allowed me to phase through solid matter. It's come in pretty handy for avoiding fights and slipping through locked doors, but even though everything *felt* the same as it normally did when I cast a spell, nada.

Fair enough. On second thought, it was probably a good idea not to phase out on a moving airplane. I concentrated and waited for lines of applied force to slice through the bands around my wrists. Once my arms were free, I could take care of the rest of the straps and figure out where I was, and more importantly, where in the Hell I was going.

Again—nothing.

I resisted the urge to scream against the rubber block. Since I started down this career path, I've spent more than my fair share of time getting my ass kicked, but it has been a long time since I've felt powerless. I didn't like it then, and I for sure didn't like it now.

Just wait, I told myself. *Something in the drugs—when that wears off, you're good to go.*

A sudden noise overcame the drone of airplane engines. The warbling tone sounded like some sort of alarm, and from the shouting involved, that was what it was.

Two voices converged not far from me, the first crying out, "He's flat-lined, get the paddles!"

I winced, wishing I could tell them, that no, I was just fine, but no one touched me. *Do they have someone else in here with me?*

"Charging!"

If I wasn't alone, this was an opportunity—if someone across from me was in the midst of a medical emergency, I doubted that much attention was being paid to me. My magic refused to cooperate. Maybe I could wriggle free?

CHAPTER 2

It was a desperate plan, but something about the feel of the slab between my teeth made desperation seem the proper response. I twisted, tugging at the straps and praying for a sudden release. All I needed was one arm. A free hand and I could get my eyes uncovered, pull the damn thing out of my mouth, and fight back. *The push will work.* The mind-control spell wasn't something I liked to abuse, but it was an old, uncomfortable ally at this point. I'd never go so far as to do so, but if anyone deserved to be ordered to dance around like a fool, it was anyone who'd blindfold and gag someone on an airplane to parts unknown.

My frustrated movements must have garnered attention from another observer, because a new voice barked, "Hey! He's waking up!"

"Shit! Put him under again!"

This time, I did scream as someone seized my left arm and jammed a needle into my bicep. The muscle cramped, and I flailed in my restraints as a soothing cold flooded up my arm from the site of the injection. Rough hands pulled on the mask, blasting cold air and who knew what else into my nostrils.

Stay awake, I told myself. *Stay awa—*

CASSIE—EARLY SATURDAY MORNING
   Western New Mexico

CASSIE HATCHER HAD ALWAYS FIGURED IT WAS NORMAL TO dislike your boyfriend's mother. Even when she'd been trying to decide whether to keep Paxton as a hands-off friend or something more back in the day, she hadn't much cared much for Helen Locke. Her sentence to federal prison for murder was icing on the cake, even though Cassie and Paxton had drifted apart after he left town.

Now, having rekindled an almost-official relationship as adults, most women would move past the high school stuff and try to build a relationship with a potential mother-in-law. And even with the convicted felon thing, most mothers-in-law weren't psychotic no-kidding witches bent on mass murder and who knew what else. That made things more complicated.

Don't forget to add kidnapping to the list. Cassie didn't bother to hide her scowl. With any normal kidnapping, she might have been able to make a run for it or signal another car for help. After only a few hours, Cassie was beginning to understand why Pax didn't like to use the *push* on anyone unless he absolutely had to. She felt mostly normal, but any moment she tried to move in a manner that would violate the command to 'sit quietly', invisible iron bands snapped into place around her entire body and pinned her in place. *He got out of it,* she reminded herself. *Somehow, some way, he broke her hold over him. Keep fighting, and you'll get the same chance.*

Helen glanced at her from behind the wheel of their stolen car and smirked. All-too-often, something in her eyes made it seem like she was reading Cassie's mind, and wouldn't *that* just be her

CHAPTER 2

luck. Paxton hadn't mentioned it as a possibility. The ability that he called the *push* allowed a spellcaster to exert their will on a hapless subject. Back in Phoenix, Helen had ordered Cassie to come with her and remain quiet, and she'd been unable to resist the witch's will no matter how hard she tried.

Cassie was also beginning to understand why Paxton's instinctive response to any situation was either sarcasm or a joke. His mother was the most humorless woman she'd ever had the displeasure to be around.

And to think I thought I didn't like her because I thought she was stuck up! If that didn't qualify as the right reaction for the wrong reason, she didn't know what did.

Despite her fear, she'd succumbed to sleep in the midst of the night, though it had been a restless one at best. She rubbed at the grit in her eyes while trying not to yawn. She suspected the logic of the spell would define that to not be quiet. The beginning of the dawn eased above the horizon before them, but the surrounding landscape remained cloaked in shadow. What little she could see didn't tell her much, though it was an easy guess that they were still somewhere in the southwest. She glanced over at Helen. *She's got to be getting tired. I'll have a chance soon.*

"We need to stop soon," Helen murmured, to herself as much to Cassie. "You must be getting hungry. Or at least need to use the restroom."

Careful to keep her voice low, Cassie said, "I didn't realize that was going to be an option." At the mention of food, her stomach reminded her that she'd missed dinner last night.

"Hardly. I can't have you pissing all over the seat like an animal. And I'm as human as you."

Cassie must have let a vestige of doubt cross her face because the other woman chuckled. "I haven't found a spell to replace bread and water, just yet, though I can go quite a while without sleep. That came in quite handy in prison, let me tell you."

Well, shit. "I see," she said.

"We'll need to change vehicles, as well, of course," Helen said. "I haven't been on the run long, but I know that much, at least. This is a nice enough car, but they'll figure out we've taken it sooner or later and start looking. Best to be one step ahead, we've got plenty of miles to go."

"Maine, right? If you wanted Pax to come find you, you didn't have to take me along. He—we—would have tried to stop you." Cassie hesitated, then went all in. "What are you trying to do, anyway?"

"All in good time, dear," Helen smirked. "The thing you have to understand about my dear son is this—he cares, a lot. It's a bit pathetic, really. If I have you, he'll be off balance, reacting rather than thinking. He stopped me once before. I need every advantage this time."

"I don't believe you," Cassie said. Helen could probably give her a brain aneurysm with one word like she had the poor owner of this car, but she didn't care. She didn't want to look back on her life and regret cowering in the face of true evil. "You could have disappeared as soon as you got the grimoire. You ditched your crew, so they must not have figured into your long-term plans. Why are you taking a risk now?"

Helen worked her mouth for a minute. With a frigid smile, she said, "Saving the world requires sacrifice, my dear."

"Saving the world? Bullshit," Cassie spat. "How many people died in prison when your little Sabrina squad broke you out? How many people have you killed along the way? You hold yourself up like you're some sort of magnanimous figure, but you're no better than a common—"

"Shut up!"

The command hit her like a slap, and Cassie's lips clamped shut. She couldn't speak, but she could still stare daggers at the other woman.

CHAPTER 2

Helen threw back her head and laughed. "I'm not surprised he fell for you, girl. You've got the same chip on your shoulder. But while you're casting me as the monster, consider this. If it was the destiny of every man, woman, and child on this planet to die within the next decade, how many would you kill to stop it? So long as I keep it under a billion, I'm calling myself the hero of this piece. Stew over that for a while."

CHAPTER THREE

PAXTON
Location unknown

THE NEXT THING I KNEW, STRONG ARMS PULLED ME OUT OF A seated position and pitched me forward. My head was too fuzzy to react, much, but I let out an involuntary cough as I hit a lumpy mattress. Coming to my senses, I realized that my hands and feet were free, and I twisted around to catch a glimpse of my captors.

I missed my opportunity. All I saw were bars covered in metal plating sliding home with an authoritative thump that rattled my cot.

Waiting until the dull echoes of their footsteps faded away, I lurched to my feet. The pins and needles hadn't gone entirely away, and I stumbled forward into the door. I slammed both palms onto it and winced. I was in a jail cell not all that long ago, and this thing looked like Valentine's people built it to hold a tyrannosaurus. The vertical bars were twice as thick as any I'd seen before. Layers of steel diamond plate covered the upper and lower

CHAPTER 3

sections, leaving a foot-tall opening for inspection from the outside. There was a slot centered in the open section—for passing meal trays through, I assumed. At the thought, my stomach rumbled. I twisted, studying the rest of my cell.

There wasn't much to see. It was ten feet square or a little smaller. A single sheet and a flat pillow covered the twin-sized cot I'd landed on. Upon inspection, the bed frame was a single piece of some sort of slick, hard plastic material. It felt sturdy enough, but I wouldn't be taking it apart anytime soon.

A combination sink and toilet occupied the far corner of the room along with a single roll of parchment ply toilet paper. I had to pee like nothing else, and that won out over my thirst.

As soon as I'd emptied my bladder, I gave my hands a quick wash, then let the water run, slurping huge gulps of water from my cupped hands until my teeth ached from the chill.

Bars notwithstanding, this place had better tap water than the last hotel I'd stayed in. I splashed a bit in my face, scrubbing away the accumulated crud and sweat of my kidnapping.

Turning away, I sat on the edge of the bed and stared at the slab of steel locking me away. I had options. A force blade would cut it, or I could simply phase through.

Standing up, I muttered to myself, "Here goes nothing." I took a deep breath, envisioned the control panel I used as a mental focus for my magic and—nothing.

I let my shoulders sag in defeat and fought the urge to scream in frustration. Whatever drugs they'd used to subdue were still in my system.

All I need is time.

Of course, the more time I wasted in here, the longer Mother remained free.

Without any sort of shower facilities, I had to settle for rinsing my clothing in the sink and hanging it over various fixtures to try. The chill of the water made me shiver as I gave myself a sketchy bath, but being cold was far preferable to being grubby. Once I'd done the best I could, I slumped onto the bed, folded the pillow over, and tried to get comfortable.

I had no way to tell how much time had passed before the sound of squeaking wheels shook me out of sleep. As I jerked myself to a sitting position on the cot, nothing in my surroundings gave me any clues, either. The blurry mix of a dream and a memory rested at the forefront of my mind as I teetered on the edge of coming fully awake. Blinking, I played it back, over and over, trying to strain the truth from the surreal nightmare imagery. *John Henry Holliday*, I heard a harsh voice whisper, and I frowned. Why was that name so familiar?

After a few moments of thinking, I shook it off and passed it off to a hangover. You'd think being drugged unconscious would keep you from being tired, but I'd slept far more deeply than I would have expected given the strange atmosphere.

The intermittent squeaking down the corridor was the first noise I'd heard all night, which seemed strange in and of itself. My gut told me I wasn't alone down here, but for whatever reason, an unnatural silence gripped the facility.

My boxer shorts were still a little damp, but I pulled them on and moved to the cell door. The concrete was chilly against my bare feet. I bent over and craned my neck, trying to get a look down the hall. The source of the noise was too far away for me to see with my limited viewing angle. Closer to the opening, the noise was loud enough for me to make out quiet murmurs of conversation accompanying each pause.

Stomach growling, I muttered to myself, "Hopefully it's breakfast."

"It's breakfast," a whispered voice confirmed, and I jumped.

The corridor across from my cell was a blank block wall, and the voice seemed to originate from my right. My neighbor, maybe? Cautiously, I ventured, "Who's there?"

CHAPTER 3

"I could say the same of you," the voice replied, then tittered a giggle made even creepier by the echo effect of the prison walls. "Call me Puck, and well met, my new friend."

"Paxton," I said, after shaking my head over his odd phrasing. Puck didn't have an accent, per se, but he didn't sound like he was from around here. "What are you in for?"

"A little of this and some more of that. Much like you, I assume. The guardians of this particular prison don't pay more than lip service to small details like charges. Welcome to the Menagerie. With luck, your stay won't be a long one—though if you're less lucky, it's off to the Pit for you."

I slid to the left, pressing my cheek against the opening in the door. The source of the noise was still out of sight, though the murmured words were becoming clearer. Two voices, it sounded like. "The Pit?"

"A place far worse than this, or so I have heard. It's nice to have a proper companion once again. The fellow to my right has nothing to say, and your cell has been empty since the Division M agents brought me here."

I frowned. "What's Division M?"

"You don't know?" Puck sounded surprised. "They are a secretive branch of your government tasked with securing your country against magical threats."

Mulling that over, I shook my head. "First I'm hearing of it. Would have been nice to have had some help, over the years. I've been taking care of magical threats on my own for a while now."

Puck didn't respond for a moment, and I worried that I'd somehow insulted him. Finally, he said, "How did you come to be here, then?"

I dug through memories slowly emerging from the drug-induced murk in my head. "His name was Valentine."

"I've not met him, but I know the name. Many say that he is both more and less than human, though few know what he truly is.

If you survived an encounter with him..." Puck's voice turned thoughtful. "That's interesting."

"I don't remember much, but I remember getting my ass kicked," I admitted. It was probably a bad idea to tell a fellow prisoner that I spent a lot of time having that happen, lest he shank me in the shower later. If we even got showers.

"From what I've heard, there's no shame in that." The click of heels on concrete joined the squeak of rolling wheels. I got a glimpse of two uniformed figures flanking a flat-topped cart.

One spoke. "Back away from the door. You know the drill." His hands were empty, but his partner held a spray-gun with a large cylinder sticking out of the bottom with the business end pointed at Puck's cell.

The pair waited, then the speaker opened the flat top of the cart and passed a covered tray through the gap in the cell. "Enjoy." After a moment, an identical tray passed through from Puck's side —the previous meal's, apparently.

They advanced to me. The speaker looked at me through the hole in the cell door. "This is your first time, and I'm only going to say this once." He pointed at the canister. "That's bear spray. You screw around with us, you get a blast to the face. Your eyes will swell shut, and that's if you can get to the sink to rinse them out in under three seconds. Takes about three, four days for the effect to wear off. You create problems for us, you lose meal privileges for the day. You catch my drift?"

I raised my hands and backed away from the door. "Catching it just fine, officer. Any chance I can get my phone call now?"

The one with the bear spray snorted a laugh. "That's a good one."

Up went the top cover, and the first guard stuck a tray through my cell door. "See you at lunch, prisoner." I eased forward slowly, cringing at the thought of high-octane pepper spray, and pulled the tray through.

CHAPTER 3

Sitting down, tray on my knees, I cocked my head and listened. The next time they spoke seemed to quite a bit further away than Puck, so the cell immediately to my left must have been empty.

I moved back over to the door and leaned my back against it while I popped the cover off the tray. If not for the difference in packaging, I could have sworn that this was a fast food breakfast. It had the same bright yellow square of eggs, circular sausage patty, hash brown, and biscuit that I'd seen more than a few times. Turning my head to cast my voice toward Puck's cell, I said, "Is this seriously McDonald's?"

He didn't answer for a moment—eating, I guessed. "There don't seem to be any cafeteria facilities on site. It's all catered. Maybe you'll be here long enough to get lucky—every once in a while, we get pizza."

"Great," I said, turning back to my breakfast. I poked the eggs and tried not to wince. They had long gone cold. *Eat up, so you can get out of here. Miles to go.*

Assembling the sausage, egg, and biscuit into a crumbling sandwich, I tried to balance wolfing it down with keeping it in one piece in my hands. I didn't know how long I'd been out, but I could tell I'd missed a few meals between Valentine knocking me out and waking up here.

The food settled into a hard mass in the pit of my stomach. Right about now was the time I'd pull up a TV show on my tablet and sip soda refills until I felt like hitting the road. Tap water would have to do. For the briefest moment I considered yelling for the guards, remembered the bear spray, and realized why the damn place was so quiet. Nobody wanted a blast in the face. I rinsed my hands off in the sink, washed cold greasiness out of my mouth, and put on the rest of my clothes. My socks had dried stiff, and my T-shirt was still a little damp, but at least they didn't reek of sour sweat anymore.

Sitting on the bed, I closed my eyes and took a deep breath. I visualized the control panel I used as a mental focus for my various spells. I couldn't help but smile as it snapped into razor focus. Whatever the drugs were, the effect had faded. I opened my eyes and held out my hand. Faint blue lines of force appeared around my extended fingers, foxfire dancing in the harsh light of the fluorescent fixture in the concrete ceiling.

Standing, I released the force blade and focused on a different sort of effect. "Puck," I said, taking a big step toward the cell door. "It's been real, but I'm blowing this popsicle stand."

Snapping out of phase, I held back my laugh. *Try and bear spray me now, assholes.* I'd bent forward to push my torso through the door to get the lay of the land when my hair stood on end and every muscle in my body twitched.

Blinking, I realized I was staring at the ceiling. The room spun and every part of me ached. When I was a kid, I made the mistake of plugging in my night light with a finger on one of the prongs. This felt like I'd done that a couple of hundred times, only all over. "What the hell," I groaned.

Even from the floor, I could hear Puck's sigh. "They don't pay much attention to their charges, young wizard, but they've spent plenty of time locking down the cells with runes. We aren't going anywhere until they want us to."

CHAPTER FOUR

Valentine—Sunday morning
   Phoenix, Arizona

The man currently known as Agent Matthew Valentine hadn't needed to sleep in well over a century. He still missed it sometimes.

On the bright side, last night's accommodations wouldn't have lent themselves to sleep even if he'd tried. Tying up all the loose ends on their cover-up of a witch coven's assault on suburbia had taken a full court press. By the the Division M crew had that in hand, it was well after midnight. It was easier, then, to move their equipment to the agency's secure headquarters in downtown Phoenix than to coordinate hotel rooms for the few agents who weren't locals.

Not that Valentine had done much of the heavy lifting, there. Once he was certain the situation was well in hand, he'd taken a vehicle and spent the rest of the night and predawn hours running a search grid of the entire Valley in hope of finding some trace of the leader of the coven, Helen Locke.

While his more fragile coworkers caught snatches of sleep in conference rooms and offices, Valentine spent his night on the phone with police departments across the southwest, praying that he'd get the opportunity to rouse his team to chase down the one who got away.

He'd taken down Helen's familiars and the witch she'd left behind to cover her trail, but not soon enough to stop her from making her escape with a hostage—ally?—and a powerful magic grimoire.

He'd had better days and more fruitful nights. None of his calls netted him any results. Division M's multi-state dragnet garnered no results. More often than not, Valentine spent his time staring at empty streets and listening to late-night conspiracy radio. They were close to right more often than they knew, but the hunch or gut feeling he sought in his own quest never came through.

Just before dawn, his stomach's frustrated growls came in stereo with his own mutters. He turned the car back toward the office until he found a Krispy Kreme, the sign alight with the promise of hot and fresh confections. He bought as many as he could carry, and the stack of boxes rode shotgun on the way back, filling the Crown Vic with the mouth-watering smell of warm dough.

Half a mile away, his phone rang. It was three hours later on the East coast, though he imagined that Director Newquist had been stewing for a while, waiting for the time to turn decent in Phoenix.

"Russ," he said simply.

"Eliot died on the plane," his boss said. "They managed to revive him, but things looked dicey there for a while."

CHAPTER 4

"Not the first time," Val said with a dismissive air. "It never seems to stick. He's a tough old boy, for a Yankee."

The director sighed. "Valentine, do you take anything seriously?"

"At my age?" He thought about it. "No."

"No sign of Helen yet?"

"Nothing so far. I've got every cop from here to Amarillo on the lookout, though—with strict orders not to engage. We get a sign of her, we'll be on her, right quick."

"What's this I hear about detainees?"

"Couple of groups," Valentine confirmed, making the turn down the road to headquarters. He cast a baleful eye on the stack of donut boxes, daring them to slide. They remained still. "Kent Sikora, a local cop. His wife, a priest from out in California named Rosado. They were all in the house, got whammied by Helen Locke before one of the other witches set the place on fire. They got out okay. Minor burns, smoke inhalation—that sort of thing. Paxton and his girl shacked up in the guest room. Next group was pretty cagey—we caught them trying to sneak around the back of the property. Esteban De La Rosa, Javier De La Rosa, Esteban Ramirez, and Carlos Gallardo."

Val could almost hear Newquist counting the names off on his fingers. "Two Estebans?"

"Yeah, one's older, the other's younger. In-laws, or something. All employees of the same PI firm that contracts Paxton Locke. They're not talking yet, but I'm planning on splitting them up and getting to that while we wait for leads."

"Pretty big crew working with young Paxton," Newquist mused.

Val pulled down the ramp leading to the underground parking garage. "Every witch has their coven, Director."

"You're still convinced he's playing for the other side?" The debate was a long-standing bone of contention between Val and his boss. If Val had gotten his way, he'd have arrested Locke a few weeks back, when he was stuck in a hospital room. Who knew how much of the current mess they might have avoided had he done so?

He waved his ID badge under the reader, then tapped his access code into the pad. As the gate rumbled to one side, he said, "Of course I'm not *sure*, but the best way to find out is to get in his head, wouldn't you say? We need to find out what he knows."

"You're playing a dangerous game, Valentine."

"Who better? Where do things stand, now?"

"We've got his powers damped down, but we'll fry his noodle if we keep pumping the juice into him. We moved him into one of the warded cells so we can interrogate him when he wakes up. I'd hold him for you, but it sounds like you're busy."

"Send me the tapes," Val said. He nosed the car into a spot near the elevator and killed the engine. "You almost sound like you admire the kid, sir."

"I've seen some of the field reports from Missouri and Phoenix." A humorous note entered Newquist's tone. "If you piss him off enough, he might be up to your lofty standards, Agent."

Val shrugged, even though he knew the boss couldn't see it. He might have taken the bait with less on his mind, but he knew Russell was just trying to lighten the mood a bit. Division M had been through a rough few days.

"A few days downstairs will soften him up. If we can't roll up the mother in the next few days, he'll be ready to talk by then." The subterranean prison beneath the Division M field headquarters in Leesburg, Virginia served as a temporary containment venue for troublesome pests until the powers-that-be made an official determination on their status. In the paranormal sense, it was the equivalent of a county jail. Business was booming, of late, and they were running out of spare cells. Plans were in motion for a much larger facility outside of Bluffdale, Utah.

CHAPTER 4

For a variety of reasons, it was a *horrible* idea to keep a prison full of monsters both human and inhuman right near one of the most populated metropolitan areas on the East Coast. When they'd first built the warehouse, heavy woods surrounded the entire complex. Despite subtle pushes back against changes in zoning, the demands of urban sprawl had turned the warehouse into an island in a literal sea of people. Out west, the facility would still be close to Salt Lake, but the population of that entire county was a fraction of the size of the DC Metro area. If they'd asked Val for a suggestion, he would have asked for Alaska, maybe, or some island they could erase from charts and GPS. As with many other official policies, he was not consulted.

"Thanks for the advice," the director said. "Keep me posted on what you get out of his friends. We can use that. We've got an all-hands-on-deck meeting tomorrow morning to roll up the task force on this side of the country. I'm pulling in all the regional heads in for a brainstorming session." His boss coughed a tight laugh. "The Attorney General is going to have kittens when he sees the bills for airfare."

"Should I take offense that you think I won't catch her by my lonesome?"

"As of this moment, Helen Locke is Division M's number-one most wanted. If Phoenix was her attempt at subtle, God help us if she goes off the reservation. I'll get you the conference link. We could use the insight."

"Will do," Val promised, ending the call. Glancing at the stack of donuts, he cursed as he realized he'd forgotten coffee.

CHAPTER FIVE

Cassie—Sunday morning
Texas Panhandle

Twenty miles out of Amarillo, something squealed under the hood of their third car.

Helen leaned forward over the wheel, squinting at the lights on the dashboard. "What is that?" she muttered. Cassie opened her mouth to answer the rhetorical question before realizing that the other woman's last order for her to remain quiet was still in effect.

"If you know something, say it!" Helen snapped.

Cassie took a deep breath, considered the noise and all the time she'd spent in the garage with her dad, then shrugged. "Sounds like the fan belt is going out. Maybe worse, if your check engine light is on."

"Lovely." Helen had used the *push* on the driver of this vehicle a hundred miles back after parking their first replacement behind an abandoned muffler shop. The previous owner, a lizard-slim guy

CHAPTER 5

with a belt buckle bigger than his head, was going on a magically-directed bender at the nearest bar.

I hope he hasn't been going to meetings, Cassie thought with a wince. After the all the hard work she'd put in to get her own sobriety token, Helen's magical puppet act and her own resulting loss of control hit close to home. "Guess we should have asked how well he takes care of his car," she said, unable to resist needling the other woman. Compared to the nearly-new sedan the witch had stolen in Phoenix, Belt Buckle's battered Ford Taurus had a vague scent of corn chips and, apparently, some bearings going out.

"We're getting off at the next exit," Helen declared, and Cassie felt the familiar tingle as the witch exerted her influence. "Speak to no one. No funny facial expressions to communicate your distress. Do you understand?"

Cassie opened her mouth to say yes, found the 'not speaking' order was already in effect, and settled for a nod. *Damn it.*

Helen signaled to take the exit. The truck stop looked pretty ratty from the highway, but it wasn't like they had a variety of choices—Interstate 40 was pretty much an ocean of flat, empty ground interrupted by the occasional city.

She'd come this way with Pax, but Cassie hadn't spent much time looking at the passing landscape on the way west. And, on the bright side, Helen's command about facial expressions helped her keep from smirking as she thought, *Sidekick, hell. You've got it bad, girl.*

Taking the turn into the automobile parking lot, Helen pulled the Taurus down to the end of the lot. The squealing under the hood had only grown in intensity. It felt like a mercy killing when the witch cut the engine and pitched the keys into the backseat.

"Do you need to use the restroom?"

Cassie considered the grimy-looking building, imagined what the facilities inside looked like, and shook her head in a firm no.

Their only luggage was the leather satchel Pax used to transport the grimoire. Helen opened it up and considered the contents. "Here," she said. She handed Cassie a twenty. "Five minutes inside, get us some supplies. Healthier stuff, if that's even possible. I'll figure out transportation."

She was halfway to the entrance before she realized that Helen had made a mistake. There was a *push* to the time limit, but she'd eased off after that. Cassie was half-tempted to buy twenty bucks worth of Reese's Cups, but that was short-sighted.

A bell tinkled overhead as she pushed her way into the small convenience store. Ignoring a greeting from the clerk, she plunged down the aisles, searching out anything coming close to Helen's request. Based on the fact that she looked even younger than Cassie due to one of her magic spells, she doubted the witch would suffer any ill effects from a poor diet. *Have to see if I can pick that spell up.* Cradling a pack of bottled water and some freeze-dried fruit chips, she was still racking her brain when she turned the corner and saw the stand for the lottery.

She'd never been much for the whole PowerBall thing, but she knew that you could get tickets one of two ways—a randomly-generated set of numbers printed from the machine, or your own chosen numbers, selected by filling in the bubbles on a form. Kind of like the old Scantron tests they took in school.

I can't talk and I can't make faces but I can damn well write.

Something inside told her that her time was running out. Setting her groceries on the floor, she grabbed a slip of paper and the stub of a pencil attached to a chain and tried to think. What could she write? The police back in Phoenix were thoroughly corrupted or had been. She realized at that moment that she didn't know if Paxton had won or not.

He did, she told herself, *and he's going to ride in on a white horse to save the day—I just have to help him find the way.*

Call it childish, call it simplistic—she'd been kidnapped by a

CHAPTER 5

witch. Telling herself fairy tales seemed like a fitting thing to do, far-fetched or not.

She scribbled across the ticket. *CASSIE HATCHER KIDNAPPED BY ESCAPED FELON. CALL DETECTIVE SIKORA PHOENIX POLICE AFTER I'M GONE. NOT A PRANK.*

Who knew if it would work or not, especially since she couldn't emphasize the note with any sort of non-verbal communication, but it was all she had time for. She collected her things and headed for the register.

The clerk was a gum-popping brunette not much older than Cassie, but after she didn't respond to her chipper, "Hey, sweetie, how you doing?" the girl went silent. The beeping of the cash register replaced conversation for a moment. "Fifteen sixty-five," the clerk announced finally.

Cassie laid the twenty on the counter between them but kept a finger on it as she took a quick look outside. Helen was nowhere in sight. Quickly, she pulled the lottery ticket out and laid it beside the twenty. She tapped the note, making eye contact with the clerk as she collected the bagged items.

"Don't you want your change..." The clerk trailed off. Cassie was halfway to the door and assumed she'd read the note. "Hey!" the clerk said.

Be cool, Cassie told herself. *Nothing happened.*

She stepped outside and looked up and down the sidewalk in front of the store. Helen stood on the corner opposite from where they'd parked, and she beckoned her forward when she saw Cassie.

Swallowing, she headed that way. At the corner, Helen led her across the parking lot for the tractor-trailer rigs. She pointed out a bright red long-nosed semi. "No more driving for us. We've got a chauffeur, now." She took the bag of supplies from Cassie, holding it open as they walked. "Banana chips, lovely. Excellent choice."

Helen led her around to the passenger side of the truck. "In the back," she said as she pulled the door open. "Say hello to Troy."

The driver was a barrel-chested guy with curly hair and a neatly-trimmed beard. Cassie saw a hint of panic in his eyes as he looked over at her. "Hello," she said, as directed, and hoped that he saw something in her eyes to give him comfort. *Hang in there, Troy. We'll get out of this.*

Helen climbed up after Cassie. "Put these away," she said to her.

The instruction at least gave her an opportunity to get the lay of the land. The sleeper was, to her surprise, pretty nice. A twin-sized bed took up one side of the area, and the opposite side had a dorm-style refrigerator and microwave, with an LCD television hanging on the wall near the ceiling.

She got the bottled water and snacks stashed in the fridge—Troy's supplies showed his fondness for Rip-Its and peanut M&Ms, then took a seat on the bed.

Helen buckled her seatbelt and adjusted the passenger seat until the fit satisfied her. "Let's go, Troy. East."

She must have silenced him, as well, because he simply started the truck and headed toward the exit without a word. Cassie licked her lips and tried to keep her breathing slow and even.

"Hey," someone shouted from outside. *Oh, no,* she thought. Helen turned to look out the passenger window. Cassie stood up and pressed her face against the small port in the side of the sleeper. The clerk stood out in the parking lot, holding a phone in one hand. She waved her other arm in the air, flagging the semi down. Troy's commands evidently didn't extend to running over any pedestrians, because he braked and pulled to a stop well short of the shouting girl. "I've called the cops! Stay here until they show up to sort all this out!"

CHAPTER 5

Helen turned and stared daggers at Cassie. "What did you do?" she spat.

She tried to hold back, but the words spilled from her lips. "I gave her a note."

The other woman laughed. "Not bad—you should have been a lawyer, girl. I want you to remember that everything after this is your fault." Turning to the enthralled driver, Helen continued, "Wait here a moment, Troy. I'll be right back."

Helen opened the passenger door and stepped down into the parking lot. Not knowing exactly what the witch would do was almost as crushing to Cassie as knowing that she'd come so close to pulling it off.

The clerk stopped waving her hands, transfixed by Helen. They were too far away to hear what was being said, but after seeing it too many times, Cassie had a good sense of what someone under the effect of the *push* looked like.

Don't hurt her, she urged, unable to speak. *Please, don't.*

Light flared out in the parking lot. Helen cradled a rolling ball of liquid flame too intense to look at directly. With exaggerated care, she held her hand out. The clerk pocketed her phone, cupping both hands together. Cassie winced, waiting for the fire to consume her, but nothing happened as the witch passed it off. She turned on her heel and walked back toward the truck while the clerk stared at the living flame in her hands with an awed expression.

Taking her seat, Helen announced, "Let's go. Be quick about it." She turned and looked at Cassie, one corner of her mouth curled up in a wicked smile.

Troy pulled the truck past the clerk. As the truck moved by, the clerk raised her head and strode across the parking lot with intense purpose. They turned right, heading back toward the on-ramp, and the bulk of the trailer behind them and the change of the angle cut off Cassie's view of the truck stop.

"Go ahead and ask," Helen said. "I'm sure the suspense is killing you"

"What did you do?" Cassie said. Her voice was hollow in her ears.

"I left her something beautiful and precious to give to some friends of mine. They're in a tough spot—somehow they managed to get trapped in the gasoline storage tanks under the parking lot."

Cassie's heart sank with the knowledge that she was complicit in the deaths of the clerk and countless others.

Halfway up the on-ramp, nose pointed to the night in the east, a new and horrible sun dawned behind them.

CHAPTER SIX

Valentine—Sunday morning
  Phoenix, Arizona

"I'm not going to lie. I'm impressed," Val said. "You guys had enough hardware in that van to overthrow a Central American government." He made a show of flipping through the pages in the folder in front of him. "Forensics is still tied up, but I'd lay even odds that the shell casings Phoenix PD found down in the cavern complex will match up with the heat you boys were packing. Thoughts?"

The slim Hispanic sitting across from him had the stillest features he'd ever seen. That, if nothing else, would have impressed Val. The file they'd managed to scrape together in the few hours since the local Division agents swept up the man and his crew was even more impressive. Back in the day, he'd have waited weeks for the type of biographical information he had at his fingertips.

Receiving no response, Val continued, reading off of the page.

"Esteban Ramirez. Honorably discharged from the Army in 2005, received California private investigator license two years later." He flipped through the pages and whistled. "Good money in that, it looks like."

Val cocked his head, but his subject just looked bored.

"So, tell me this, then, Esteban. Why does a San Diego private eye come to Phoenix at the beck and call of a white-haired punk with delusions of grandeur?"

That got a reaction. The other man's eyes narrowed, and he leaned forward in his chair. The handcuffs holding his wrists to the table complicated that somewhat, but he didn't seem to mind. "First of all, asshole, the only person who calls me by my given name is my *abuela*. Second, you're so in the dark you can't even recognize light."

"Enlighten me, then."

"Doesn't work that way. This isn't the kind of thing you can tell."

Val pushed down the smirk. Esteban was right, of course. He debated for a moment, trying to decide the best way to keep him off balance, then said with a shrug, "I agree. Even then, I've seen a lot of men freeze when they *do* see. The mind locks up. Can't reconcile the image in front of you with the stories your mama told you your whole life about there not being any monsters under the bed."

Frowning, the other man gave him a considering look. "What's your name?"

"Agent Valentine."

"My boys call me Scope. And I'm not telling you a damn thing until I talk to a lawyer."

"I'll get back to you on that." Val closed the folder and rapped his knuckles on the door for the agent on the other side to open it. Halfway into the hall, he called out, "How's that coffee coming?"

As soon as Agent Jared Anjewierden closed the door, Val

turned and gave him a wink. The baby-faced member of the Phoenix crew shook his head and tried not to laugh. In spite of his youthful appearance, the one-time Air Force SP was second-in-command of the Phoenix office.

"Remind me not to get on your bad side, sir."

Val gave him a crooked grin. "Just having some fun. Next one?"

"Right here," Anjewierden pointed out. "The elder De La Rosa."

"Ah, the family scion. Wish me luck."

Val pulled open the door and stepped into the interrogation room. It was identical to the one next door, down to the bland baby-poop green paint color on the walls. The agency had probably gotten the shade on a bulk discount. Division M was one of the few, if not the only, branch of the government that invested the majority of its budget dollars into core requirements over fancy decor.

Esteban De La Rosa might well have been on Val's side of the table, given his dignified air and ruler-straight posture. His demeanor made sense, considering he'd retired as an Illinois State Police detective before joining the family business.

Val took his seat. "Fancy seeing you here, Detective."

The elder Esteban's eyes narrowed. "Have we met?"

"Not as such, but there's enough in here to give me a grasp of the man, I suppose." He raised the folder.

"Fair enough. You have questions?"

"I do."

"I have answers, but there are conditions."

Val leaned back and raised an eyebrow. "Such as?"

"We got close enough to see Kent's house on fire—are my friends safe?"

He considered quibbling but guessed the detective would see through it. "The Sikoras and Father Rosado are under observation in a hospital. Smoke inhalation, some minor burns. They'll be fine."

"Cassie? Paxton?"

"The young lady seems to be on a road trip with Paxton's mother. As for the young man, himself...well, he's not in a great place, to be honest."

De La Rosa's nostrils flared in anger, but he closed his eyes and took several deep breaths to calm himself before responding. "Look, I know you think that you're helping, but you aren't. We're not the bad guys here."

"Oh? Between the piles of bones left out on the city streets and what we found under the gymnasium at Upward Path, I've got at least a hundred bodies. If you're not the bad guy, here, please, enlighten me."

"I don't know what kind of game you're playing at, here, but if you know about Upward Path, you know about the boys we—" De La Rosa caught himself, then seemed to decide that he didn't care about pesky little things like self-incrimination. "The boys that we helped Paxton save. I sure didn't see any of you FBI pricks around."

Val chuckled. "Oh, I'm not FBI. Here's my problem, though. We got the story the boys gave. And it paints a pretty compelling picture. The problem with that is, I've got a wizard with the known ability to compel people to do or say what he tells them to. So how do I know he didn't lay the mojo down on all of you and make you tell whatever story he dreamed up?"

"Known wizard?" Esteban's face worked through a half-dozen expressions as he processed the fact that Val had made the statement with no hint of irony. "What agency *are* you with?"

"That's neither here nor there," Val assured him. "We're here to find out what side you're on. And by extension, what side Paxton is on."

The detective tried to throw his hands up, but the cuffs interrupted the motion. "Whoever you work for, they must not screen for intelligence. You're a damned fool if you think Paxton Locke is some kind of monster."

"Why?" Val pointed out. "You used to. I've read Patrick Locke's murder book. You had Paxton tabbed as an accomplice in his father's death. That makes me more than a little suspicious when I see such an abrupt change of heart."

"If you read my notes, you know why." Esteban shrugged. "There were a few things I glossed over, but I followed the evidence. Evidence says the boy didn't do it. DA even offered the mother a deal if she'd say he was in on it, and she laughed in the man's face. It's ironic, in a way. Pax was haunted long before he ever talked to ghosts."

"What did you gloss over?"

"It's kind of hard to rationally explain the skin-crawling terror one feels while examining certain artifacts. That woman had some bad mojo laying around." He cocked his head to one said and gave Val a canny stare. "But you know what I mean, don't you?"

"I—" Val started, but the fist banging on the door cut him off before he could speak. He rose and rapped lightly in return. Once the door opened for him, he slid through and tried not to slam it closed in frustration. "What?"

"We got something," Anjewierden said, voice tight with tension. "Last night in Amarillo, a truck stop burnt to the ground when the underground fuel tanks exploded. Local cops were interviewing witnesses and enough weirdness popped up that the read-in portion of the department called it in. We've got a confirmed sighting."

"I'll track down Morgan and George," Val said, annoyance immediately dispelled. "Get us a chopper to Luke, I'll make some calls on the way and see if I can rustle up a jet." Damn the cost—they had a witch to hunt.

CHAPTER SEVEN

Cassie—Sunday, before dawn
Oklahoma

Restricted to sitting quietly, it was no surprise that Cassie fell asleep. The hum of the big rig's wheels on the highway and slight swaying of the sleeper on air shocks led her to lie down. Visions of the store clerk's fate chased her into an uncertain sleep that was still better than the intermittent snatches of sleep she'd caught while riding shotgun with Helen.

Carried by inertia, she rolled toward the front of the cab as they came to a slow stop. Catching herself, she managed to keep from falling out of bed and sat up.

The natural thing to do would be to ask what they were doing, but the spell remained indefatigable. She took a deep—but quiet—breath. *You can do this. Don't give up.*

"... go ahead on to your original destination, dear. As soon as we're out of sight, I want you to forget that you ever saw us. As for why you've gone so far out of your way, you had to take a detour to avoid that horrible incident at the truck stop in Texas. Understood?"

"Yes," the driver said, his voice dull. A surge of hope rose in Cassie at the realization that her captor might be letting him off none the worse for wear.

Why they were stopping already was another question. She crossed her fingers that Helen was feeling chatty.

"Grab our things, Cassie. We'll need them, where we're going."

The nice thing about her body being on a magical autopilot was that it gave her plenty of time for introspection. While her hands pulled the water and bag of snacks out of the truck's mini-fridge, she was considering the momentary view she'd gotten out of the front windshield. Save for the cones of illumination projected by the headlights, it was dark as far as she could see. Spits of intermittent snow drifted across the beams. She'd only spent a few days in Phoenix, but the warmth in the Valley had almost been enough for her to forget that Thanksgiving was only a few weeks away.

A lump rose in her throat. *I hope my dad isn't going out of his mind.* Since leaving with Paxton, she'd kept in regular contact with him, if only by text, but she couldn't remember the last time they'd spoken. It had to be going on two days at this point. *Will it be better if he never finds out where I am, or if he knows I was taken?*

This time of year had always been tough without her mom, but the two of them had pushed through it together. She wanted to think that her dad would go on if something happened to her, but the way he'd quizzed Pax in the hospital made her doubt he'd so easily accept it.

Shit, girl. Quit moping and put on your big girl panties. If you do something about, it isn't going to be a problem.

The wind of the semi's passage ruffled her hair, and she shivered as she realized she now stood outside in the chill air. The snow was thickening, with no care that it was unseasonably early.

She found herself walking beside Helen on the side of the road. The other woman cupped another ball of flame in her hand. This served more for light than as a weapon. With the truck gone, the darkness wrapped them. Combined with the chill, the night struck Cassie as particularly oppressive, and the hairs standing on the back of her neck told her that something was watching them.

Helen's grin was wicked in the firelight. "Feel that, do you? You can speak. There's no one around to hear."

"Something's giving me the creeps," Cassie agreed. "Where are we?"

"Beaver Dunes, Oklahoma."

"I thought we were going to Maine," Cassie said.

"We are. We're taking a shortcut." Helen turned her head and gave her a look. "I shouldn't have done that in Texas."

"Is that why you let the driver live?"

"What?" Helen stopped walking, face contorted in obvious confusion. Catching herself, she laughed. "No, I'm not talking about the deaths. As I said, a few here and there are a drop in the bucket. I'm talking about attention. That was a huge signal to Division M. If we stuck with the truck, they'd have caught up to us sooner rather than later."

Keep her talking. "Division M?"

Helen turned off of the main road and headed down a lightly-graveled track. "A secret government agency tasked with securing the country against supernatural threats." She looked back over her shoulder. "Fascinating history, really. Been around as long as the country itself, in one way or another."

"How about that," Cassie said. The shiver that crawled up her spine then was only partially due to the cold. "Mulder and Scully are real."

"Who?"

She tried not to laugh. Helen was calm at the moment, and she didn't want to do anything to change that. "Never mind. TV show

CHAPTER 7

—I don't remember if Pax liked it or not." Helen led them off the path. Patchy scrub grass grew out of sand, of all things. The snow collecting on the ripples of sand seemed out of place. Somehow, the weirdness seemed right given the turn for the strange her life had taken the last few weeks. "Guess these are the dunes. Where are the beavers?"

Helen ignored the question. "In the mid-1500s, the Spanish explorer Coronado led an expedition from Mexico through what's now the southwestern United States." She laughed derisively. "He was looking for gold. He struck out there." The other woman stopped. She turned, waiting for Cassie to catch up. "I wonder how he felt about some of the things that he did find." She waved a hand at the darkness behind her. "The Native American tribes living in this area knew to avoid this area, and they tried to warn him about the dangers. But Coronado didn't listen, and several of his men disappeared without a trace during the course of their journey across what's now called Beaver Dunes State Park."

Cassie swallowed. "What happened to them?"

Wiggling her fingers, Helen whispered, "Vanished without a trace. Ever since then, people have gone missing in this area. Others have reported seeing strange lights and hearing mysterious sounds." She grinned. Combined with her youthful face, the expression made her look like an exuberant teen telling ghost stories.

The fact that Cassie was fairly certain this particular story was true shattered the illusion. "You know all the secrets of the universe, what's the real story?"

Helen turned in place. She seemed satisfied with their location. She gave the ball of light a soft, underhand toss that lofted it into the air. A few feet above their heads, the fire stopped, lending the entire area the atmosphere of shadows dancing around a campfire. Nothing about this particular patch of grass and sand looked any different from any of the others Cassie had followed Paxton's mom through.

"Here's the deal," Helen said finally. "The Edimmu opened my eyes to a lot of the unseen gears and mechanisms of the world around us. That's all that magic is, really—tapping into the primordial energies that forged existence itself. When I say reality, what 's the first thing you think of?"

Cassie rubbed her arms, wishing for a heavier coat, and said, "I don't know. Earth, I guess. Life, and everything that comes after."

Helen dug through the brush until she found a short length of wood, then used it to trace a circle around them. "The universe, to put a picture into your head, is like the ball pit at Chuck E Cheese." She raised a finger, cutting off Cassie's response. "What we consider our reality, our plane of existence if you will, is one of those balls. But there are countless other planes, all rubbing together in the pit. Sometimes certain realities touch, sometimes they don't. There are places, then, where the surfaces of the balls in the pit, are a little closer to—elsewhere." Circle finished, Helen inscribed strange symbols around the perimeter, muttering under breath as she went.

"You got all this from a shadow monster imprisoned in a clay pot?"

"Such a gross simplification. The creature was not of our world, but able to exist in multiple realities at once. The shadow, as you call it, was simply an aspect of that."

"So when Pax stopped it, did he really kill it?" Cassie knew that was giving him more than a little credit since Pax himself believed a no-kidding act of God was what stopped the thing and its human host. It was a long shot, but who knew—maybe his mother would drop whatever it was she was doing if she thought that her son could foil her plans.

"Who can say? The shadow was truly that—a vague impression of the thing's true form. I don't know that you could call it eternal or even immortal, but it counted its life in terms that would make our own seem the blink of an eye."

If anything, the night was growing colder, the wind whipping stinging sleet against her exposed skin. Hugging herself, Cassie opened her mouth to keep asking questions, but Helen brought a finger to her lips.

"Quiet, now," she said. "We don't want to spook our pathfinder." She drew the grimoire from the satchel and let it fall open. If it worked for her the way it had for Cassie and Pax, it didn't matter where she looked at it—in Pax's experience, the book showed him what was on his mind, conscious or not. For Cassie, it had been less generous. Every page she'd opened had been the truth spell, which felt less and less useful every minute she remained in Helen's clutches.

She had a sneaking suspicion that the book worked just a little better for the other woman. Holding it up to let the light from her unearthly fire illuminate the pages, the other woman read in a steady voice too sonorous for her frame. Her words came as though from some malevolent megaphone. For a moment, even the wind stopped, surrounding them with silence.

Cassie didn't see the glowing greenish orb at first. The flame over their heads washed it out, even against the ink-black night. She saw it on its second circuit of the perimeter Helen had described, and her breath caught in her throat.

Something about it seemed to sing to her, and she took one step, then two, toward the edge of the circle, wanting nothing more than to reach out and touch it as it zipped by. She first regarded the sickly green color as something poisonous and sepulchral, but just as quickly a little voice in the back of her mind whispered that it was beautiful, the color of polished jade. *One touch, won't that be nice?*

She reached out, then jerked back to her senses as Helen seized her wrist mere inches from reaching out to the light. "Not yet," Pax's mother whispered. "Seductive, isn't she? The will-o'-the-wisp isn't evil, really—she's a thing of instinct and emotion. More curious than cruel. To keep on with the earlier analogy, they're the children playing in the ball pit. Shame." The pitch of her voice shifted, and Cassie shivered as she recognized the *push*. "Stop."

The green orb froze along its circuit, hovering in front of Helen. A screaming sound, right above the range of Cassie's hearing, made her flinch. The other woman chuckled.

"She's not happy with her chains. Haven't had that problem before, have you? Don't fret. I need you to take us somewhere."

The squeal rose and fell with the wind. *Push* or not, the light seemed to be arguing the point. Stowing the grimoire in the satchel, Helen crossed her arms.

"This isn't up for debate. You are bound—if you want to regain your freedom, you will take us where I want to be, at the next spring equinox. *Now*." The magic-powered fury in the final word made the grains of sand at their feet vibrate, and Cassie felt as though she were sinking.

The will-o'-the-wisp recoiled from the perimeter, brightened, then circled them. Faster and faster it moved, until a solid band of green light surrounded them at chest level. "Take my hand, Cassie," Helen said, and the wave of gratitude that went through at the almost-human expression elicited a surge of self-loathing. If the witch was aware of the storm of emotion running through her, she didn't let on. She continued, "Imagine the poor, hapless conquistador or hiker, coming across such a being. Entranced, making contact—cast into alien dimensions. The luckiest of them would die quickly. From what the Edimmu said, our plane is an island of sanity in a sea of torment."

Cassie swallowed and blinked at the band of green. It was thickening, and she could make out vague shapes through the haze. Trees, perhaps? A squared-off silhouette might be a cabin, but further examination ceased when daylight burst across her face. Recoiling, she covered her face with her free hand even as she cried out.

Chuckling, Helen said, "The where, of course, is as important as the *when*."

Eyes adjusting, Cassie blinked.

A circle of sand-covered snow sat in the middle of a lush green forest. The chill she'd felt vanished in the warm breeze, bringing with it the sound of chirping birds and the crisp scent of pine.

Cassie jerked her head around, spinning in place. The incongruous sand and topography of Beaver Dunes were gone, replaced by a forest straight out of central casting. "What is this?" she demanded.

"I release you," Helen said to the glowing spark. Its light was much diminished, either by the sunlight or the exertion of their journey. It flickered, then vanished entirely. "You're not asking the right questions, dear. Welcome to Maine—the woods outside a small town named Randolph, to be precise. As for when? It's March 20—the spring equinox. The moon is full tonight, and we have a lot of work to do before it rises."

"Why?"

"Enough questions," Helen snapped, and Cassie's lips slammed shut.. "But the answer is a simple one. The police can't catch if they can't find us. As far as they're concerned, we're a cold lead four months old. Come along, now. We need to be ready for my son and his friends."

CHAPTER EIGHT

Valentine—Sunday morning
  Outside of Amarillo, Texas

As much as he wanted to continue the interrogations, an active lead on Helen's whereabouts took priority. With Eliot in the hospital, he tabbed Anjewierden to accompany him, leaving Morgan and George to continue quizzing the detainees.

On the bright side, at least the young agent had the presence of mind to snag a box of donuts on their way out the door. The Air Force C-21 they commandeered out of Luke didn't have much in the way of meal service.

The closest Division M field office was in Dallas. Rather than inconvenience any more agents than he already had, Valentine settled for renting a car at the Amarillo Airport. He doubted they'd be keeping it long. Locke had been keeping a low profile for weeks now. No matter what had caused her to lose her cool in Texas, she'd be in the wind again.

Valentine, though, had an ace up his sleeve.

CHAPTER 8

Even without lights, he got the rental car up into triple digits as soon as he got out on the Interstate. The second time he whipped around an insufficiently-fast car in the left lane, he glanced at the younger agent and raised an eyebrow at his pale expression. "Problem?"

"For God's sake, sir, the scene isn't going anywhere. And we'll never see it if you kill us in a wreck."

Val smirked, then decided to drop down to ninety-five. He liked Anjewierden. The kid had spunk. And slowing down was simpler than telling him that he'd been driving since the kid's grandfather was a glint in great-grandpap's eye. Finally, he said, "The scene's not going anywhere, sure. Her signature's a different story."

"How so?"

He signaled and whipped around a rusted-out pickup truck adopting delusions of grandeur in the passing lane. "You've been through the basic thaumaturgy classes, right?"

"Sure. But you know those just brush the surface, if that."

He did. Val, in fact, had pushed for that policy long ago. Division M had a strange relationship with magic users. Those who'd proven reliable, like Morgan, were worth their weight in gold. The agency had a collection of material and artifacts sufficient to train an army of magic-wielding agents but refrained from doing so. There'd been a few incidents in the past, demonstrating that when it came to the supernatural, Lord Acton's maxim about the corrupting influence of power held doubly true.

Val himself thought it was more the chicken than it was the egg. The type of person who sought to empower themselves was probably not the sort you wanted having it. His team was a perfect example of that—in various ways, he, Eliot, George, and Morgan were all victims of mystical circumstance.

But Anjewierden wasn't cleared for that, so he moderated his answer. "Right. Look at it this way, a magic-user acts as a conduit for power from somewhere else, shaping its application. That act leaves a trace on the affected person or object. And we can track that trace."

The junior agent hummed in interest. "Do I want to know?"

Despite himself, Val grinned. "No, you do not."

"Fair enough."

The site of the incident became obvious as they got closer. A couple of Texas DPS cruisers sat at the top with their lights flashing. A quick flash of Val's ATF credentials got them waved around.

He'd been expecting bad, but the sight laid out before them as they cleared the roadblock made his jaw drop.

A burned-out frame was all that remained of the truck stop. The pavement in front of it had cracked and rippled in the heat. There was no sign that there'd ever even been gas pumps, though the huge crater in the blacktop in front of the ruined building made that obvious. The responding police and fire had cordoned the area off with traffic cones and yellow warning tape, for obvious reasons. The crater was deep enough that Val couldn't see the bottom, even from near the top of the off ramp.

"Holy shit," Anjewierden said finally, as Val pulled the rental up behind one of the dozens of official vehicles surrounding the site. "I don't know what I was expecting but it wasn't *this*."

"Never underestimate a witch with a burr in her saddle," Val replied. He thought back to fights that over the years that he'd very much rather forget, along with men and women he wanted to remember and suppressed a shudder. Shivering in front of the kid would be bad for his image. "Let's go."

Most of the activity seemed on the downward slope. Looking at the site, Valentine could understand why. If there'd been any mundane clues left to dig through, the explosion or fire had taken care of that. The cops and firefighters were here to pick up bodies and keep prying eyes away. It was shit duty, but Texas cops were better than most. He scanned the immediate area until he saw a middle-aged man wearing a Texas Ranger uniform. It was more likely than not that he was heading up the investigation, so he headed that way with Anjewierden following in his wake.

The old boy had skin the color of tanned leather, and he wore his steel-gray hair short enough to see scalp. He saw Val coming not long after they left the rental car, but his expression remained implacable until he navigated the now-corrugated parking lot and offered his hand while displaying his credentials. "Agents Valentine and Anjewierden, ATF."

The Ranger's eyes flicked back and forth between the two men. One of his eyebrows ticked up a fraction as he read Val's name on the badge. "Valentine, eh? Been to Texas before?"

"More than a few times," Val said. It was even something approaching the truth. He glanced down at the Ranger's name tag and added, "Captain Murphy."

Murphy nodded and shook Val's hand. "Old partner of mine, Ernie Hidalgo, told me some wild stories about some work he did with the ATF. Mentioned an agent by the name of Valentine. I'm guessing that's you."

Val kept his face blank, though he did take a quick look at Anjewierden. The other agent, thankfully, was distracted by the blast crater and not paying as much attention to their interactions with local law enforcement as he should have been. He was of a mind to let that slide, especially since it would prevent any more questions from the inquisitive young agent. He considered his answer carefully. Division M didn't like to go around advertising their existence. They were a black, off-budget line item in the ATF's ledger. While a lot of what they did required close cooperation with local authorities, security requirements meant they couldn't exactly advertise with every officer in every jurisdiction. They were more judicious—reading in those who had up-close and personal experiences, or often Federal retirees who moved down to local law enforcement to double-dip on their pension.

There were a couple of Texas Rangers in the know. Murphy, to his knowledge, wasn't one of them. It seemed as though old Ernie had taken that upon himself. "Good man," Val said, finally. "Talks too much, though."

"He did, at that," Murphy allowed. "Been dead going on ten years now."

"I'm sorry to hear that," Val said, and meant it.

The Ranger gave him a tight nod. "Not sure how much there is here for y'all. We've got witness interviews, but most of them were too focused on the fireball to see which way she headed." He doffed his hat and ran his fingers through his hair. "No security footage, all the cameras melted in the blaze and there's no off-site backup. We did put in a warrant to pull all the credit card transactions a couple hours before the event, and we'll run down names and registrations as soon as it comes through. Might come up with something there."

Val nodded. It was probably a dead end—Helen would either kill the driver or switch vehicles by the time they ran down which of the customers had given her a ride, but he wasn't in the business of dismissing long shots. Sometimes they paid off, after all. "I've got some specialized equipment I'd like to try if you don't mind."

"Be my guest. You planning on taking this over on an official basis?"

With a shrug, Val replied, "There's not going to be a trial. And you don't want one of your men catching her."

"'bout what I figured, from what Ernie said. It true y'all roasted up some of that critter?"

Val grinned. "I couldn't choke much of it down. Sucker got big too fast, turned the meat tough."

"And here I thought you were going to say it tasted like chicken." The Ranger dipped his head in farewell. "Don't take this the wrong way, Agent Valentine, but it's not usually a good sign when your folk come around. If I didn't see y'all again, I think I'd be much happier for it."

"Understood. We'll be out of your hair soon."

"Good hunting, sir."

He continued toward the blast crater. Anjewierden stepped up beside him and murmured, "What was that all about?"

"Ancient history. Don't worry about it." At the edge of the hole, he knelt and slipped a hard case out of the inner pocket of his suit coat. It was small, perhaps three inches by six, and right at an inch thick. "Got that compass ready?"

"Yes."

"Good. Watch this." He flipped open the top of the case with no fanfare. One of the most powerful artifacts in Division M's possession lay nestled in the foam lining the interior. Roughly the length of an unsharpened pencil, the metal rod came to a sharp point on one end, with the opposite rounded over. Val braced himself and plucked it out. He'd kept the case close to his body for hours now, but the rod still held an unnatural cold that tugged at the skin of his fingertips. "It stays a good forty to fifty degrees below ambient. If you have to use it in the middle of winter, wear gloves. It'll stick."

He plunged the pointed end of the rod into the top rim of the crater, where the asphalt had blown away to reveal the dirt below. Val held his breath for a few nerve-wracking seconds. When the metal under his skin turned comfortably warm, he grinned viciously.

"Oh, Helen, you fool." He pulled the rod out of the dirt. As soon as the point was clear, the tip swung up on its own volition and pointed north-northeast. Val took a quick look around to make sure none of the first responders were paying attention before fully releasing it. Powered by the residue of the magic Helen had used to cause the explosion, the divining rod hovered six inches above the pavement. When he prodded the sharp end with a finger, he might as well have been trying to move a brick wall. "Take a compass reading."

For once, Anjewierden didn't have any questions. The young agent leaned over, got his compass lined up with magnetic north, and compared lines. "Right between twenty and twenty-one degrees. Call it halfway."

"Close enough," Val said. He brought the opened case up underneath the rod. As soon as the foam touched it, the energy dissipated and it moved freely. "Let's go."

He'd cajoled a regional map out of the clerk at the car rental agency. It took him a moment to unfold it on the trunk of the rental car to highlight the panhandle and Oklahoma to the north. "Compass," he said shortly. The other agent laid it on the map and he poked it around a bit to get it lined up. It was a pitiful thing, really—clear plastic, stamped and mass produced on an assembly line somewhere. Probably put together by machines. He'd had something to put it to shame, back—

Val shook off the thought. The past was moot. The mission was everything, now, and if he couldn't respect the craftsmanship of the compass, he had to admit that it was accurate.

He snagged a pen from Anjewierden's shirt pocket without asking, then used the case as a straight edge to line up their location. The revelation was anticlimactic for Val—as soon as the rod pointed north, toward the eastern side of the Oklahoma panhandle, he'd known in his gut. "Shit," he said, as the line slashed through the legend 'Beaver Dunes Park' printed on the map. "Let's move. We don't have much time."

CHAPTER NINE

Aleister—Monday morning
  Leesburg, Virginia

NEW KRISTIN PULLED OLD KRISTIN'S SEDAN INTO THE parking lot of a Harris Teeter grocery store. The shopping center sat in a convenient location off the main highway on the road leading to the building the American government used to conceal the Menagerie and, more importantly, their secure vaults of various eldritch artifacts.

Rolling hills surrounded the Division M facility. Developers had planted high-end houses and business developments on postage stamps of land throughout most of the surrounding area. Enough wooded area remained for Aleister to stroll through. In recognition of the fact that people didn't usually go hiking in business casual, Knight had forgone his usual ensemble in favor of a plaid shirt, khakis, and low boots. The stiffness of the new fabric combined with their unfamiliarity doubled down on his discomfort, but if all went well, he'd be changing into traveling clothes sooner rather than later.

He pulled a pair of items from his satchel and presented them to his partner. The first, a glossy 8x10 photograph, pictured an age-darkened section of wood lying next to a ruler for scale. A series of numbers in Knight's own, mechanically-precise handwriting lined the back.

"The artifact should be identical to the one in the photograph," he said. "If you have any difficulty extracting its location from the men in the vault, the lot number on the back should help you to find it." He'd expended an immense amount of capital, both mystical and monetary, to gather intelligence about the facility and its contents. The payoff would be more than worth it.

Liliana studied the numbers with a frown, then flipped the photo back over. "This isn't a wand," she muttered. Her eyes went a little wide, and she stared at Knight. "This is a piece of the Spear, isn't it? I thought it was a myth."

"There are myths, and then there are myths," he said with a wave of his hand. "Don't try to renegotiate terms now—we have a deal."

"I'm not looking for a sweetener. I'm concerned about my own skin."

Knight grinned. "You'll be able to touch it. You shouldn't need to. It'll be in a storage case."

She considered that with a predatory gleam in her eyes. Knight felt certain that her duplicate had never worn such an expression. For all her bravado, dear departed Kristin had been a kind, trusting soul by all accounts.

It made her an excellent target.

"Fine," Liliana agreed. "Anything else I happen to bring along is mine and mine alone."

He frowned. That was a change in the terms of their bargain, but not an enormous one. "Fair enough, so long as it doesn't impact

CHAPTER 9

your timetable." He nodded to the second object. About the size of a hardback book, he'd wrapped it in burlap secured by twine. In spite of the innocent appearance, she handled it as though it were a live bomb.

Which wasn't too far from the truth.

"How long do I have?"

"There's enough energy bound up in the building to put an aircraft carrier on the moon. As soon as you step inside, the spell in the package will begin to siphon some of that. After about twenty minutes, the vessel will reach capacity. I'd advise you to be out the door by then if nothing else."

"Perfect," she said. "I'll see you in the woods, Aleister."

He stepped out of the car and waited for her to drive off. As soon as her taillights joined the flow of traffic along the secondary rode, he slung his satchel over one shoulder and set out himself. There was a well-situated hill less than a quarter mile from the Division M annex.

Knight grinned. He'd never understood the American fascination with fireworks, but he found himself looking forward to the show.

Kevin—Monday morning
Leesburg, Virginia

"We need to put batteries in the thing," Kevin Menard insisted, trying not to pound the workbench with his balled-up fist. The unruly piles of high-end electronics and priceless artifacts guaranteed he'd knock something off, and that was more paperwork than he wanted to deal with right this moment. The spectacular failure of Division M's pride and joy in the field had put enough scrutiny on him and his department.

His counterpart, research partner, and constant foil folded his arms across his chest. Doctor Hans Schantz was Kevin's opposite in almost every way. Where the lead engineer was short and muscular, the physicist was tall and slender. Menard was blunt and to the point—Hans was far more diplomatic. The only point of commonality the two men shared was their dabbling in realms far outside the boundaries of what most would call science.

The blueprints on their table described the subject of their debate. In person, the massive suit of armor measured ten feet from the bottom of its broad, cross-shaped feet to the top of its barrel chest. It had no head to speak of, but Menard and Schantz had mounted a pair of optical sensors approximately where eyes would be. Piloted by Division M agent George Patrick, they'd designated the creation 'Troll-1.'

George, for some mysterious reason, referred to it as Beatrice. After seeing the whimsical expression on the normally-acerbic agent's face at the declaration, Hans and Kevin went with it.

Less acceptable was the revelation of a critical flaw in their design. Designed to even the playing field between the more mundane Division M personnel and the creatures they confronted, the machine was heavily-armed and armored enough to stand up to pretty much anything encountered in the history of the agency. So, when Helen Locke the fugitive witch cut Troll-1's strings with a wave of her hand, it was time to go back to the drawing board.

Hans sighed and ticked the points off on his fingers. "We're at the limit of current servomotor technology. We add more weight, we slow the next generation down and reduce effectiveness. And with the weight and power draw, if you want any sort of endurance, you're talking a lot of mass devoted to batteries. Which means we'd have to cut armor."

Kevin frowned. He rubbed his chin thoughtfully. "I'm listening. How much are we talking?"

The doctor tapped into a calculator for a moment after consulting the design notes lining the edges of the blueprints. "A third, at least."

Wincing, Kevin said, "That's not horrible. That still makes most stuff survivable."

"Sasquatch?"

"Shit. Probably not."

Hans traced his finger along the list of runes they'd inscribed into the Troll's exoskeleton. Powering a machine with a mysterious energy that defied all known laws of science offended the physicist's sensibilities. He liked to tell himself that which everyone else in the agency dubbed 'magic' was just another form of science. That, he'd once told Menard, kept him from curling up and rocking back and forth in a corner. Squiggly lines and marks shouldn't have been able to provide kilowatts of electrical power—but somehow, they did. "It seems to me that it would be easier to determine what weakness allowed the wi— Helen Locke, that is, to interrupt the power supply. There must be some way to implement a tamper-proof seal, for lack of a better term."

"Agent Morgan consulted on the original glyphs," Kevin said. "I wonder if she has any experience with this sort of thing."

"Never hurts to ask, but she's been out of town with the rest of the fearsome foursome."

Kevin leaned over the blueprints, studying the glyphs. "I hear Locke hurt Eliot pretty bad. Maybe we shouldn't feel too bad about her taking down the Troll."

"Good point," Hans agreed. "I don't see where we messed up, and that's what—"

The main door leading into the lab buzzed. Kevin glanced over and tried to keep a goofy grin from spreading across his face. He'd had a low-grade crush on Kristin Hughes ever since she'd transferred into the Leesburg office a few years back. Dating amongst coworkers was usually a big-time policy violation, but the ultra-secret nature of Division M had led the powers that be to loosen some of the restrictions. It was much easier to maintain secrecy when both partners in a relationship were already read into the nuances of a black organization.

"New artifact from one of the field offices, gentlemen." She lifted a flat, rectangular object wrapped in burlap and twine. "Needs to go in the vault."

Kevin took a quick glance at Hans. The scientist wore a puzzled frown. "Not the process, Miss Hughes. We need a copy of the incident report so we can do a volatility assessment. *Then* it goes into a vault."

She gave the two men a dazzling smile and strolled across the lab. The subdued click of her heels on the linoleum sounded like thunder in Kevin's ears. His cheeks flushed with heat as a sweet fragrance filled his nostrils. He wondered what sort of perfume was pungent enough to smell halfway across a room, but the scent overwhelmed his thoughts and left him with a pleasant buzz. "Uhh," Kevin said. "I, um..." Further conversation failed him—he shook his head and laughed. Hans snorted laughter of his own as Kristin stepped up to their table.

She glanced at the blueprints before depositing her artifact on top of them. "We don't need all that silly paperwork today, do we? I wouldn't mind taking a look around the vault, though. How about it?"

Hans wobbled back and forth, then clamped one hand on the table to steady himself. "Not, uh, procedure." He took a deep, shuddering breath. "Menard. Call ... security."

Kristin pouted. "Party pooper." She snagged Hans' tie with one hand and pulled him closer. Away from the support of the table, he wobbled back and forth drunkenly. "Kevin, sweetie, can you open the vault by yourself, or is it a two-man job?"

He puffed his chest out with pride. "I can do it."

"Marvelous." Kristin put a hand on each of Hans' cheeks, then twisted violently. In spite of their size disparity, the physicist's neck rattled like popcorn as she twisted his neck far beyond its normal limits. He crumpled to the floor like a puppet with its strings cut.

A small, still voice in the back of Kevin's mind screamed in horror, but a fresh rush of Kristin's heady scent blurred his vision. After what she'd done to his friend, the crimson fingernail she traced up his throat and under his chin should have reduced him to hysterics. Instead, he stood there, knees trembling with suppressed ecstasy as she brought her lips close to his ear and whispered. "Open it for me, Kevin."

Voice thick with desire, he croaked, "Yes, of course." He stumbled across the lab. His body burned and ached all at once. He wanted nothing more than to strip out of every stitch of his clothing, and some subtle undercurrent in Kristin's voice told him that if he pleased her, she might let him do just that. Conscious thought slipped away, replaced only by animal instinct, and a vast, gnawing need to satisfy his mistress.

The vault consisted of a pair of massive safe doors set into an interior block wall. Open, Kevin knew without looking that he'd find stainless steel walls, floor, and ceiling. Regularly-spaced glyphs were the only irregularity in the gloss finish of the massive metal cube's interior. The magic symbols strengthened the walls and prevented penetration by otherworldly means. As far as earthly means, it would take some doing to punch through twelve inches of solid steel.

As he drew further away from Kristin, his muddled thoughts cleared a bit, and he considered how nothing in the vault was all that dangerous. The contents were items either for study and testing—often recent acquisitions in the course of Division M investigations—or tools the staff used to craft and maintain their own magical arsenals. The enchanted chisels they'd used to inscribe the runes of power on the Troll, for example. As far as stockpiles went, this one wasn't much to speak of, and Hans had told him that the real mother lode was—Kevin froze, the sight and sound of his coworker's snapping neck running through his mind. He opened his mouth to cry out, but Kristin pressed her chest against his back, wrapping her arms around his torso. Her fingers traced lines of heat down his chest and stomach, then playfully continued along the front of his thighs.

"We're so close," she whispered, nibbling on his earlobe. That overpowering perfume overtook him once more, and he nodded, a dumb grin spreading across his face.

His fingers felt thick and clumsy. It took him a few tries before the door accepted his code and withdrew the massive locking bolts lining the perimeter. He heaved, and the lights on the interior came on automatically as he turned to display the contents of the vault to Kristin.

"That's lovely," she said. The peck she gave him on the cheek caused his eyes to go crossed, and he was on the floor before he realized he'd collapsed. Fuzzy, he lifted his head and watched as she walked the perimeter, studying the contents of each shelf before moving on. Toward the back of the room, she plucked a storage cylinder reminiscent of the pneumatic carrier tubes used by banks. Tucking it under one arm, she returned to the entrance and knelt at his side. "You poor thing. You're about to burst from all the excitement, aren't you?"

He couldn't coordinate his lips and tongue to form words, so he settled for a sheepish grin.

Kristin tousled his hair. "Thanks for your help, Kevin. I want you to wait here for a while, okay?"

"Okay," he managed.

"Good boy," she whispered, and a thrill went through him at the praise.

Each click of her departing heels seemed to coincide with the heavy lassitude that overtook him. Body tingling, the dissipating aroma of her perfume carried him into an exhausted sleep.

Liliana—Monday morning
Leesburg, Virginia

. . .

It took everything she had to leave the human behind. He was well-marinated in the juices of his lust, and Liliana was *starving*.

She hadn't survived in a world that had claimed so many of her brothers and sisters without an exceptionally well-developed sense of survival. That, combined with her own personal knowledge of how matter-of-fact Knight tended to be, lent more than a little urgency to her steps as she hustled the artifact out of the building. More than anything the wizard was prone to understatement. She expected that the building was not long for the world.

Nearly home free, she ran into a crowd at the building entrance. She dug through the harvested memories of her host form, cringing ever-so-slightly as she realized that the powerfully-built human clearing the security checkpoint was the Director of Division M, Russell Newquist, along with his security detail and assorted hangers-on. At first, she feared discovery, but a memory of an ongoing high-profile case bubbled to the top, and she relaxed. They were meeting, not about her or Aleister Knight, but rather the human witch, Helen Locke.

Liliana held back a cruel smile. *Fools.*

The director smiled as he saw her. "Kristin! You didn't have to meet us down here. I'm sure you've got plenty to attend to before the conference."

Kristin's mannerisms and voice tasted bitter in her mouth, but she reminded herself that she'd be able to shed the disguise, and soon. "Guilty, Director—I actually forgot something out in the car. I'll see you shortly."

He smiled and nodded, turning away to another member of the group as she hustled past. Once her back was to the herd of sheep, she let down her guard and allowed herself to smile. It was so nice to work with professionals. Knight never failed to present

CHAPTER 9   63

her with a challenge, but he also backed it up with enough research and planning to make even the hardest job silk smooth.

She hit the button on Kristin's keys to pop the trunk. Slipping the strap of the Division M agent's cheap purse off of her shoulder, she pulled the artifact out and deposited the purse, keys and all in the trunk. They didn't need the cutesy little shit box of a car, anymore, and she fully intended to replace it with something low and *fast*.

As soon as she got something to eat.

ALEISTER—MONDAY MORNING
   Leesburg, Virginia

THE GROUND UNDER HIS FEET SHOOK, AND A SECTION OF THE massive building's roof bulged before rupturing and venting gouts of flame into the sky.

Aleister allowed himself a small smile of pride. It had been a difficult bit of magic, packing something so powerful into a portable package, but it wasn't the first time he'd used something of its like. Depending on how thoroughly Division M maintained its records, there was a possibility they'd be able to link the device to him.

By that point, he would more than likely hold the completed Spear and wouldn't give much of a damn. The thought of them scrambling around, hair on fire, when they *did* realize who'd hit them, brought more than a little joy to his heart.

Leaves rustled, and he turned. *Right on time.*

Liliana had already shed the trappings of their first victim. Walking naked across the forest floor, her body rippled and tightened into a familiar blond-haired ice queen. She remained nude for two steps before skintight leather formed to complete her appearance.

Even knowing what she was, the sight of her lithe, erotic form brought a rush of blood to otherwise forgotten areas. He pushed the urge down—as enjoyable as the experience might be, he'd likely not survive it, given the reddish cast to her eyes.

She proffered the containment cylinder with a sarcastic grin. She likely felt his subdued attraction, though she respected—or feared—his own abilities enough to refrain from doing anything about it. From a normal human, even a bit of interest was like blood in the water to a shark for one of her breed.

The buzz that went through the case as he accepted it brought a smile to his face. *Three down. One to go.* "Your fee is in the normal account," he said, bowing his head politely. "It's always a pleasure."

Liliana smirked. "I'll keep quiet—for a price."

He was accustomed to her foibles, but he still felt a hint of annoyance at even a joke about extortion. "Tell anyone you care to, love. When you're ready to pay the price."

"If the humans find out what you're up to, they'll move Heaven and Earth to stop it."

Knight raised an eyebrow. "You don't know the half of it. Which tells me you don't have any idea what I plan to do with it, either." He winked. "And I know you wouldn't stoop to dealing with the mortal authorities. Unless I'm mistaken, they have your kind listed as kill on sight, no?"

She laughed. "I do so enjoy our business ventures, Aleister. Call me again." Liliana waggled her fingers in farewell as she headed back toward the main highway in a languid strut.

His smile faded, his face turning as hard as his thoughts. *Once I'm done, I'll have no need for such as you, creature.*

CHAPTER TEN

PAXTON
Location unknown

I couldn't cut or phase my way out of the cell, but that didn't mean that I couldn't get ready to attempt an escape.

After the beating I'd gotten from a trio of witch's familiars, I'd spent most of the past few weeks limping around, trying to build my strength back up. Say what you will about being stuck in an eight-by-ten cell. It was a prime opportunity to rest up.

The food wasn't plentiful enough to go overboard, but after the first meal on wheels, I settled into a routine. I'd eat, then turn the focus of my healing spell inward. The last time I'd used it, I'd nearly drained myself dry, melting pounds of weight off my body that I didn't need to lose. The sight of my cheekbones and ribs in stark relief after I woke up in the hospital was shocking, to say the least. I'd spent much of the intervening time gorging myself and groaning at the aching of healing bones.

Magic turned out to be a pretty decent diet plan. And tiring myself out made it easier to sleep through the occasional odd noise in the otherwise pervasive silence.

I'd made the mistake of asking Puck what a noise was, at one point. Part of me hoped that he'd been pulling my leg, but I was starting to doubt it.

Every time I started to believe that I'd found the bottom of the magical rabbit hole, I discovered something else. As though ghosts weren't bad enough, Puck and I were apparently a few cells down from a griffin. If the roar was anything to go by, an eagle's head on a lion's body did weird things to your vocal cords.

The quiet had done wonders for my hearing, and tired as I was, as soon as the subtle squeaking of the food cart trickled into my cell, I opened my eyes and sat up on my bed. Last night had been cold enough that I'd left my clothes on, and I bent over and laced up my shoes. 150 laps around the cell made for a mile and promised to bore me to tears, but it wasn't as though I had a hopping social calendar.

I smiled, remembering Cassie urging me out of bed to go running with her. *What I'd give to be able to tell her I'm coming...*

The lights flickered.

Leaning closer to the opening in the door, I said, "Hey, Puck. Does that—"

I didn't get the chance to finish my question. A wall of flame shot down the hallway toward my cell with a freight-train roar. I flinched back, barking my elbows on the concrete floor as I dove for the bed. The room went dark as the lights went out for good, then brightened as flame shot through the hole in the cell door. My cell went from the edge of too cold to sweltering in the span of a few seconds.

The floor shook, bouncing me up and down a few times. A heavy impact pushed the mattress down on top of me, and I squirmed closer to the wall, hoping the entire mess wasn't about to come down on me. When I turned my head, I saw that the room had gone almost completely dark, save for a sliver of light at one side of the cell door. I squinted, trying to understand what I was looking at.

My heart leaped in my chest. The earthquake or whatever it was had twisted the door out of true, and one corner sagged out into the hallway. Was that enough of a gap to exploit?

The disaster seemed to be over, and muffled screams filled the abrupt silence. I slid out from under the bed and headed toward the light. If the electricity was off throughout the cell block, there was only one place where it could be coming from.

The gap wasn't big enough for me to get my head through to look, but what looked like sunlight originated from the right side of my cell, back toward the entrance. I took a step back and looked at the ceiling. The previously-smooth slab of concrete was spider-webbed with cracks, and more than a few chunks had fallen out. For the moment, it seemed stable, though who knew how long that would last.

The dust in the air made the soft blue light of my force blade even brighter. I braced myself for the shock as I stuck it through the opening between the door and the wall, but nothing happened. With the structural integrity of the room compromised, it seemed as though Division M's spells were kaput. I brought the blade down to cut through the bottom hinge. As soon as the metal parted, the door shifted further out, and the ceiling cracked and popped with it.

"Shit!" I wrapped my fingers around the open edge of the door and pulled, trying to keep it from moving any further. *Didn't think that through, did you, dipshit?* Then a pair of heavily-muscled hands appeared above my own, shoving the door back as I pulled, and I screamed.

In my defense, a stubby but wickedly-curved claw tipped each finger on those hands. That would have been frightening enough

CHAPTER 10

on its own if the skin of the hands wasn't a mottled brown-and-green pattern reminiscent of military camouflage.

A face appeared in the gap, and it was as much a horror as the hands—flat, with a broad slash of a mouth filled with needle-like teeth and a pair of parallel slits for a nose. A pair of surprisingly-normal looking brown eyes looked at me from under a heavy brow ridge that rose into a bald pate, all framed by a pair of bat-wing ears.

"Calm, wizard," the thing said, and I realized that the creature was my neighbor. "Hold the door steady, or it will crush us both."

"What—" I started to say, then took a deep breath to steel my nerves. "No offense, Puck, but what are you?"

He laughed a familiar wheezing chuckle. "We call ourselves 'the people', but you humans have to have a name for everything. Division M calls us pukwudgie. Can you make it through the gap?"

I eyed the space and shook my head. "No, but I can do something I should have tried from the get-go." Releasing my grip on the door, I went out of phase and stepped through the metal. I tried to avoid the strange creature, but I passed through his side on the way through. He laughed again.

"Tickles, wizard." He studied the door, then released it. "Should hold long enough for us to move. Come!"

He scrambled down the hallway, bouncing over and around intermittent piles of rubble. Seen in full, his appearance proved to be stranger. He was short, no more than four feet in height, and bow-legged. His arms were long and muscular, and he ran more like an ape than a man, resting on his knuckles to lever himself up and over anything in his way. What skin I could see was the same mottled camouflage color as his hands, though he wore a red and black plaid shirt over a pair of cutoff khakis. *I never thought a goblin or troll would look like it stepped out of an L.L. Bean catalog.*

Puck stopped and turned back to look for me. When he saw I hadn't moved yet, he shouted, "Run, wizard! Division M will be coming!"

I wasn't able to move so fast as my strange companion as I picked my way around chunks of concrete. Taking the occasional glance at the cracked ceiling, I crossed fingers that it would hold long enough for us to make our escape.

Some of the other cells hadn't been so lucky. The door on the third cell from Puck's had fallen completely inside. Blood seeped out from the wreckage, mixing with the dust. I could make out a hint of tawny, golden fur through the opening, but little else. If I'd had any remaining doubts after seeing Puck that more than a few of the inhabitants of this mysterious underground prison weren't human, that settled it.

Further down the hall, my companion muttered something inaudible. Even without being able to make out the words, I could tell that he was annoyed.

"Yeah, yeah, keep your pants on," I said, moving forward. Further down the hall, it brightened significantly, until I could make out a massive gash in the upper half of the prison wall. Dirt mixed with concrete had fallen inside, forming a rough ramp. Outside, I could hear the vague sound of sirens. Puck was right—we needed to hurry. I could probably make myself invisible, if not now, for certain once I was outside, but I didn't know if he could say the same. He may have looked weird, but he'd saved my life, and that counted for something.

Another, closer, groan stopped me. I turned away from the opening. After looking into the sunlight, it took a moment for my eyes to adjust, but I finally made out the crumpled shape of the food cart, buried under a massive slab of concrete—along with one of the guards. I didn't see the other, but something told me hadn't been as lucky as this one. Part of the frame of the cart kept much of the debris off, but chunks of rubble pinned one exposed leg.

CHAPTER 10

I pulled on one end of the cart. It moved easily—the slab had stopped on other chunks of concrete, which was probably good for this guy. Sheet metal and aluminum wouldn't have stood as much of a chance.

The guard was the one who'd brought breakfast on Saturday, the talker. He blinked at me as I knelt beside him and tossed chunks out of the way. "How bad is it?"

The dust-streaked name tape on his uniform read STOCKER. He took a shaking breath and replied, "I can't feel anything below the knee. Don't know if that's a good sign or a bad sign."

Wincing, I held back my comment. With most of the smaller stuff out of the way, I had the guard's upper body freed. If not for his leg, I could pull him out of there and help him outside.

Abruptly he shouted, "Holy shit!"

I spun in place, then relaxed. Puck stood nearby, bouncing nervously from foot to foot. "Leave him, wizard. We have no time."

"You're with that thing?" Stocker demanded.

I looked back and forth between the two of them. "Okay, no offense, man, but you're the one running the top-secret black site here. Still waiting on my phone call, by the way."

"That thing *ate* three campers," the guard wheezed. "It deserves to be locked up."

I gave Puck a wary glance. "Is that true?"

His nervous shimmy told me everything I needed to know before he spoke. "They were on the people's land but left no offering. I had every right!"

Blue light flared, and Puck's eyes widened at the force blade I'd brought up between us. "That's not how things work, Puck," I said slowly. "You can't just go around eating people."

"Kill it," Stocker blurted. "We don't have any way to subdue it."

"I saved your life, wizard. Foolish. I should have expected betrayal from a human." He lifted his chin in defiance. In spite of his monstrous features, I couldn't help but see a bit of wounded pride, there.

I banished the blade. "Go," I said. "In thanks for my life."

Puck blinked and took a glance at the light. "Truly?"

"Truly," I echoed. "With one condition." Taking a deep breath, I *pushed*. "You will never kill, injure, or eat another human."

He squealed in frustration, and the sound made the hair on the back of my neck stand on end. Somewhere, I'm sure, dogs were howling. "Unfair, wizard! But I will heed your bond."

"Go home, Puck," I said. "I'll take care of this guy."

He spat onto the floor, disgusted. "They don't deserve your kindness. They will capture you again and use it against you."

I shrugged. "Maybe. But I've got bigger fish to fry right now. Can you get out of here without anyone seeing you?"

Wheezing another laugh, my strange friend shook his head. "Of course. Until we meet again, wizard." He turned, hurtled up and out of the hallway, and vanished from sight.

When I turned back to Stocker, he was staring at me with wide eyes. "What have you done? That thing's dangerous!"

"Not anymore," I said. "I *pushed* him—you heard that, right? I don't like to use it on people, but—"

"That's *not* a person," he interrupted.

I rubbed my forehead and tried not to sigh. "Whatever. You want to get into a semantic argument, or you want to get out of here?"

He closed his eyes. "There's nothing you can do."

Studying the slab of concrete, I only half-heard him. "Maybe. Maybe not." Phasing myself through the blockage wouldn't do anything, but what if I phased *him*? I'd never tried it. Up until a few weeks ago, I'd always considered the spells I'd learned to be good for one thing. Cassie had pointed out the possibility of using spells in fashions other than the way I had been. The effect I

CHAPTER 10

called force blades was simply a telekinesis spell, applied a little differently. When I'd first gained the ability, I'd thought it useful only for grabbing drinks out of the fridge.

As the saying went, sometimes you needed a second set of eyes. "Try to relax," I said. Wrapping both hands around Stocker's knee, I closed my eyes and took a deep breath. When I'd healed Cassie, I'd sort of pushed outside of myself while. If I did the same thing with the phase spell—

Stocker gasped, but I forced myself to ignore it and focus on what I was doing. His leg felt lighter, less confined, somehow, and I pulled. Halfway through the motion, I opened my eyes in time to see a horribly-crushed limb phase through the slab of concrete. I didn't want to overdo it, so as soon as I saw that he was clear, I killed the effect.

Blood spurted instantly—I resisted the urge to curse as the guard screamed in agony. The pressure had kept his wounds closed, but without it, the sleeping limb was coming back to life while Stocker bled out.

I didn't hesitate—I grabbed his knee again. The sense I got of his body as I began to heal it made me wince. His leg was the worst injury, but he had broken ribs, a slight concussion...

The leg was the most pressing issue. The last time I'd done this sort of thing, I'd put myself in the hospital, so I had to walk a fine line. I couldn't fix him completely, but I had to do enough to keep him stable. I shook with fatigue as I felt shattered pieces of bone drift back together, while blood vessels and veins sealed.

He was still hurt, and probably bad enough to be permanently crippled, but Stocker was no longer in any danger of bleeding out. I forced myself to stop, yanking my hands away from his leg. His screams of pain had become soft sobs. I wanted to tell him it was going to be all right, but my throat was terribly dry and my stomach rumbled with hunger.

"What did you do?" He stared down at his leg. When I'd

phased it out of the concrete, it had been a lumpy, flattened mess. It still didn't look so hot, but the bones, at least, were straight, and his foot stuck up.

"Fixed it, as best I could," I said. "Come on." I got around on his bad side and threw his arm over my neck. "You're going to have to help me some, dude. I'm about to fall over here."

Using his good leg, he was able to get up onto one foot with my help. He winced as we stumbled toward the exit. The incline up and out was steep, but I bore down. Escape was my first priority. I could rest up later. Stocker banged his injured leg a couple of times and bit back screams, but to his credit, he didn't stumble or fall.

Blinking in the sunlight, I took a quick look around. The building behind us was a two-story block construction that had the look of a converted warehouse. We'd come out on the back side—I could hear the sirens, but the grassy area in front of me didn't have a parking lot. A couple of concrete picnic tables told me this was probably some sort of community lunch area. The grass rose up into a small hill peppered with trees. It was green enough that I knew I wasn't anywhere close to Arizona, but I'd already figured that much out.

I helped the guard to the ground and leaned him against the wall. A massive plume of smoke rose overhead from closer to the front of the building. "Any idea what happened?" I said.

He shook his head. "No clue. We were doing the normal rounds, then boom."

"Same here." I started to rise, but he snapped a hand out and seized my wrist.

"You aren't going anywhere, kid. You're still a prisoner."

Staring down at him, I saw more than a little fear in his eyes. He'd put on a brave tone, but it was all a show. *What is he afraid I'll do to him?* "I am not the bad guy," I said, taking my time with each word. "One of your coworkers got a bug up his ass and threw

CHAPTER 10

me in here, but there's someone bad out there that I need to stop. Keeping me locked up in here isn't going to help that happen."

"I don't know your story, and I don't care. You can take it up with—"

"The judge? You guys wouldn't give me a phone call, remember? Last I checked, this is still America. Ever hear of the Constitution, asshole?" My hands tingled with the urge to do something, but I pushed it away. I was right to be angry, but that didn't mean I needed to escalate things. I went out of phase, and Stocker's hand passed through my wrist as I took a step back. He couldn't chase me, not with that busted-up leg, but he could cry for help. Even over the sirens, someone would hear him, eventually.

The move was obvious, but I hesitated. I could use the *push* to make him forget he ever saw me, but that came too close to the sort of meddling Mother was fond of. I wasn't that person, no matter how hard it made things on me. "Damn it," I said, to myself more than Stocker, then *pushed*. "When I snap my fingers, you're going to fall asleep for a few minutes. When you wake up, you tell whoever you need to tell to make it happen that you need to talk to Valentine. Tell Valentine that Paxton Locke is on his side, but he's not helping matters, much. Got it?"

He wobbled back and forth, his eyes a little out of focus. Recovering, he said, "Yes, but—" I snapped my fingers and cut him off. I'd considered making him sleep until someone came upon him, but who knew how stable the building. I'd hate for it to collapse on top of him right after I dragged him out of there.

As for me, it was time to run. The direction didn't matter so much as getting away. I turned, picked a point on the hill behind the building and took off.

My legs didn't hurt anymore, which helped, but I was tired and hungry. I needed to find someplace to rest up, muster some strength. I needed to find out where I was, and figure out how to get back to Phoenix. From there, I didn't know yet. I had to track

Cassie and Mother down, somehow. The De La Rosas and I hadn't had any sort of plan of action if I up and vanished on them, but I hoped that they'd stayed in the wind. If I could get my hands on a phone, I could get some help.

"Miles to go before I sleep," I muttered. Throwing up my invisibility spell, I plunged into the trees, bound for the top of the hill.

CHAPTER ELEVEN

Valentine—Monday morning
   Phoenix, Arizona

The reactions of his fellow agents as he stomped into the office erased any doubts Val had whether the expression on his face matched his thunderous mood.

The trip to Oklahoma had been a colossal waste of time. Worse than that, he couldn't understand *why* it had been so. The ironclad reading they'd gotten at the truck stop had turned into mushy confusion once they reached Beaver Dunes. His jaw had dropped on the side of the road as he pulled out the tracking device. Deployed, it pointed toward the center of the park for the barest moment before swinging one way, then the other, until finally settling into a slow orbit like a sped-up hour hand on a clock.

It was the mystical artifact's best approximation of a shrug.

Anjewierden, to his credit, had weathered the initial storm of his rage with a stoic expression. After Val vented his spleen, the younger agent had asked, quietly, "Need me to drive back?"

His anger bottomed out, then, only to crest after they made the return trip to the Phoenix office. He marched into the conference room his team had taken over and slammed the tracking artifact on the table.

Morgan lowered the report she was reading and offered him a single raised eyebrow.

"Check it," Val growled. "Piece of shit spazzed out on me."

"All right," Morgan agreed. She opened the container and studied the needle from several angles. With a shrug, she said, "It's fine. If you want to wait a few hours, I can dig a little deeper, but the surface enchantments remain intact."

"Explain to me, then," Val said, composing himself, "why it gave me a strong signal toward the Oklahoma nexus, but after we got there, it had *nothing*. I've seen uncertain results before, but I've never seen it spin around in circles."

She frowned. "The only way it would do that would be—" Morgan frowned, then said, "Oh, dear."

"What does that mean?"

Flipping through stacks of paper, his fellow agent didn't verbally respond, though she did lift a single index finger. Val sighed. He'd seen Morgan do this sort of thing before, and it never paid to interrupt her while she arranged her train of thought.

Several minutes passed, then she pushed herself away from the table with a pained groan. "*Mallacht Dé ort*," she spat. She trailed off into muttering even more mysteriously until Val rapped his knuckles on the conference table.

"English, Morgan."

She snapped back into focus and gave him a dirty look. "I've listened to enough of your Southern invective over the years. You can let me slide on this one." Morgan stood and leaned over her side of the table. "It's all connected."

CHAPTER 11

He pulled out a chair and sat down. With his arms crossed, he said calmly, "I'm listening."

She ticked the points off on her fingers. "Helen Locke makes her escape from prison. Her shield spell has a sigil identical to that used by the Sisterhood of Salem during the Second World War."

"Right," Val interjected. "They were a group of *volksdeutschers* from the eastern US who relocated to Germany with their families during the Depression. And they're all stone-cold dead. You know that." Unbidden, an image of fire and stone came to him, along with the metronomic echo of dozens of pairs of boots marching in precise lockstep. He didn't like to think much about the past, but it was hard to forget a frequent nightmare rerun for over seven decades.

"We don't have much information about them beforehand, but surely if they were as powerful in the United States as they were when they set up shop in Heidelberg, we'd have some record of their existence. Where'd they get their juice?"

Val sighed, wishing he'd grabbed some breakfast or at least a cup of coffee before storming in. "All we ever got was rumor and hearsay, but the common story going around was that a Nazi officer serving under Rommel found a book in the desert and sent it home. We were in 'blow shit up' mode and didn't take any time to find out."

"Right." Morgan plucked a folder from out of her collection. "We've got what's supposed to be a complete list of everything Helen Locke acquired using her position at the University of Chicago. Between us and the local police, we recovered maybe three-quarters of it." She plucked a sheet from the folder and handed it over. "Check out what I highlighted."

Val read the entry. "Book, leather-bound, Sumerian cuneiform, unknown origin." He was about to ask what the big deal was, but he cocked his head to one side. When she'd used a Division M agent to communicate with Director Newquist, Helen had told them she was trying to recover a grimoire from her son. "You think this is what she's been after all along?"

"I do, but not only that—it's not a grimoire, it's *the* grimoire. She got it on loan from the Pergamon Museum in Berlin. They have an extensive Mesopotamian collection, but this was never exhibited to the public. I sent out a few feelers but didn't get much on the record. Off the record, the museum doesn't care all that much, because they always regarded the book as a curiosity and possible late forgery."

"Why?"

"Sumerian only existed as a common written language until the first century. Paper was invented in China, thousands of miles away and two hundred years later."

"So, they transcribed it?"

"On paper that remains flexible, with a leather binding that remains intact, almost two *thousand* years later?"

"Shit," Val said. "Okay—so the grimoire made it to Berlin, then into Helen's hands. She hasn't made any *blitz soldat,* thankfully. And she used the familiar spell before getting the book back, so that's just standard-issue nasty work. What are you worried about?"

"Before, I was going to say that the only way for the tracker to react in the way you describe would be if the target was no longer in this dimension. Even if they're dead, it'll point you to the body. That sort of reaction means that she's not *here.*"

"Beaver Dunes is a nexus," Val said slowly. "But anyone unlucky enough to get caught up in it has no control over where they're going—right?"

"While you were gone, I did my rounds with the detainees. The San Diego guys are a bunch of hard-asses, but I think Detective Sikora was a little loopy on pain medicine in the hospital. He couldn't talk much before he started coughing, but I got enough."

"Smoke inhalation is tough," Val agreed. "What did he have to say?"

"Helen left them a message to pass along to her son. She wanted him to know when and where she'd be."

"So they *are* working together," Val said. "Ha!"

"I very much got the impression that this was not a friendly invitation. She wants Paxton to confront her in Randolph Forest during the Ides of March. Randolph, Maine, makes the nexus in Oklahoma look like a pinhole. It is, without exaggeration, the most malleable point on this continent. Maybe even the world."

"Why is this the first I've heard of it?" Val frowned. "I've been around as long as you have."

"No offense, but it's not exactly your department. But Division M thaumaturgy has it warded six ways from Sunday. Tighter than the White House. You haven't heard of it *because* we locked it down hard enough that we don't have to nuke the entire state. And even *that* builds on top of the work started by the Penobscot tribe and continued by the Pilgrims."

"You're not exaggerating."

"If those safeguards fell, the eastern half of the United States could be sucked into another dimension. Worse—something might come through."

"'In his house at R'lyeh, dead Cthulhu waits dreaming,'" Val quoted.

"Lovecraft was an optimist," Morgan replied with a shake of her head. "I'm not sure what the timing signifies, but at least we've got—"

A shout from outside cut her off, and a few moments later George wheeled frantically into the conference room. "I just got a call from headquarters," he gasped. "Someone just bombed the Menagerie."

CHAPTER TWELVE

Paxton—Monday morning
Leesburg, Virginia

Finding a place to hole up was easier said than done.

When I reached the crest of the hill, I turned to look back. The building over the underground prison was rectangular and utilitarian. From this vantage point, I could make out no identifying marks to give me a clue about how Division M presented themselves to the world at large.

The plume of smoke and the number of emergency vehicles in the parking lot were both large enough that I'd likely be able to find some mention of it on the Internet, at least. I moved on.

The holding facility lay in a hollow, surrounded by hills and trees. Looking out, I'd initially suspected that I was stuck in the middle of nowhere. To my surprise, I found that a subdivision of ostentatious-looking homes surrounded the building. All things considered, it was about the worst place to put a clandestine magical prison, but from Puck's attitude, I guessed my mysterious enemies didn't have to worry much about escapes.

At mid-morning, most of the homeowners were at work. Those who weren't crowded the edges of their property, gawking at the plume of smoke and gossiping with the other rare neighbor. That, at least, made it easy to ignore the occupied houses. Wrapped in invisibility, I moved on, with the gawking onlookers none the wiser.

Of the first four empty houses I checked, three had conspicuously-placed security monitoring services signs and the other had a doghouse. Maintaining the cloaking spell was starting to wear on me, and I grew more and more frantic with every passing moment.

I jogged across a suburban street after I waited for a slowly-moving car to pass in front of me. Yielding the right of way gave me the opportunity to check the license plate, at least. It seemed that I was in Virginia if the car was local. I tried to consider how long I'd been in the plane, but the drugs had thrown off my judgment of time. It didn't feel like I'd been in the air all that long, but then again, I'd been unconscious for most of it.

Three streets over, I struck pay dirt. The house was the same design as every other home in the area, but the grass was a little bit too long, and two rolled-up newspapers lay on the front porch. Forcing myself to be patient, I did a slow circuit of the home. Seeing no visible signs of an alarm system or dog doors, I went for broke. I walked up onto the porch, did a quick scan behind me to make sure there was no one in sight, and dropped the cloak. Just as suddenly, I went out of phase and stepped inside.

It's a pain, not being able to use two spells at the same time. But in the grand scheme of things, it's a minor issue. Even if someone *had* seen me, would they raise an alarm? Or pass it off as a figment of their imagination? In my experience, people are more than willing to lie themselves into acceptance of any number of weird things.

In the daytime, at least. Once the sun goes down, the lies are harder to swallow.

Back in phase, I kept my footsteps light as I advanced through the foyer. The drapes throughout open throughout, providing a good bit of light, but also creating a concern. I'd need to be careful moving through the house, lest some neighborhood busybody spot me.

Someone had arranged newspapers and a pile of mail on a side table. I flipped through the envelopes and noted that the mailing address was in Leesburg, Virginia. Score one for license plate poker. There was also a week's worth of postmarks. Jack and Nora Davis, who I assumed were the homeowners, had been gone for a while, and it had been a few days since anyone had checked their mail for them.

It would be my luck that their house sitter might stop by at any moment, but that just lent more of a sense of urgency to my movements. I did a quick walk-through of the house to make sure I was alone, though I didn't bother with the second floor. If anyone moved up there, I'd hear it long before they'd be in a position to see me. The stairs descended into the foyer in view of the living room, and there was little of interest to me in either place.

The kitchen was at the back of the house. I told myself before I opened the refrigerator that they'd probably cleaned it out before leaving, but I couldn't help but feel disappointment at the empty shelves. A couple twenty-ounce bottles of Mountain Dew hung out in with the ketchup, mustard, and mayo on the inside of the door. I pulled them out and toasted the air after guzzling a good bit of the first bottle. "You're a true connoisseur, Jack."

The cabinets were more promising, and I assembled a smorgasbord of crackers, peanut butter, a few granola bars, and a box of Cheerios wobbling on the threshold of going stale. It wasn't what I'd hoped I might find, but beggars—or thieves—couldn't be choosers.

Forcing myself to chew slowly, I took inventory. I'd regained my magic, at least—without it, I was an easy target. As far as physical possessions went, I didn't have much. A pair of sneakers, khakis, a plain gray T-shirt, and a long-sleeved button down. That was just about right for Phoenix in November, but in my quick trek outside, I'd been more than a little chilly. Then there was the fact that everything was grimy and a little gross. I'd get suspicious side-eye from the staff of any stores I walked into.

Which was a problem in and of itself, since I no longer had a wallet. No ID, no credit or ATM card, no cash. *Shit.*

Meal complete, I bundled up the trash as neatly as I could, jamming the granola bar wrappers and an empty cracker sleeve into an empty soda bottle. I'd sipped the second more slowly, but it was nearly empty as well, and I left it out while I put the jar of peanut butter and the other boxes back where I'd found them. Other than a few crumbs on the kitchen island, there was little overt evidence of my passing. I brushed the crumbs into the sink and called it good.

Stomach full, sugar and starch singing in my bloodstream, I cast an appraising eye toward the ceiling.

I didn't feel like I had time to do a load of laundry, but if I was quick about it, surely I could get a shower. If Jack was close enough to my size, maybe I could even get a fresh set of clothes, too.

Pushing down a nagging sense of guilt, I pulled a spare trash bag from under the sink, finished the last Mountain Dew, and headed upstairs.

The layout of the second story was simple. The master bedroom sat at the rear of the house, over the kitchen. Smaller bedrooms flanked the stairs. Washington Nationals memorabilia filled the room on the left, and a massive television set across from a pair of recliners. The opposite room was more understated, frilly almost—a small sofa, bookshelves, and a desk with an all-in-one computer. His and her caves, I guessed. I headed for the master.

The same taste evident in the woman-cave continued into the bedroom. The king-sized, four-poster bed bore a heavy burden of pillows and a patterned comforter. Framed photographs lined the walls. Jack and Nora didn't look that much older from Cassie and I. They glowed with happiness in the pictures, and from the looks of things they were the sort to spend their vacations outside doing things rather than relaxing. In one photo they posed in ski gear, another, scuba masks.

I saluted the photo closest to the attached bathroom. "Thanks for the hospitality, folks. I'll pay you back, someday."

Picking through the closet, I found that Jack and I shared a waist and inseam, but his outdoorsy lifestyle had blessed him with a serious upper body. His shirts would all be baggy on me. Tucked in and layered up, it wouldn't be a big deal.

My own clothes went into the trash bag, while I was careful to take the more casual clothing showing wear. Hopefully, I wasn't stealing Jack's lucky hockey shirt or anything. Naked, I carried both loads into the bathroom. After hemming and hawing whether to leave the door open, I finally just went with it.

Living out of an RV, bathing usually consisted of a quick shower in the miniature built-in stall. Every so often I'd use the rental stalls at truck stops, just to stand up straight and take more time to enjoy the hot water. Here and now, I split the difference. I lathered up nearly as fast as I did in the RV, but I took a few minutes to let the hot water beat down on my head and blast away some of the accumulated funk.

It wasn't as relaxing as it should have been. I kept imagining shouts from below over the spray of the water. Once, certain I'd heard something, I cut off the water and listened intently.

I remained alone in the house.

Look at it this way. Surely the house sitter has a job. Why would she come over at—I checked. *Ten in the morning? That's it?*

"Wow," I said to myself. The way the day had started, it wouldn't have surprised me if it had been closer to noon. Time might fly when you're having fun, but it crawled under intense pressure.

Wiping the condensation from the mirror, I took a look at myself. My hair went bone-white the same night Mother killed my father, and I keep it cut short enough that it didn't need much in the way of maintenance. Other than the color, it looked fine. The dark stubble on my face was another thing entirely, and with a little guilt, I dug around in the drawers and medicine cabinet until I found a razor.

I had to laugh at the image of myself shaving with a bright-pink razor, but Jack seemed to be the electric shaver type, and he'd taken it with him. My eyes kept going back to my hair, and when I realized why, I bit back a curse.

Surely this mysterious agency would try to enlist the help of police around the country. Any description of distinguishing features would include my young age and incongruous hair.

I dug through the cabinets again, but the rich black hair Jack demonstrated in his family photos was all-natural. However you sliced it, the dude had hit the lottery of life.

"Something else to take care of," I muttered with a shrug. Personal hygiene attended to, I relaxed and pulled on the clothes from Jack's closet. As I'd figured, the shirt was loose, but not by much. Tucked in and covered up by a baggy hooded sweatshirt, I no longer looked like a homeless person.

The bed was a tempting sight, but I shook my head and forced myself to leave the master. Sleeping uninvited in a couple's private bedroom seemed like more of a line to cross than stealing food and clothing.

Secure for the moment, I wandered into the room with the computer on the desk. I needed to get back to Phoenix. Without an RV or even my motorcycle, my only real option was to fly. I considered stealing a car, but that posed its own set of problems. With no money, how would I get gas? Then there was my lack of a license, the possibility of a manhunt by this Division M, traffic cameras, and any number of complications.

As lousy as my last flight had been, another one was my best option. Crossing my fingers, I found the power button on the computer and waited for it to wake from sleep. A wallpaper of a kitten clutching a tree branch with the caption 'Hang in There!' greeted me on the desktop. "Bless your trusting soul, Nora," I said as I opened up the Internet browser. I'd feared a password, but with an open system, I could do a bit of planning before heading on.

That bit of luck seemed to use up my supply. I figured my best chance for slipping onto a flight unnoticed was later at night when there should be fewer people on the plane. The last flight out of Dulles en route to Phoenix left before six in the evening. Not only was that too early, the trip was also over five hours long. That was a great deal faster than driving it, but that was a *long* time to keep up the deception. I wouldn't be able to hold the invisibility spell for that long, and if I happened to nod off, I didn't know if I'd maintain it. That was something that bore experimentation, but something told me that sleeping would be a pretty effective off switch.

I could *push* any of the flight crew or fellow passengers who found something amiss, but that wholesale abuse of power was the kind of thing I was trying to *stop*. It struck me as the sort of thing Mother would do, and logical or not, that automatically made me bristle at the thought.

Of course, that all depended on getting to the airport. Jack and Nora's house was, according to Google Maps, only a twenty-minute drive to the airport. Tracing the route with my finger, I determined that there was no easy way to walk to it with a couple of major freeways between me and Dulles.

"What a pain in the ass," I muttered. I closed my eyes and rubbed my forehead. Like it or not, I was going to have to get a ride, which meant I'd have to use the *push*. "Magic book four inches thick. Do you learn how to fly or teleport? No, you had to talk to ghosts. Idiot."

Closing my browser windows, I put the computer back to sleep. With my immediate needs met, I sat in the chair and stared off into space, unsure what my next step should be. Finally, I stood and moved to the window. Peeking through the curtains, I looked up and down the street. There were hardly any cars in sight—if their neighbors were anything like the couple that owned this home, I imagined they were all at work. Short of going door-to-door in search of a stay-at-home mom, I didn't have much choice other than to wait. When I saw cars trickling back into the neighborhood, I could keep an eye out for men or women who lived alone. If I had to *push* someone to give me a ride, I'd rather not have to mess with an entire family.

I debated calling a cab or an Uber, but that sort of thing left an electronic trail, even if I used my magic to get out of paying. Would my former captors be keeping an eye on that sort of thing, to try and track me down? This house was close enough to the holding facility for me to see that the plume of smoke was gone. If the fire department had completed their job, someone was presumably combing through the wreckage, and if Stocker hadn't told them I'd gotten out yet, they'd learn sooner or later.

With no plans coming to mind other than waiting, I gave Nora's small sofa an appraising glance. It had about eight pillows too many, but after I kicked my shoes off and moved the excess to the floor, it was the most comfortable place I'd rested since the last night at Kent's house.

Telling myself to keep listening for the house sitter, I closed my eyes and promptly forgot about the reminder as I drifted off.

CHAPTER THIRTEEN

Aleister—Monday evening
 Washington Dulles International Airport

THE BLOKE IN THE SUIT MOVED WITH TOO MUCH CARE TO BE completely sober. When he plopped into the seat next to Knight outside the terminal gate, the slight slur of his speech confirmed that assessment. "Going or coming?"

He considered ignoring the guy, but drunks were like puppy dogs—they tended to not want to leave you alone absent a strong reminder. The last thing he wanted to was garner attention from TSA by sucker-punching a drunk, so Knight gritted his teeth and played along, "Headed home."

"Ah, a Brit! Headed over for a conference, myself. What were you up to in the States?"

"Business trip," he said, a curt dismissal. The other man did not take his hint.

"Things go well?"

CHAPTER 13

Despite himself, Knight smiled broadly. "Oh, you could say that."

"Stellar," the American slurred. "What are you in? Wait, don't tell me." He made a show of looking Aleister up and down. Knight had worried about bringing his walking stick through security, but he needn't have bothered—every one of the personnel checking passengers at the metal detectors had treated him with kid gloves, assuming he was handicapped. The drunk stared at the stone sphere topping the cane, blinked, and snapped his fingers. "I've got it! Antiques."

"You have me," Aleister said with a smirk. "I am known to acquire the odd thing, here and there."

"I'm in consulting," the other man said. "But in the end, it's all about reading people—taking their measure, knowing what they're looking for. Take antiques, for example. You need to know the best way to negotiate with whomever you're dealing with. Some people want to haggle, others don't want their time wasted."

"I'm definitely in the latter category," Aleister said, but the drunk didn't pick up on the subtext.

"Let me give you my card." The other man fumbled through the inside pockets of his suit jacket. "Location, business field—it's all about the people. Give me a chance, I can save fifteen percent in the first year. That's over and above my commission."

"It's a rather specialized realm," he demurred. "I'm established, and not interested."

"Hey, man, don't kid a kidder. Everyone's interested in saving money." The drunk shoved his card into Aleister's hand. "You can't afford *not* to work with me, friend."

Static crackled and the gate attendant spoke. "At this time, we'd like to begin boarding our first-class passengers aboard British Airways flight 216 with service to London Heathrow."

"That's my call," Knight said. "Some other time, perhaps."

"Ah, we have time. Five minutes, that's all I'm asking."

Knight pushed his annoyance and impatience into a ball, then reached out and shook the other man's hand. "Thank you, no." Power surged through the skin contact, and the drunk yelped, pulling his hand away.

"What the hell?"

"Static electricity, I'm sure."

"Yeah, maybe. I—" The other man winced, then clutched his stomach. He was, Aleister knew, currently in the throes of some severe stomach cramping. It wasn't the most powerful spell in his arsenal, but it was an effective one. "Oh, man." The consultant shifted in his seat, and a wet sound followed as the cramps led to something—*embarrassing*.

He'd been using magic for over six hundred years. Juvenile or not, the aftereffects of the enchantment never failed to amuse Aleister. "Seems as though you should hit the head before takeoff. On your bike, now."

The other man didn't answer, but he rose and rushed away toward the head. Based on the typical length of the spell's effect, the drunk was about to miss his flight.

"Which should make things right peaceful." He crumpled the business card and tossed it in a nearby bin. Rising from his own seat, Aleister threw the strap of his carry-on over one shoulder, turned to head to the gate—and froze.

For those of a mystical bent, hunches and insight often expressed themselves in less abstract ways than those lacking power. Depending on the power level, Aleister often knew at a glance if a fellow practitioner was worthy of respect or disdain.

Walking into Walter's shop in San Francisco a few nights back, every hair on his body had stood on end from the presence of Helen and her coven. Just being in the same room as Liliana gave him a twitchy feeling.

Here and now? He felt as though someone had walked over his grave. His palms were suddenly damp and his stomach clenched.

CHAPTER 13

Frowning, he looked up and down the concourse, but saw nothing of interest. *Sodding fool*, he told himself. *You're going soft in the head.*

Even so, he kept glancing over his shoulder until he was safe and secure in the belly of the plane.

PAXTON—MONDAY EVENING

Washington Dulles International Airport

The sound of the front door opening woke me up. As I blinked my eyes at the shadows on the wall, my heart went into panic mode. *How long have I been asleep? Am I too late?*

An analog clock on the wall informed me that it was after two in the afternoon. I hadn't missed the flight, but the house sitter I'd worried about had just shown up. Wrapped in my invisibility spell, I eased out to the landing. I hadn't noticed the floors creeping underfoot in my time upstairs, but better safe than sorry.

The woman unloading an armful of mail onto the side table by the door had a bit of a familial resemblance to Nora—an older sister, maybe. I stared at the open door, waiting for a voice from outside or something else to throw a wrench into the outrageous plan that popped into my head.

The chance of success wasn't the part that made me hesitate. Magic in the equation meant that my crazy idea would work. That didn't mean that it was the *right* thing to do.

The *push* was the power I'd had the longest. It was also the one I feared above all others and used least of all. Maybe I was naive at sixteen, but once I realized the sheer destructive potential of being able to control others, I swore to myself that I'd never abuse my gifts. When in doubt, follow the tao of Spider-Man— with great power there must also come great responsibility. All temptations aside, I'd stuck to my guns for a decade. And now I was about to throw it away for a ride to the airport.

I didn't have much time. The house sitter's hands were empty, and she turned back to the open door. Decision made, I dropped the invisibility and stepped forward before she could walk out of the house.

"Close the door," I *pushed*, "and don't scream."

She followed the mystical instructions, though she turned to stare up at me after doing so, face pale. The command not to scream didn't prevent her from asking, in a quavering voice, "Who are you?"

Shame coursed through me, and I hesitated. I'd crossed a dark line, but that didn't mean that I had to keep going. As awful as what I'd done was, I had an opportunity to ease the damage rather than make it worse. That didn't make the action any better from a moral standpoint, but it was something I could focus on the next time I tried to sleep.

"I'm Paxton," I said, then *pushed* again. "I'm not going to hurt you. I'm a good person in a bad spot, and I desperately need your help." That, at least, wasn't all that different from times I'd used the *push* before to calm frightened homeowners and assure them that yeah, I really was there to help them with their haunting problem.

It was funny to think that I'd much rather be out making house calls, again. I'd thought dealing with ghosts was bad. It wasn't nearly as nerve-wracking as this hero stuff.

She blinked a couple of times, then smiled. The magic convinced her, utterly and totally, that I was telling the truth. And that was the sneaky, seductive part about the *push*, in the end. You could make anyone into whatever you wanted them to be with a few words—a friend, a lover, a slave. You could command them to stand still while you plunged a knife into them, over and over, and they'd do it. Screaming inside all the while, and venting unheard impotent terror. On the outside, at least, she looked curious and intrigued. "Oh, my. And here I was thinking this day was going to be boring."

I hoped that the person inside her agreed, and it wasn't prose borne of magic.

Somehow, her smile helped. And, over the next few hours, as I gave her the bare bones of what was going on and what I needed from her, I couldn't help but wonder if it hadn't been more than a little genuine.

Nina was, yes, Nora's older sister. A freelance software developer, she worked from home, or whatever place drew her fancy at the moment that had a usable Internet connection. It was the sort of vagabond lifestyle I could appreciate.

Now, less than an hour before the flight to Phoenix was scheduled to leave, we sat in her car at an off-site parking lot intended for those coming to pick up arrivals who didn't want to pay a parking fee. I'd been a nervous wreck for the entire drive. On the bright side, that wasn't because I was afraid of anyone recognizing me. I was antsy because of the strange feeling on my scalp. The hair dye Nina had fetched at a nearby pharmacy was dry, but I still had to keep telling myself not to test it lest I invite scrutiny.

"Are you sure I can't drop you off at the terminal?"

I glanced at Nina. "This is fine," I said. "I can find somewhere to go invisible between here and there where no one will see. If I do it right at curbside check-in, someone's bound to notice."

She grinned. "It's been interesting, Paxton Locke."

"For what it's worth, I'm sorry. I don't like laying the whammy on people like that, but I was desperate." I paused for a second, then said, "If you want, I can make you forget that I was there." It was doubling down on a wrong that had thankfully turned out right, but the least I could do was offer.

"No, I want to remember. I was afraid, at first, but you're right. You're one of the good guys. If you hadn't put a spell on me from the beginning, I'd have thought you were crazy, but I've got all the proof I need, don't I?"

I considered that for a moment, then shook my head. "The worst part is, this isn't the strangest conversation I've had today. Thanks again, Nina."

"Wait!" She reached into her purse and pulled out some bills folded over a business card. "It seems strange, but—let me know how things go."

"I can't take your money," I protested.

"Pay me back after you rescue your girlfriend and clear your name."

I tried not to laugh. "You realize that if I don't stop my mother, it's likely going to be catastrophic, right?"

"Then it's a win-win. You save the day, I get my money back. If you don't, it doesn't matter, anyway."

Marveling at her optimism, all I could say as I pocketed her money and her card was, "Sounds like a deal. I'll do my best."

I cut across a couple of long-term lots and headed for the main terminal. The air was crisp with cold and alive with the rumbling vibration of jetliners taking off and touching down. It all lent strange energy to the air—nothing magic, but rather a sense of a great machine with a singular, momentous purpose. You didn't get that sort of feeling on the open road, but then, you couldn't haul the sort of arsenal I'd kept in my RV in a suitcase, either.

In a dark corner of a parking garage, I went invisible, then joined a line of pedestrians walking across the shuttle and drop-off lanes. After all my trepidation and concern, my goal was in grasp, and I was mere moments away from taking step one in my rough plan to fix everything.

I didn't fly much, but Dulles looked more worn-down than I'd expected. Forgetting my spell, I stood and stared in front of the automatic doors and nearly blew the entire thing. A rushing man in a business suit nearly bowled me over. As I scrambled out of the way of traffic, I couldn't help but notice the confused look on his face as he tried to figure out what he'd run into. Thankfully, that didn't last long, and he planted his cell phone against his ear and resumed his march toward ticketing.

I need a new phone, at some point. For now, there was no purpose in doing anything about it, so I filed the thought away and got my bearings. Not having to worry about checking in saved me time. I found the gate number for the flight to Phoenix and headed that way.

The security checkpoint was more daunting than I'd expected. Even this late in the evening, a line of passengers snaked back and forth, waiting to pass through the inspection stations. I pressed my back against the wall and studied the angles, trying to figure out where the best point to go through was. There were broad gaps on either side of the x-ray machines for luggage, but getting to them was the hard part. If there were fewer people in line, I could just duck under the straps, but I had to slide along the wall. A family with young children and a stroller forced me to pause and back up, as they came close enough to the wall to effectively block it off to me. The vast majority of the other passengers seemed to be people traveling alone, though, and I made it to the point of the line closest to the checkpoints and ducked under the flexible strap.

This part was a lot easier. I waited for the TSA agents working this side to step out to wand a passenger, then stepped through their workspace and into the terminal beyond.

I'd held the invisibility spell for a while, and my hands shook. Forcing myself to keep my pace at a brisk walk, I tried to ignore the fatigue. The flow of passengers in this part of the terminal was light enough that the squeak of my sneakers on the floor would seem out of place, and I wasn't exactly equipped to answer any official questions.

Ducking into a bathroom, I did a quick scan to make sure I was out of sight, then dropped the spell. The only thing I had to worry about now was some eagle-eyed security person manning the closed-circuit cameras. Would they question seeing me walk out of the bathroom without walking in, or just let it go?

I was banking on the latter. Shoving my hands into the pockets of my sweatshirt, I walked out of the bathroom and headed down the concourse. After spending the last nerve-wracking fifteen minutes trying to be sneaky, strolling as though I didn't have a care in the world was a hard task.

That act became more difficult as I realized I didn't have a bag. Would any of my fellow passengers or security notice my lack of a carry-on? I glanced around as I took the stairs down to the underground tram to my gate and relaxed. Everyone around me was more focused on their phones or travel companions than they were on me. *Act casual—if you don't give anyone a reason to pay attention to you, they won't.*

I was tempted to whistle, but I refrained. Best to remain unremarkable, a gray everyman in a sea of those with far more important things on their minds. In a way, that was almost as good as an invisibility spell.

Forgoing a seat, I clutched a vertical rail and held on as the

CHAPTER 13

tram whizzed through an underground tunnel. My stop was second to last, which gave me plenty of time to watch the passengers who departed and those who replaced them after the first stop. A hum of conversation filled the tram, in more than one language, and I continued to relax, secure in my cloak of anonymity.

As the train stopped at the terminal before my stop, every hair on my body stood on end. I fought the urge to shiver, and my knuckles turned white on the rail as I tried to look around to see the source of the sensation. I'd felt something similar before, in the presence of ghosts, but this far surpassed any mystical alarm I'd ever experienced. It took everything I had to remain still, and when the train accelerated away from the second terminal, the tingle on my skin vanished.

Maybe, I smiled to myself, *the airport is haunted. It wouldn't be the strangest thing I've ever run into.*

Joining the stream of travelers, I rode an escalator back up to ground level and strolled toward my gate to do a walk-by. I was happy to note that the waiting area at the gate was less than half-full—if that luck held, I had a fair shot at finding an open seat, or even an entire row of them.

With time to kill, I kept walking. There were several restaurants and shops along the concourse, and I decided to grab a burger and fries. Framed magazine covers of all the regional awards they'd won decorated the place alongside sacks of potatoes for their fresh-cut fries. The price stung, and took a chunk out of the cash I'd taken from Nina—*borrowed,* I told myself firmly—but it was a pretty damn good sandwich. I ended up feeling, if anything, a little stuffed.

The wait for my meal hadn't been too bad, and I headed back toward the gate, looking for blind spots along the way. An empty gate held potential, though a couple of college-aged kids had plugged their laptops into the outlets in the wall. I nodded to them in greeting as I walked up to the windows, pretending to be studying the runway. From the beeps and buzzes, they were too involved in some sort of computer game to pay me any mind. I couldn't help but shake my head at their obliviousness.

It worked for me, though. I put my back to the window, checked to make sure no one was looking at me, then went invisible.

If I'd thought getting through security was nerve-wracking, waiting for an opportunity to get on the plane was even worse. If I went too soon, there was the chance I might take a ticketed seat. If I waited too long, I wouldn't be able to get on at all. Watching and trying not to make any noise, I spent the next few minutes bouncing in place as the crew at the gate began boarding the plane. The waiting area had filled up in the meantime. It seemed that I wasn't the only one who'd taken the opportunity to grab a bite. I hoped that there'd still be room on board.

I got lucky. With only a dozen passengers left to board, there was some sort of issue with the boarding pass scanner. The delay held up the line, and I slid around the gate. Heading down the jetway, I kept looking back until I was out of sight from the terminal, then dropped the spell. I'd held it nearly as long as I had when I'd crossed through security, though the food helped. I didn't feel as drained as I had before.

The flight attendant at the bottom smiled as I approached. Here was the moment of truth. If she asked me for a boarding pass, I was going to have to resort to the *push*. Bracing myself, I smiled, myself and said, "Good evening."

"Good evening to you, too, sir," she said, then waved me on.

I tried not to sigh in relief. The assumption on her part was obvious—if I'd gone through the gate, the other crew had scanned my boarding pass. It went to show that if you acted as though you belonged, most people were going to believe that you did.

Fake it till you make it.

CHAPTER 13

I made my way down the aisle. The delay back at the gate seemed to be over now, as other passengers were coming in behind me. I kept moving toward the rear. The row in the very back looked empty, and I crossed my fingers that it would stay that way. There were more than a few empty seats sprinkled throughout the plane, but I didn't want to chance grabbing one only to have someone come behind me and kick me out.

The flight attendant in the back was a man about my height, with a slim build and frosted tips on his close-cropped hair. As I approached, he frowned, then said, "What's your seat number?"

The nice thing about the *push* was that it wasn't necessarily the volume of my voice but the power behind the words. Under my breath, I said, "I'm supposed to be here, relax."

His shoulders came down and he smiled and backed up a bit.

"Is anyone sitting there?" I pointed to the back row.

The flight attendant checked his clipboard. "You're in luck, this row is empty." Looking back up, he cocked his head to one side. "Everything all right? Usually, people hate sitting in the back. If there's a problem with your seat, I'll be happy to help."

"I just want to stretch out," I said, and it wasn't entirely a lie. "It's been a long day."

"As long as the fasten seat belt sign is off," he said, winking.

My grin was genuine. I'd tortured myself with visions of robotic, mind-controlled flight attendants, of having to *push* everyone on board to forget me, but things were going far smoother than I'd expected. "I would never," I replied.

"Blanket and a pillow?"

"Please," I said. Sliding over to the window seat, I flipped the armrests up and tried to get comfortable. A bulky, balding man in a business suit occupied the seat in front of me, and he already had it cranked so far back that the magazine pouch brushed my knees. He turned and stared when my legs hit his seat.

"Somebody gets sick in the bathroom, you'll regret sitting here.

The only reason I am is that my company's too damn cheap to let me fly any other airline."

"I'm not too worried," I said. "My nose is a little stopped up and I'll probably sleep most of the way."

Disinterested in further conversation, he grunted and turned back to his laptop.

After the delivery of the promised pillow and blanket, the thunderous beating of my heart slowed to something more normal. I was still a little on edge, but the little milestones in the journey ratcheted me down a notch as each passed. The flight attendants sealed the cabin doors, the ground crew towed us from the gate, and the captain's smooth voice filled the air, punctuated with beeps and tones.

By the time the takeoff acceleration pushed me back into my seat, I relaxed enough to jam the pillow between my ear and the bulkhead. Closing my eyes, I fell into a deep, dreamless sleep.

CHAPTER FOURTEEN

VALENTINE—MONDAY EVENING
Joint Base Andrews, Maryland

A lone agent waited as Val, George, and Morgan descended the cargo plane's ramp. The streaks of dust on his rumpled suit combined with the fact that he didn't recognize the other man doubled down on the bad feeling he'd had in the pit of his stomach since they left Phoenix.

"Agent Dylan Prather, sirs. And ma'am." Val's sense of age wasn't always the best, but the other man looked to be in his early thirties, with a tall, wiry build.

He stuck his hand out, and Val shook it automatically. "What department are you in, Junior?"

Prather bristled at the nickname, but Val didn't particularly give a shit. *Everyone* he worked with was a damn kid save for maybe Morgan. "Assistant director of the southeast region. Came aboard from Jacksonville PD six years ago."

"That explains it," Val said with a shrug. Under the circumstances, he couldn't find it in himself to force a smile. "I try to stay out of the heat and humidity as much as possible."

"How bad is it, Agent Prather?" George interjected.

"Pretty bad." His shoulders sagged. "Do we want to talk about this here?"

"Talk as we walk," Val ordered. "Take us to the car."

"Right." Turning to lead the way, Dylan continued, "Director Newquist is in the ICU." Lights flashed on a black Chevy Suburban as he unlocked the doors using the fob. Glancing nervously back at George, he pulled open the rear passenger door. "Can I help you get in—"

"I'm fine," the bald agent growled. He wheeled up to the SUV, stretched for the grab handle, and pulled himself inside. "Put the chair in the back, rookie."

"I'm not a—"

"Just go with it," Morgan interjected, stepping around to take the front passenger seat. "It's all relative."

Val pulled open the cargo hatch and waited while Agent Prather struggled with the collapsing latches on George's wheelchair. Once he figured them out and got the chair down to a more stowable configuration, he murmured, "How bad off is the Director?"

"It's touch and go. A good chunk of the building collapsed. It looks like his detail got him under a conference table in time, but enough debris hit it to buckle it down on top of him." Agent Prather looked down at his hands, and Val realized they were as dirty as his suit. Comparative newcomer or not, he'd apparently been digging his fellow agents out on the scene. The kid rubbed at one spot but did little more than smear it around to make an even bigger mess. "I've seen worse in my time—but not by much."

Val winced. "Jimmy and Kyle?" He had a strange relationship with the former Army Rangers assigned to protect the Director. He respected their abilities; they regarded him as a threat with the potential to go off at any given moment.

Well, they weren't wrong.

CHAPTER 14

"Didn't make it."

"Damn it." Val followed the other agent around to the driver's side and took the seat next to George. "What happened?"

"We're still trying to figure out how she did it, but someone set off a pretty serious bomb in the vault." The Suburban's tired chirped on the tarmac as Prather gave it some gas, heading for the exit.

"She?" Morgan echoed.

"Kristin Hughes, she is—or was, rather—in operations for the annex. We've got her walking into the vault and—" Prather gulped. "I don't understand what I saw, to be honest."

"Use your words," George growled. "You don't need to understand it to describe it."

Prather flushed and gave the other agent a dirty look in the mirror. "Kristin was maybe five-six. A little extra weight, but a looker." He cringed. "Sorry, Agent Laffer."

Morgan's tone was as dry as the desert they'd just left. "I'm familiar with the male propensity to think with the lower head, Agent. Do continue."

"She walks into the lab, and Dr. Schantz and Agent Menard look like someone hit them with a baseball bat. You'd have thought Kate Upton walked in. They talk for a bit, then she reached out and broke the doc's neck with her bare hands. After that, Agent Menard helped her open the vault. She took something and left him there. A little bit after that, whatever she brought in exploded and took out the cameras."

"On the bright side, the dangerous stuff is in off-site storage," Val sighed, thinking back to the truck stop. "Morgan? What do you think?"

"I've got a few ideas, and none of them are good."

"Doppelganger?" George wondered.

"I was thinking succubus. Pheromones would explain the behavior Agent Prather describes, and doppelgangers have human-normal strength. Did we send anyone to Agent Hughes' house? A succubus would eat any evidence of foul play, but there'd still be blood and signs of a struggle."

"We've got most of our manpower digging through the rubble looking for survivors and keeping the FBI from shouldering their way onto the site."

"They don't have jurisdiction, it's our facility," Val exclaimed. "What's their excuse?"

"Joint Terrorism Task Force," Prather explained. "And we don't have any senior-level agents around to play bureaucratic games with them, so we've been stalling."

"Good Lord. Were the casualties that bad?" Morgan whispered."

"The initial task force meeting was this morning," Val said, with dawning horror. "Russ said something about having all hands on deck." He closed his eyes for a moment to compose himself. "Who's next in line?"

Prather shook his head. "The timing couldn't have been worse. The only regional SAC to make it out was Carter, from Seattle, and he's in the ICU, too. With him out of the way, well—Agent Laffer, if we're going by seniority." He had the good grace to look embarrassed. "No offense, Agent."

Morgan smirked. "I'm too old to be bothered by mentions of it, kid. But I'm just a team leader. This is war, now. We need someone with a little more gusto."

As one, everyone save Prather turned to George. "General?" Val said.

The other man scowled. "You want something blown up, I'm your man. I'll lead the boys in the field all day long. But quit dodging it, Valentine. You're up to bat." He shook his head with a crooked smile. "You'd have been running this show years ago if you didn't prefer fieldwork."

There was more to it than that, of course. The one thing that men like Newquist and all those who had come before him had in common was diplomacy. It wasn't so much that Val couldn't turn on the charm and schmooze his way through any situation. He was a Southerner; that sort of thing came with the territory. It was the fact that after doing this for so long, the various iterations were so damn predictable. *I'm one hundred and sixty-seven years old, and if I've seen a dozen bureaucrats stymie our core mission for their own personal fiefdoms, I've seen fifty.* This wasn't a situation for diplomacy or negotiation. Right now, Val didn't give two shits about jurisdiction. When they found out who was responsible for this incident, every resource Division M could bring to bear was in play to rectify the issue. To hell with the consequences.

"I'll take care of the FBI," he said, bowing to the inevitable. Then, with dawning horror, he said, "What about the holding facility? Did we do a head count?"

Prather nodded. "It didn't go well. We lost most of the subjects. A few survived, and we had two escapes. We've got a team looking for the escapees now, but they're short-handed."

Val closed his eyes and tried not to curse. "Who escaped?"

"The pukwudgie and Paxton Locke. We've kind of given up finding the puck, the damn things are impossible to see even in the daylight, but surely we'll be able to—" Prather caught the look on Val's face and fell silent.

"No," he said through gritted teeth. "You won't be able to find him, not now."

"What's our priority, boss?" Morgan asked.

He considered it for a moment, then shrugged. "Pull the search team back. Paxton Locke's on the back-burner for now. We need to track down our bomber and figure out what we're going to do about Randolph. Unless I miss my guess, the kid will turn up right on time to be a pain in my ass."

CHAPTER FIFTEEN

P AXTON—M ONDAY EVENING
Sky Harbor International Airport

After the nerve-wracking experience of getting *into* an airport, getting off the plane and heading for the exit of the airport in Phoenix was relaxing in comparison. Not having to concern myself with lost or missing luggage was a big part of that, of course, but I'd also been nervously anticipating what awaited me at the top of the jetway.

Visions of hard-faced government agents in dark suits waiting to take me into custody kept chasing me out of my sleep. The third time I jerked awake, I gave up and flipped through a SkyMall catalog. I didn't pay much attention to the assortment of gadgets, but it gave my hands something to do while I ordered my thoughts.

My worries turned out to be for naught—as I walked through the airport, I didn't see much of anything except other passengers rushing toward the exits or awaiting their turn in the air.

Now that I had both feet on the ground, I stewed over the fact that I had no knowledge of the situation on the ground. I glanced

CHAPTER 15

at television screens as I walked by them, half-expecting to see a picture of myself.

The death of Donald Thibodeau at my hands and the flight of the shadow demon Tlaloc had broken the hold they'd held over their cultists and the leadership of the Phoenix police department. I had no way of knowing how much the survivors remembered if anything. Either way, I doubted that the precarious position Kent had put himself into by bringing me out to help in his investigation persisted after the fact. The cultists hadn't appreciated my intrusion into their territory and had threatened my friend's career in an attempt to get me to back off.

The question was, how would Division M treat someone who was, ostensibly, a fellow law enforcement officer? After everything I'd seen in DC, I doubted they'd go for cooperation. Based on my treatment, Kent's relationship with me would tar him with the same brush.

In the end, it only mattered to the extent of finding my friends. I hadn't been an official consultant, and given that the incident in Sikora's neighborhood was only tangentially connected to the kidnapped boys I'd helped bring to safety, my help there wouldn't get me far.

On the flight, I'd come to the conclusion that my first step needed to be Kent and Jean's house. I knew Mother had taken Cassie, but the status of the Sikoras, Father Rosado, and the De La Rosa brothers remained a mystery.

Getting there, of course, was the fun part. Phoenix might not have had the traffic congestion of DC, but it sneered at the nation's capital when it came to urban sprawl. Kent's house on the far north side was over forty miles from the airport. I considered the cash remaining in my pockets and knew a cab was out of the question. Even if I could afford one, I wasn't sure it was a good idea. Would the agency pursuing me stake out possible places of interest? In their shoes, I would. I was also pretty sure that taxi companies kept records of fares, even when they paid cash. In this day and age, that might invite even more scrutiny than I'd like.

It's a good thing your hair's already white or paranoia would take care of that. I smiled at my reflection in the big windows near the baggage claim and tried not to shake my head.

With my limited budget, public transit was the way to go—even if the bus route stopped well-short of my eventual destination. If it came down to it, I'd walk. Given the proximity to the interstate, I thought that I might be able to hitch a ride, especially if it was only a few exits north. *No push*, I told myself. I'd escaped from prison and crossed three-quarters of the country. It was time to take myself out of desperation mode.

Outside the terminal, I fed some of my dwindling supply of bills into a machine and bought a transit card. Bit by bit, I was replacing the lost vestiges of my modern, first-world lifestyle, though this was a smaller step than most, to be sure.

All things considered, I'd much rather have a set of car keys. Or a credit card.

The buses came frequently enough, every twenty minutes or so, that I didn't have to wait long after I figured out the route I needed to take. I'd ride west for the first leg, then take the 19th Avenue bus north to Happy Valley Road, parallel to I-17 the whole way. I hoped my final stop would be a good omen.

The crowd on the bus was light, and most of the faces wore expressions of fatigue or focus. I was, I noted, one of the only people on the bus not wearing headphones or looking at sort of device. The bad part of that was that I had little to occupy myself other than my own thoughts, and after the fitful bits of rest I'd caught on the flight, it became a struggle to stay awake.

The rustle of paper caught my attention. Turning, I saw that the man on the bench behind me had occupied himself with a newspaper rather than earphones. I raised a hand to get his attention, then asked, "Mind if I take a look at the front page?"

CHAPTER 15

He shrugged, passed it over and returned to the sports section.

Unfolding the paper in my lap, I looked down and tried to keep the smile off my face. Anyone who saw a happy expression combined with the subject matter of the headline story would likely draw the wrong idea. The last thing I needed was for an offended soul to shoot my photo out into cyberspace. Hashtag: #CheckOutThisCreep.

MISSING TWINS FOUND, the headline read in bold lettering an inch tall. Below, it continued: *SWAT TEAM RAIDS REHAB FACILITY. POLICE SPOKESMAN DENIES CLAIMS OF RITUAL MURDER.*

"Deny all you want, fellas," I whispered under my breath. "Doesn't change the truth."

The photographer had framed the shot well—Evan and Ethan, stepping out of the back of an ambulance. They were grimy and hollow-cheeked, but Evan wore a huge grin and was flashing a thumbs-up to someone outside of the frame. His twin had his head down, staring at the ground with his brother's arm wrapped around his shoulders. The second boy hadn't made so much as a peep during his rescue and return from the ancient catacombs below the cult's rehab facility. Knowing that he remained haunted by unknown terrors tempered my sense of accomplishment. Yeah, they were alive, but had I gotten to them as fast as I could have?

I stared at the picture, trying to sear it into my memory. I approached life with a chip on my shoulder and more than a bit of sarcasm, but that was just a defense mechanism to keep me up and moving past the things I'd experienced. If I was going to keep at this business of being a wizard, I had to remember that not everyone could brush insanity and impossibility off. For many, it left a very a real mark. Me? I could always turn invisible and phase out of harm's way.

My stop was next, so I handed the paper over and hit the button to signal the driver. When I swung off the bus, the cooling air hit me in the face and pushed away any thoughts of sleep. Moving helped as well, and I trotted along the sidewalk to the next bus stop. Shortly thereafter, my connection came along, and I repeated the process of swiping my card and finding a seat. Much like the westbound bus, most of the passengers were in their own worlds, and that worked for me. I was going to the end of the line, so I tucked my head up against the window and closed my eyes.

The fits and starts as the bus proceeded from stop to stop took a bit to get used to, but I drifted off into a strange quasi-sleep. It was only when the bus went through a wide turn, pulling my head away from the window, that I opened my eyes. I was alone on the bus, and I met the driver's eyes in the mirror.

"End of the line unless you missed your stop," he called out, and I gave him a thumbs up as I slid out of my seat. Brakes squealed, and the doors opened with a hiss.

Exiting the bus, I felt like I'd stepped off the edge of the world. The south side of the road was well-lit, occupied with various buildings and businesses. The opposite side was empty desert scrub, undeveloped save for a Circle K gas station on the northeast corner of the intersection.

The temperature had dropped even further during my trek north, and a sudden cold wind out of the east made me shiver. I shoved my hands into the pockets of my appropriated sweatshirt and wished I'd grabbed something more substantial. It was moot now, but I mentally added a warmer change of clothes to a shopping list that had far outpaced my available resources. "Baby steps," I told myself. I headed west toward the freeway. If I remembered right, there were a couple of big box stores and a shopping center there. That would be a better place to thumb for a ride than here in the boondocks.

I'd only gone a few blocks when I heard echoing footsteps behind me. Taking a quick glance, I saw a skinny figure in a hooded sweatshirt and ratty pants. He was far enough back to not be an immediate threat, but something about his demeanor instantly raised the hair on the back of my neck. Stepping faster, I gritted my teeth as the sounds of his own movement increased. *I don't have time for this shit.*

I wheeled off the sidewalk into an empty parking lot. The festive pink stucco of the building bore murals of dogs, cats, and birds on either side of a pair of glass doors. The steel security shutters rolled down behind the entry would have made a formidable barrier for anyone but me, but I was done running. Turning around, I planted my back against the wall of what looked like a veterinary clinic and awaited my pursuer.

He hesitated at the entrance to the parking lot, looking both ways as though expecting a trick. Finally, he surged forward. I got a look at a pitted face surrounded by stringy blond hair as he moved into the halo of illumination cast by the roof-mounted security lights.

Metal clicked, and light flashed off the edge of the switchblade he pulled out of his pocket. "Empty your pockets and hand over your wallet."

"Are you serious right now?" I said. My heart thumped in my chest. Even though I knew intellectually that I was in no danger, more primal instincts screamed at me to run.

He stepped forward and raised the knife higher. "This look like a fucking joke to you?"

I pulled my own hand out of my pocket and smiled. The lighting was good, this close to the door, but it wasn't bright enough to overcome the blue lines of the force blade extending a good three feet from my balled-up fist. "Mine's bigger. And a hell of a lot nastier."

His knife hand shook, and he took two steps backward. "What the hell?"

"Stop," I *pushed*. He froze, and a look on panic spread across his features. I grimaced and resisted the urge to command any further. I stepped closer, imitating the position he'd taken earlier with his own knife. "Throw yours up on the roof," I said. I didn't put any magical command behind that, save for the implied threat of the force blade.

"Okay, okay." He leaned back and heaved. I heard metal click on the tiles, then silence as it came to rest behind the knee wall. *A little curiosity for the maintenance man to find, someday.*

Banishing the force blade, I crossed my hands over my chest. "What have we learned about mugging people?"

He blinked. "Not to, uh, do it?"

"Correct," I grinned. "Now—empty your pockets and hand over your wallet."

I got a good look at a mouthful of rotten teeth when his jaw dropped. "Are you serious?"

"Does this look like a fucking joke?" I snapped. "Pockets. Wallet. On the ground."

It took him several attempts with fumbling hands, but he eventually threw a rubber-banded roll of cash, a plastic baggie, and a Velcro wallet on the ground. Frowning, I collected it. Pocketing the cash, I held the baggie between two fingers and studied the brownish powder inside.

"What's this?"

"What do you think it is, man?" He squirmed in place. "Keep the money, just let me have the crystal." The hint of a whine seeped into his tone toward the end.

I ignored him and tore open the wallet. The driver's license picture showed Darrell Goetz in healthier, presumably non-drug abusing days. When I shifted it to take a better look, a plastic picture holder flipped over. A gap-toothed blond girl grinned at me. "This your little girl, Darrell?"

He swallowed audibly. "Yeah, that's right."

Closing the wallet, I stared at him. "You do right by her?"

"What is this?"

"Answer the damn question!" My anger frightened even me, but at the same time, part of me *liked* it, and I felt a little dizzy as I considered the rush I felt at holding power over another person. Was this what it was like for Mother? Is this what drove her to such atrocity? *Take it down a notch.*

"I try to," Darrell said, both hands out toward me. "I know I'm a mess, you think I don't know that? I stay away from her and my old lady, that's what's best for them."

I closed my eyes and tried to bring my sudden fury under control. The uncharacteristic rage boiled deep down in my gut.

When I'm not using it to create force blades, the telekinesis spell is pretty wimpy. Focusing on the raw emotion coursing through me, I pushed that into the spell, focusing on my target. The resulting effect had more than enough oomph to shatter the glass of the entry doors when I flicked my fingers. Immediately, a siren sounded from behind the roll-up shutters.

I heaved and threw the plastic bag of crystal meth out into the night. "Here's the deal, Darrell," I said. "You're going to sit here in front of the door and wait for the cops. When they show up, you're going to admit that you've been mugging people. You broke the glass to see if there were any drugs inside." The *push* had him transfixed, and I looked away. I didn't like the glazed, half-aware look in his eyes.

It was too close to what I'd seen in my dad's eyes when Mother killed him.

Taking a deep breath, I forced myself to continue. "You need help, Darrell. You're going to take whatever deal they give you, but you need to go to rehab. And when you go, you're going to go all-in. You're going to get clean, and you're never going to abuse drugs ever again." I waved the wallet in the air. "You've got a kid who needs a father. Maybe you haven't been the best in the world up until now, but you've still got time to fix that. For better or worse, you're going to be better. Got it?"

The haze went out of his eyes. He licked his lips and nodded. "Okay. Should I sit down now?"

"Sure," I said. I handed back his wallet. "Be good, man."

The cops might have ignored a lone figure walking away from a crime scene, but I didn't take the chance. As soon as I stepped out of the parking lot, I went invisible and kept moving until I heard the squeal of tires on the pavement behind me. Looking back, blue and red lights flashed on the pink stucco.

I allowed myself to smile as I watched them cuff Darrell and ease him into the back of one of the squad cars. The man who'd been ready to stab me for my wallet had a different manner about him, as though a great weight had come off his shoulders.My pledge to refrain from using the push hadn't lasted long. I couldn't decide if I should feel guilty or shrug it off. Yeah, I'd usurped another person's free will, twisting to bend to my own—but if he was better off, wasn't that a *good* thing?

The wind picked up, then, and something about the rising pitch of it reminded me of the ghostly voice of my father in the hospital after Cassie and I beat Melanie and the Edimmu. He'd warned me about regarding people as tools.

My ensuing shiver was only partly due to the chill in the air.

CHAPTER SIXTEEN

Valentine—Monday evening
   Walter Reed Army Medical Center, Maryland
   Visiting hours were long over, but if you had the credentials to access the areas of the hospital restricted to Presidents and covert agents, the nurses and security didn't get too up in arms.
   Even so, he came bearing gifts. "Lucky Luciano from the Don's, people?"
   The MP at the nurse's station raised an eyebrow. Val didn't recognize him, but the two nurses had worked the top-secret ward for a few years. He slid the top box off of the pair he carried and let it rest on the counter.
   Delia, the brunette, shook her head as she spun the pizza box around. "And it's still warm! One of these days you've got to tell me your secret route." Don's Wood-Fired Pizza was nearly thirty miles away in Sterling, but Val's only shortcut was a heavy foot and flashing lights.
   He winked and laid a finger alongside his nose. "Top secret, ladies and gentlemen. He in the usual room?"
   The redheaded nurse, Patty nodded, pulling paper plates out

from one of her desk drawers. "Being his normal cooperative self." The MP looked less dubious now, accepting a plate from the nurse. The cafeteria was pretty good, but it wasn't like a top-secret facility could order-in anything better.

Val strolled down the hallway. Only a few of the rooms had closed doors. Every room with an open door remained dark and empty. On the others, the nurses had labeled the charts and patient information with cryptic code names. The third door from the right bore the legend 'Mr. Red.' Val balanced the pizza, opened it with his other hand, and walked inside.

Eliot looked a damn sight better than he had just a few days ago. That wasn't saying much, since the fight with Helen's coven and their familiars had left him on death's door.

"Kids today," Val said in mock-complaint. "A few bumps and bruises and they just lie down and whine."

"Piss off, you old fart." Eliot wheezed as he tried not to laugh. He fumbled for the controls on the side of the bed and raised the angle so he could look the other man in the eye. "When's the last time you saw your intestines, smart guy?"

"Been a few years," he had to admit. He laid the pizza box down on the wheeled table next to the hospital bed. "Brought you a Sicilian Hit. I thought you might appreciate the irony."

"All these years, you're still not funny." His partner eyed the box with an expression serious enough to be considering the meaning of life.

"Think about it all you want," Val said. "I'm eating." He grabbed a slice and plopped down in the chair. The TV was blank, which was typical Eliot. *Have to see if he wants any books.* He felt bad that he hadn't seen his oldest living friend since he'd been in the hospital, but it wasn't like he'd been resting on his laurels in the meantime.

Eliot finally made his decision. "Screw it. If it hurts my guts,

CHAPTER 16

I'll get over it." The pie Val had kept for the two of them was heavy with pepperoni, sausage, ham, and meatballs.

Should have grabbed some Tums. Grinning, Val said, "That's the spirit."

They ate in silence for a few minutes before Eliot spoke up. "I heard about Leesburg."

"Yup. Boss ain't looking so good."

"You running things in the meantime?"

Val raised an eyebrow. Eliot shrugged. "Logical choice."

"If you say so. I'm just a trigger-puller."

"How about Locke? You get a line on her?"

"We had a solid lead in Texas, but she slipped away." He made a disgusted face. "Freaking *magic.*" He cocked his head and thought back to the cop he'd talked to in Amarillo. "Remember the last time we went to Amarillo?"

Eliot thought about it, then nodded. "Giant snake. Good times."

"What did that hippy say when we blew up the *culebron* with George's bazooka?"

"Far out, man," his partner quoted.

"Heh, that's right." Val leaned back in the chair. "I ran into one of Ernie Hidalgo's trainees out there. Guess he's been dead for a while."

"Comes for us all, in the end. Well, most of us. Think he's still yapping in the coffin?"

In point of fact, Hidalgo had never shut up. That was impressive, considering the end of their joint mission had seen the extermination of a rampaging *culebron* with high explosives. The giant snake started out sampling longhorn cattle from the local herds. By the time Val and the gang got wind of the situation, the beast had gotten a taste for human flesh, stalking and consuming four hikers in as many days. "I didn't think much of the '60s, but at least they didn't have camera phones."

"Lot easier to confiscate or destroy film," Eliot agreed. "What's got your goat, old man?"

Val sighed. "Too many moving pieces. I don't know where everything fits, yet. We've got a Division M employee on video killing Dr. Schantz and planting the device—"

"Hans is dead, too? Shit."

"Yeah, Menard, the director's security detail. Bunch of office staff. Most of the Menagerie is flatter than a pancake, including about half of the occupants." He groaned. "That reminds me, I need to sign a bunch of condolence letters."

"Who planted the bomb?"

"It looked like Kristin Hughes, but it wasn't. We got a science division team to her house and found blood all over the place. Matches her type, and there's enough that she shouldn't have been able to walk out of there."

"Skinwalker?"

"We're thinking succubus. Menard died, uh, happy, if you know what I mean."

Eliot grimaced. "I thought we wiped all those things out like disco."

"Around here, yeah. Betting this was a Euro-trash import. We're running facial recognition scans of incoming and outgoing international flights for the last couple of weeks. The thing that sticks in my craw, though is the timing of the whole thing. We get our hands on Paxton Locke, haven't had a chance to properly interrogate him yet, and bam, we get a breach in one of our most secure holding facilities and he escapes quick and easy as you please."

"Tough trick to pull, calling in from help from inside the prison. You think the mother was behind it?"

"I am starting to believe," Val said slowly, "that she doesn't give much of a damn about him. She could have taken him in Phoenix, but all she wanted was his grimoire. Yeah, she took the girlfriend, but she's just a hostage."

"We sure about that? Maybe she was playing both sides."

Val shook his head. "Up until a few weeks ago, Cassie Hatcher was a college student with a part-time job at Target. Different university from Helen's crew, and different crowd."

Eliot sat silent, and Val let him think. His partner was a much better pure detective than he'd ever been, and he saw things from a perspective that sometimes led to leaps of understanding. Finally, the other agent met his eyes. "It's a coincidence. The timing doesn't work, no matter how you slice it. The Menagerie is tight enough that there's no way that the boy could get word out. How would the mother coordinate that from across the country, while trying to evade capture?" He cocked his head to one side, eyes distant, and then a pained expression crossed his face. "Hell."

"You all right?" Val reached for the call button, hoping the pizza hadn't irritated Eliot's healing insides.

"I'm fine. I just realized—we've got a third player to concern ourselves with."

"Whoever was behind the bombing," Val said. He rolled the idea over in his head, then added, "Shit."

"Succubi are anything but intellectual. We're talking about someone with the power base to be able to hire or intimidate one into working for them. That's not Paxton Locke, no way, no how. Maybe his mom? But I doubt it. Not unless she's been spending time in Paris between serving jail time."

He replayed the surveillance video in his head. "She took something out of the vault. We're going to have to cross-reference the last inventory with anything about the size of a shoe box."

"Hope the boys kept good records. But you can delegate that. What's your next move?"

"Apparently, Helen wanted her son's friends to pass a message along to him. If he wants his girlfriend back, he needs to find her in Randolph Forest during the Ides of March."

"Maine? That's not good."

"Seriously?" Val exclaimed. "Am I the only one who doesn't know about this place?"

Eliot grinned. "Well, as you said, you are a trigger-puller. Timing and hostage would point toward some sort of ritual."

"Morgan thinks she's going to try and bust the wards."

His partner went paler than usual. "Good God, why? What does she stand to gain from that?"

"I don't try and psychoanalyze, bub. Like you said, I just shoot 'em." Val grabbed another piece of pizza. "I'm headed up there tomorrow morning to try and get the lay of the land. I'm bringing Morgan along to try and track her, but she thinks it's a waste of time. She thinks whatever method Locke and her hostage used to slip out of our grasp is going to keep her hidden until spring, but I don't buy it." He gave Eliot a serious look. "Rest up and get better, brother. I need you watching my back. Something tells me this is going to be a real cluster."

"Working on it. Few more days, I'll be up and at it."

"I'm going to hold you to that when I get back, old timer."

PAXTON—MONDAY EVENING
Phoenix, Arizona

It ended up costing me a tank of gas, but I found a couple of fraternity brothers making a pit stop on their way back to Northern Arizona University. They were more than happy to let me hitch a ride in exchange for covering their fill-up. Flush with Darrel's cash, it was more than an even trade to my mind.

After exchanging fist bumps and handshakes, I promised the bros I'd bring my girlfriend to their next keg party and left them to finish their own trip. Hands in the pockets of my sweatshirt, I started walking before they pulled onto the on-ramp. I wasn't much concerned about them spotting my face on the news and reporting that they'd given me a ride—I wouldn't be here for long.

Returning to Kent's subdivision was a surreal experience. Had it only been a few days since the De La Rosa brothers and I filled a cooler with drinks and ice at this gas station before heading to Upward Path? I'd crossed the country twice, and even though I'd grabbed snatches of sleep at every possible moment, I still had to hold back a yawn as I considered the street leading to Kent's house.

Rather than head straight in, I went south for another half-block, looked around, then turned invisible. From there I cut across a few yards until I came out onto my friend's street where it curved down and around.

I stood in front of the Sikora house for a few minutes to take it all in. The emergency vehicles were gone, and all that remained of the place my friend had called home was a sidewalk, a driveway, and piles of rubbled blocks. The wreckage no longer smoked, but the area still smelled strongly of fire.

Someone had shoved metal bars into the ground to support

long strands of yellow police tape. I ducked under the obstruction and walked slowly around the perimeter. Away from the road, I judged it was late enough that I could drop my cloak. The windows of the homes on either side were dark, and the shadows were deep enough to conceal my presence.

"Stop stalling," I muttered under my breath, then shook my head. I'd spent so much time focused on what I *had* to do over the last frantic hours that now, presented with the moment, I hesitated.

Keeping myself from knowing wouldn't change the truth. Coming back here seemed to clear my memories of that night a bit, and I remembered some discussion of survivors.

But that didn't mean that everyone I'd left behind had made it to that point. I took a deep breath, steeled my will, and *pushed*. "Is anyone there?"

Ashes stirred in the breeze. I thought I heard the far-off barking of a dog, but I remained alone. *Good.*

A girl stood directly behind me when I turned to head back to the street, and I nearly jumped out of my skin at the sight of her. She wasn't the first ghost I'd ever seen or even the worst-looking, but her sudden appearance prompted an involuntary, high-pitched squeal of alarm. *Big, bad wizard.* I shook my head ruefully. *Squeak like a chipmunk when you spot a ghost.*

She'd been short in life, maybe an inch over five feet, and stocky. Her face was classically beautiful—high cheekbones, full lips, and a dusting of freckles. Despite the breeze, her red hair remained perfectly still, without a single curl out of place.

"I don't know you," I said, keeping my voice low. "I'm sorry to bother you. If you want, I can—"

I know you, Paxton. Well—I knew your mother, I should say.

I fought my fight-or-flight urge and tried to keep my tone even. "You're one of ... Mother's little helpers, I guess?"

CHAPTER 16

She smiled a little at the joke. *I'm Roxanne. We called it a coven, but we were never equals. She used us.*

"Not the first time she's done that sort of thing, Roxanne," I said. "You were here when it all went down?"

Yes.

"Are my friends all right?"

I died before the house burnt down—I didn't see that part.

"What happened here?" Something about the ghost of the girl was off. Ghosts weren't usually lucid. They're the echo of a living, breathing soul; a psychic snapshot imprinted on the universe by the agony of a horrific death. There are various levels to it—individual definitions of horror do tend to vary from person to person —but as I liked to quip, ghosts weren't all there. It could have had something to her being a witch, and wasn't *that* a disconcerting thought? If there were ever reasons to wish to die in your sleep, not ending up as a ghost had to be one of the biggest.

Helen used a tracking spell to find you. We came for the grimoire, but right as we arrived they attacked.

"Who? My friends?"

No, she shook her head. *Helen said it was Division M. There was a, I don't know, a werewolf or something. Plus some guy in a massive suit of armor. I took the werewolf out, but the suit of armor killed Giselle before the familiars could take it down. After that...* She shrugged. *I died. I watched the glowing man kill Kelsey, but I didn't realize what I was until later.*

"Glowing man? Werewolf?" I shook my head slowly. The little voice in the back of my head whispered that I knew exactly who the glowing man was, but I pushed it down. "I don't have time for this. I've got to find my friends." I gathered my will. The ability to speak to ghosts works with the *push* and allowed me to pull back the curtain on reality. When ghosts learned the truth of their existence, their energy faded away. It's a melancholy practice for me, but their pain seems real enough.

If I had the power to relieve that while keeping them from haunting the living, is it so wrong to make use of it?

As though she sensed what was about to happen, the girl ghost blurted, *Wait! I don't know where to find your friends, but I know where they took the motor home we came in. Maybe yours will be there, too.*

I cocked my head and gave her a suspicious frown. "How does that work? Did you follow them, or something?"

I can't explain it, I just feel it. She shrugged. *Some of my things are in there, and I feel this connection to them, I guess you could call it. It's been going away, but for now, it's there.*

"I've got a partner already. You helped my Mother kidnap her," I pointed out. "After you and your crew broke her out of jail."

Must be nice to have never made a mistake in your life.

"That's not the point. Losing a cell phone or getting into a car accident is a mistake. Turning frat boys into brainwashed clones is not a mistake. Throwing fireballs around and burning buildings down is a really poor life choice, to say the list." I spread my palms wide, reminding myself to keep my voice down, lest I rouse the neighbors. "You and all your friends received a gift that millions of people out there would do anything for, and you squandered it. Do you *know* what my Mother wants to do with the grimoire?"

Her silent voice, if it was possible, was very small. *No.*

I reached for the words, flinching as the images I'd seen when I'd taken a glance at the spell popped into the forefront of my memories. "She's going to end the world," I said, finally. "The stuff I saw makes an Emmerich movie look like a fairy tale."

Then you need all the help you can get to stop her, right?

"What's in it for you?"

What, you don't believe in redemption?

I stared at her partially translucent form and considered. It wasn't like anyone else would see her. I'd have to watch myself more than her, to make sure I didn't speak out of turn when anyone else could hear. *Slap a Bluetooth earpiece in, no one will notice.* I shook my head, holding back laughter at the thought, then shrugged. "Fair enough," I agreed. The thought of heading *back* into town was annoying, but maybe I could find a similar deal that had gotten me up here.

At some point, I was going to have to find a place to hole up to sleep, which complicated things. The night simplified my movements, but public transport didn't run twenty-four hours a day. "Which way?" I asked, finally.

The ghost—Roxanne, I told myself—hesitated, then pointed generally southeast.

Well, that eliminates the west side of town, at least. I checked my watch and tried to remember the route schedule from the bus. The same route I'd taken north would be running for a few hours, and it was close enough to the Interstate for me to walk. If I could make it there before the last run of the night, we could head south and take periodic bearings. When her instinct told her directly east, or somewhere close, we'd start heading that way. Just thinking of it sounded tedious, but I didn't have much choice unless I wanted to resort to stealing someone's car.

There's already a target on your back. Doing something like that is the equivalent of jumping up and down and screaming, "Hey, come and get me!"

"I guess we'd better get going," I said, finally.

CHAPTER SEVENTEEN

Paxton—Early Tuesday morning
Phoenix, Arizona

By the time I found someone heading south who was willing to give me a ride, we'd missed the last bus route for the day. But sometimes it's better to be lucky than good.

The guy who finally agreed to give me a ride, Marvin Donaher, had one condition. He was heading to his late shift at Honeywell, and he couldn't drop me off on Happy Valley Road, where I'd caught my first ride. He did, however, take us further south to Deer Valley, his normal exit.

Roxanne 'sat' in the backseat—though I suppose you could more accurately describe it as hovering in place. As soon as Marvin got off of the exit and headed east, she bounced in place. I'd never seen barely-restrained excitement from a ghost before. I had to force myself to look away to keep from laughing.

Marvin pulled over in the parking lot of one of the Valley's ubiquitous Circle Ks. "This work well enough?"

"This is perfect, sir, thank you." I dug a twenty out of my pocket and tried to hand it over, but he waved it away.

CHAPTER 17

"I can't take your money, son. This is on my way as it is. I hope you track your friend down and get your keys back."

The comment threw me for a split-second before I remembered the little white lie I'd used an excuse for the ride. "Well, thank you again. This sort of thing never happens when you've got your phone. I appreciate the help—don't work too hard tonight!"

He winked. "There's a reason I prefer the late shift, it's nice and slow. Take it easy, kid."

I stayed silent until he'd pulled out of the parking lot, then said, under my breath, "What's up?"

The direction changed. It's straight east, now.

That was an unexpected boon, and I shrugged and went with it. The way things had been going the last few days, I figured the universe owed me a little luck.

Following the sidewalk, I headed that way. This late, the streets were mostly abandoned, all the businesses shut down save for periodic fast food joints. My stomach growled at the sight, but I forced myself to push on. If Roxanne's RV was in some sort of impound yard or evidence lockup, my best bet was to get to it before the start of the workday, so I could take my time to search without concern for anyone seeing me.

The negative little voice in the back of my head chose that moment to bring up something I'd been trying not to think about. *And what if my RV is there, too?* That would mean that Division M had caught the guys, and I was well and truly on my own, save for a ghost of uncertain reliability. I crossed mental fingers. *This will all be a lot easier if Carlos and the guys are somewhere waiting for me.*

If it was there, I doubted that I'd be able to retrieve my own vehicle. Even if I got the opportunity to do so, it wouldn't make sense. The Thor was too slow and too obvious. What I did have, though, was a Kawasaki Vulcan 750 motorcycle strapped to a rack on the back. If my luck held out, the spare key I kept stashed inside my motor home would still be there, and I'd gain a set of wheels. The bike was common enough that it shouldn't raise any eyebrows, even after my adversaries noticed its disappearance.

"What would be in your RV, anyway?"

Clothing and food mostly. That won't be much help, but there's a folder, a Trapper Keeper, with all the spells we were able to collect. I don't know what you can do, maybe there's something in there that will give you a better chance against Helen.

"Trapper Keeper?" I chuckled. "That's great—what kind?"

My Little Pony—Twilight Sparkle. If a ghost could sound sheepish, Roxanne fit the bill. *The tracking spell Helen used to find you might be in there, too.*

I shrugged. "I'm not getting my hopes up. I'll be happy to throw together a travel bag and get my bike back." *After that, food, sleep, and in the morning, I need to get a phone and figure out a way to get in touch with the De La Rosa brothers.*

I'd half-hoped that I'd find some sign of their presence at Kent's house—nothing so overt as a trail of breadcrumbs, but something to give me a clue where they might have gone off to. If Roxanne's tracking spell panned out, that was an opportunity. If the authorities had taken the trouble to tow Mother's vehicle to whatever lay in front of us, surely they'd gone through it looking for evidence. Would they have taken a Twilight Sparkle binder? I guessed yes and hoped not.

Half an hour later and over two miles down the road, I was ready to throw in the towel. Gut feeling or not, there was no sign of anything like a police impound and the buildings were starting to become few and far between. I told myself I'd go a bit further, and if we didn't find anything, I was turning around and hitting the Taco Bell by the interstate.

Shortly thereafter, when I saw the building complex and the fence surrounding it, I had to resist the urge to slap my forehead. Even in the predawn hours, many of the office lights burned inside

CHAPTER 17

the glass-and-stone building. At first glance, I might have assumed it was an ordinary office building, albeit with better than normal security. Bits of metal missing from the stylized copper sign on the concrete pillar out front created a stylized fingerprint, and the legend on the sign read 'FBI Phoenix Division.'

"Well, shit," I said. Glancing at Roxanne, I raised an eyebrow. She nodded and pointed to the rear of the building.

Back there, somewhere.

It didn't change things all that much. I'd planned on going invisible until I was behind cover, anyway. Taking a look around to make sure no cars approached, I went ahead and threw up the cloak. I started walking again, but the need to hurry lent urgency to my steps.

The parking lot on the west side of the building remained empty save for a few sedans. Another entrance lay on the west side of the building, and as I approached I stiffened. A well-lit guard station secured the entrance on that side of the complex, and two serious men sat inside. Slowing my steps, I eased around one of the arms in an unconscious pantomime of how I'd entered the Upward Path campus. I'd had backup then, but the lack of cavalry in my current situation didn't entirely explain my discomfort. Tangling with cultists and monsters was one thing—I really, really didn't want to pick a fight with Federal law enforcement. I didn't *like* this whole 'man on the run' shtick. The fact that they'd started it meant that I might not get my choice.

The road curved back to the west around the rear of the building. Roxanne had no problem seeing me despite the invisibility spell, and every time I looked to her for clarification, she'd nod or point onward. One way or another, I was on the right track.

A secondary fence, interwoven with plastic strips to create a visual barrier, stood past a trio of loading docks. I didn't need Roxanne to show me the way now—the familiar upper half of *my*

RV was visible above the fence. "Damn it," I whispered. "If it's here, where are they?"

There didn't seem to be any obvious surveillance cameras in view, but I found a shadowed section of the fence before I dropped my cloak and phased through. The eclectic collection of vehicles in this secondary lot made me wonder if the other vehicles were from other crime scenes. You didn't see a canary-yellow Lamborghinis parked between a Range Rover and motorhomes every day, after all.

That's ours, Roxanne said, pointing. I didn't recognize the model off the top of my head, but it was a larger, more luxurious one than my own. A massive impact had punched the big window at the rear of the coach out of its frame. Familiar-looking streaks of black viscera surrounded the gaping wound. Someone had taped heavy plastic sheeting over the hole and the stained areas—to preserve any evidence, I guessed.

From the looks of the impact crater, I *really* didn't want to stick my head inside of the other RV to see what sort of stomach-turning gazpacho the hit had made of the familiar. On the bright side, my sidekick of the moment didn't have a sense of smell. "Can you check it out?"

Roxanne stared at the rear of the RV for a moment before shrugging. She faded out of sight as she walked toward the vehicle. I considered waiting for her to complete her search, but I decided the less time we spent back here, the better.

I moved around to the side and phased through the door. I'm no neat freak, but I keep things in their place. The piles of stuff thrown around inside told me that the Feds had searched the place. I hadn't owned this vehicle long enough to add the same hidden storage that I had in my previous RV, so didn't expect any of my backup weapons to remain. After a quick check, no pleasant surprises were forthcoming.

On the other hand, pretty much everything else *was* still

inside, though it took a bit of work to sort through the piles to find what I wanted. Checking the refrigerator, I rolled my eyes when I saw that someone had taken all the Mountain Dew I'd left in there. "Cheers, I guess," I muttered. I popped open a Tupperware container I'd stashed among the condiments in the door and breathed a sigh of relief when I saw that no one had taken my spare motorcycle key.

After a few days with little more than the clothes on my back, I took a strange satisfaction in packing up my own toothbrush, miscellaneous toiletries, and outfit selections that would work in any number of climates. Shouldering my backpack, I munched on a Pop-Tart and took a final look around to make sure I hadn't forgotten anything. Nothing else jumped out at me, so I grabbed my helmet and phased back through the door. Roxanne stood outside, but to my credit, I didn't flinch this time.

"You could have come in," I said, forcing a grin. I headed around to the back and started working on the straps and pins that held the Vulcan to the tailgate rack.

Didn't want to impose, I guess.

Straining, I had to find a balance between letting the bike roll down the ramps and keeping it from making too much noise. I usually didn't pay much attention to the racket, and I winced now as metal rang off the pavement. The quiet of the night made it stand out that much more. I crossed my fingers and prayed that if the guards heard it, they'd pass it off as street noise. Propping the Vulcan on its kickstand, I went through the process of stowing the ramps and straps. If my luck held, maybe no one would notice the missing bike for a day or two. "Any luck?"

Roxanne made a face. *It's nasty in there. I didn't see any of our stuff.*

"Kind of what I figured," I said. The trio of cloned familiars I'd faced when I'd first had a run-in with Mother's crew had left pretty disgusting messes behind. I felt a sudden swell of pity for the poor crime scene investigator who had to clean that black, cloying goop off Roxanne's magical Trapper Keeper.

What now?

"Now to see if we can get out of here." I gave the fence an appraising look. "If I can pull this off, the night isn't a total loss." When I phased, my clothes and anything on body came along for the ride—would the same be true of something larger? There was only one way to find out. I pushed the bike over to where I'd phased through the fence, took a deep breath, and ...

Oh, man, I thought. Not only did it take me longer to feel the effect come into play, but physically speaking it felt like I'd just tried to bench press a refrigerator. I leaned forward on shaking legs and pushed the front wheel through the fence. There was no going back now—I'd never tried it, but I figured it would be pretty bad for the engine if I phased pieces of chain link fence into it.

As soon as the Kawasaki was clear, I cut the spell short. Waves of exhaustion rolled over me, and I barely got the kickstand popped out before I collapsed onto the ground. Quivering, I met Roxanne's eyes as she stepped through after me. "For future reference," I managed. "That is not recommended."

To make matters worse, I wasn't out of the woods yet—I still had to get past the gate guards. Rather than double down on phasing, I dug another Pop-Tart out of the box I'd stashed in my backpack and downed it while I waited for the shakes to pass.

You can really hurt yourself that way.

"No shit? You don't say." I was going for subtle sarcasm, but the comment came out far nastier than I'd intended.

She frowned, cocked her head as though considering whether to speak, then continued. *We almost did the same thing until we learned to tap. Your mom taught us how to reach outside of ourselves—there's plenty of energy in the world, you just need to know how to get to it.*

I finished off the Pop-Tart and considered that for a moment.

If nothing else, that explained Mother's ability to use her magic so effectively. The first time I used the *push*, I passed out and woke up in the hospital. So far as I could tell, Mother had never so much as broken a sweat.

"Nothing I can do about that now unless you can teach me how to do it."

She frowned. *I can feel my magic, but without a body...* she waved her hands in frustration. *Nothing happens.*

"Great." Balling up the wrapper, I stashed it in my pocket. Worn out and ready to crash, I considered the insane and stupid idea of starting up the bike and riding away for a few moments before I shook it off. *Suck it up*, I told myself. I got to pushing.

I saved my mystical strength until I got closer to the guard station, then went invisible. It was a bit of a strain to increase the radius of effect, but not as bad as phasing had been. I could handle this for more than long enough.

The guards didn't so much as look up as I wheeled the bike past. Sweat dripped down my forehead as I rolled out onto the street and kept pushing. I wanted to be out of their direct line of sight before I dropped the spell, and after a few more nerve-wracking moments of pushing, I looked back and couldn't see them.

Throwing a leg over the seat, I inserted the key and twisted it. After all that, it would be just my luck that the battery would have gone dead in the interim since I'd last ridden. But the engine roared to life, and I let myself smile as I reveled in the sense of freedom that controlling my own mode of transportation gave me. Checking both ways, I did a U-turn in the middle of the street and headed back toward the interstate.

I'd earned some well-deserved rest. When the morning came, it was time to double down.

CHAPTER EIGHTEEN

Valentine—Tuesday morning
Randolph, Maine

They hadn't yet arranged for another cargo plane to haul their mobile command center back from Phoenix, but it was for the best. In a small town like this, the thing would stick out like a sore thumb. Commandeering the agency's Gulfstream to fly to Portland, Maine, and renting a car was as low-key as Val was willing to go.

On the plane, Morgan had said, semi-jokingly, "Maybe you should drop the Men in Black routine. Try some plaid." The look he gave her ended any further discussion on *that* particular topic, though he had at least foregone a tie. After so many years, he felt naked without a suit coat, and the good people of Randolph, Maine, weren't likely to react well to a stranger carrying a quartet of holstered pistols, badge or not.

Less than two hours after they'd landed, Val pulled their rented sedan to one side of a picturesque suburban street and growled in frustration. There were two main roads in town—Water Street, which ran along the Kennebec River, and State

Route 226. They'd made a circuit of each, pausing every so often for Morgan to take a sounding with the tracker, but the mystical divining rod didn't behave any better for her than it had for Val.

"Could it have, I don't know, worn off?"

Morgan shook her head as she turned the rod over in her hands. "No, once you have it locked onto a target, that's it until you set it to another."

"All this stuff you can't touch drives me crazy. Give me something tangible any day of the week."

"Or shoot," Morgan smirked.

Val ignored the jibe. "Allow me a moment to go off into the weeds, here. If Helen was able to manipulate the nexus to move her between two points in space, what's to say she couldn't go through time, too?"

"I'm not saying I'm disagreeing, but know that every time manipulation spell I've ever seen was of limited utility. We're talking back and forth hops of something like five minutes. Months or more would be so far beyond the pale, I can't imagine the energy requirement. Then there's the fact of accounting for physical displacement."

"How's that?"

"The Earth rotates and travels through space at the same time. We perceive this as a fixed point, but we're in motion in a multitude of vectors. If we don't account for that in the geography of the casting, there are any number of things that could go wrong."

He cocked his head to one side, imagining it, and grimaced. "Like what, appearing over the river, or something?"

"Or inside a hill, or outer space. Like I said, lots of flashing red letters and warnings. The magical equivalent, anyway."

He gave her a sidelong glance. "I don't recall anything like that in the archives."

Morgan's expression remained placid. "There's a reason for that. We're not meant to know certain things. I didn't trust *myself* to learn any of the incantations, much less potential researchers at Division M."

Val shrugged. "Fair enough. Since I don't see Helen sticking out of the ground around here, I'm going to assume the worst. Let's say she was able to jump across months-long periods of time. For that matter, why wouldn't she just go *back* to last March?"

"If she had, I'd assume we'd be seeing some sort of sign of that. Unless we stopped her then."

He laughed. "That'd be a fun trick, considering we don't know how to do what she did, ourselves."

"All kidding aside, I think it has to be a jump forward if she wants her son there. How else would she expect him to make it on time?"

"Which begs the question, what's the point?" He waved a hand outside the window. "If she needed him for the ritual, why not take him instead of the girlfriend? Why goad him into coming after her? Does she *want* him to try to stop her?"

"We never did determine what sort of ritual she was trying to perform when she killed the husband in front of the son. Maybe it's a reenactment, and she needs him in the audience again."

Val frowned. "How does that work?"

"Powerful emotions can supercharge a spell, far beyond the metaphysical abilities of the caster. Killing her husband in front of her son? That's a double whammy—betrayal *and* horror. Maybe the depth of a relationship between a girlfriend and boyfriend doesn't compare to a father and son, but it has to come close. Then you've got the repeat performance aspect of it. He already has strong emotional reactions to her mere presence. Putting him back into the same sort of scenario? That's akin to a walking nightmare, and doing it *here*, in a nexus?" She shuddered. "It won't be good."

"I know you say this is a nexus, but it looks like a standard-issue cozy northeastern small town. Why here? I expected more Silent Hill and less Cabot Cove."

CHAPTER 18

"George plays enough console games in the command center that I'm familiar with the first reference. The second one is over my head."

"*Murder, She Wrote*," Val said with a frown. "And if you tell anyone else in the Division, you'll regret it."

"Oh, your fascination with Angela Lansbury is safe with me," Morgan said. Unable to contain herself, she giggled.

He tried to glower at her, but he couldn't hold it, and he ended up shaking his head. "Fine. Answer the question."

"The warding does a lot to keep things wholesome, I guess you'd say. You can't completely close a nexus, so something's going to pop out every now and then, but the spells keep it from opening any further and encourages the creepy crawlies to move on. Which, admittedly, leads to people seeing and hearing things that puts Randolph on a list of Maine's haunted places." She shrugged. "But it's better than the alternative."

Val drummed his fingers on the steering wheel. "So, we're in a holding pattern until she pops back up. We've got the field office in Portland—we have any agents assigned to observe and report the conditions up here?"

"Not really. There are a couple of guys in the police department who are read-in. If they spot anything, Portland's less than an hour away by helicopter."

"I almost want to park some people here, but who knows where to tell them to watch. Think Helen would spook if we set up in force?"

"After what she pulled in San Francisco? I doubt it."

"Right," Val frowned. "This small a town, the cover-up would probably be harder, ironically enough. Everybody knows everyone else. I think our best alternative is going to be to leave some pictures of Helen and Cassie with the local police and have Portland loop us in on any reports they get. I hate being reactive, and it's not ideal, but it's the best of a bad lot. What's the exact date?"

"The Ides of March? March 15th—it corresponds to Julius Caesar's assassination. We have some time, yet—what do we do for the next few months?"

Val put the car in drive and pulled back on the road. "I want you to go home for a bit and shake the trees. See what falls out. It's looking like it wasn't local talent that hit us, but they damn near decapitated the entire agency. Figure out who, or what, we're up against. With the Lockes on the loose, we don't have time to deal with anything else."

"If I'm right about what she needs him for, you need to track the boy down. He's a pawn."

"We didn't get off to the best start," Val admitted.

Morgan laughed. "I'm shocked that you rubbed someone the wrong way, truly. But seriously, Val—I'm not going to be around forever. The more I learn about him, the more I think that Paxton Locke looks at himself as some sort of superhero. We could use that, especially now."

"You planning on retiring?"

"We're all in the same boat—we don't get that option. But I'm not lucky enough to be able to shake it off after the medical teams shovel my guts back into place like you and Eliot. Sooner or later, my number's going to come up."

"I'm not that lucky," Val murmured. "Sometimes I think I'm playing with loaded dice."

"Decidedly ironic, given your history, wouldn't you say?"

CHAPTER 18

P<small>AXTON</small>—T<small>UESDAY MORNING</small>
Phoenix, Arizona

I bent my *push* rule to convince an annoyed-looking clerk at a Days Inn close to the interstate to let me pay cash for a room without scanning in a credit card or driver's license. The look of suspicion he offered up made me think he suspected I was going to use the room to cook meth or something. After the night I'd had, my idea of a wild party was a sack of tacos, a ridiculously-long shower, and crawling under the covers. The mattress wasn't the most comfortable thing I'd ever slept on, but it was a damn sight better than the one in Division M's holding facility. I was even tired enough that Roxanne's presence in the room didn't keep me from falling asleep. As I drifted off, I half-considered asking her if ghosts needed to rest, but I slipped into dreamless oblivion before I could muster the effort to speak.

After sleeping a solid eight hours, I took another shower—I was bound and determined to get my fifty bucks worth out of the place—put on clean, familiar clothing, and headed out for the day.

One of the workers at a nearby Denny's pointed me toward the closest department store. Less than an hour after my late breakfast, I sat down in the snack bar of a Super Target and went through the process of activating a prepaid cell phone. A few purchases and the hotel had put a serious dent in the cash I'd taken off Darrell, but all the same, I felt like I was marking things off of my mental checklist. It was time to touch base to see if I could track down the De La Rosa brothers. This whole thing would be smoother with corporeal backup. Roxanne had been a great help thus far, but there wasn't much she could do to watch my back. And I had to sleep, sometime.

What's our next move?

I gave her an annoyed look and held back my response. The last thing I wanted to do was become 'the weird dude talking to himself in the snack bar.' The more attention I drew to myself, the greater the chance of Division M catching up. She laughed at my expression—she'd known I couldn't respond.

Great, I'm hanging out with a ghost that's a bigger smart-ass than I am, I thought. Thankfully, the store had all the accessories I needed. The Bluetooth earpiece was neither charged nor synced, but it didn't need to be. I just needed it to be there to serve as a red herring to any curious onlookers. Pulling it out of the package and hooking it in place, I said to Roxanne, "I'm glad you're having fun with this."

Give me a break—I'm dead. It's not like there's much else for me to do.

"Fair point," I agreed, gathering all my trash into a plastic bag. "I'd probably be worse than you." Given my calling, it was a foregone conclusion that my death would be horrific in some way. The people who die peacefully in their sleep don't generally go in for haunting, and for good reason. The spell that granted me the ability to speak with and summon ghosts had explained that they weren't departed souls at all, but rather the psychic afterimage of trauma. Knowing that they were semi-sentient copies of formerly living people lessened the guilt I felt at banishing them, but not by

CHAPTER 18

much. It still felt like needless cruelty applied on top of prior trauma.

My focus on my new electronics must have bored my companion, because she turned and strolled through the seating area, pausing to snoop over the shoulders anyone piquing her interest. I shook my head and murmured, "Whatever floats your boat."

Without my old phone, I honestly had no clue what any of my friends' contact numbers were, but the way that the De La Rosa brothers had set up their cell phones worked out in my favor. Using the store's free WiFi, I hit their homepage and selected the 'Contact Us' link. They'd purchased their phones in a block from their provider, even the cell phones. Seeing the main office number flipped the light switch in my noggin. The next number in series was the person I needed to talk to, Karen Gallardo, but I was going to have to be careful about it. Any agencies that were looking for me would know of my association with the brothers, and they'd have the phone lines tapped. Calling the main switchboard with my new cell phone number was a surefire way to get myself caught. A text message was the best way to go, but I couldn't drop my name in there, either. I was going to have to make a reference that both she and I would get. As I considered my options, I realized that we had history on our side.

Carlos' wife, and Esteban's niece, Karen took it upon herself to be an honorary big sister over the years. I've lost count of the number of friends she'd set me up with, and most of the dates were pleasant enough. The problem with dating was more on my end—in the years immediately after gaining the *push*, I didn't trust myself to lose control and abuse my powers. So for the most part, I cut things short before they had the potential to get serious. There were a few ruffled feathers, but none of the blind dates topped the one that made me pull the plug on any future hook-ups.

I don't know if Becca Evans saw me as some sort of challenge, or what, but by the end of our second date, she dragged me into a jewelry store in the mall and proceeded to marvel at the engagement rings. As far as signals went, that was the equivalent of a raging bonfire.

Later that night, when I told her in what I felt was a gentle way that I had no interest in continuing our relationship, the crying and carrying on that ensued was as impressive as it was baffling. When it didn't stop for over half an hour, I turned and left her alone in *my* apartment. It was that or use the *push* to make her leave, and I wasn't prepared to do that.

Over the next few hours, I'd swing by the parking lot, check to see if her car was still there, then leave to go somewhere else. I ended up spending the night on Carlos and Karen's couch, and the next morning, Becca was gone. She wasn't destructive, as far as I could tell, but I thanked my lucky stars I didn't have a pet rabbit and proceeded to throw away my toothbrush and other assorted toiletries. Just in case.

A wizard's life is a thing of wonder, truly.

Carlos found the situation hilarious, and while his wife was mildly disapproving, she let it slide. Karen still didn't stop trying to set me up, though after the Becca experience I was much firmer in refusing.

I tapped out a quick text, crossed my fingers, and hit send.

Hey, it's Duffer. I lost my phone and all my contacts. Do you still have Becca's number?

If there was anything I was worse at than dating, it was golf. I hoped that Karen remembered the nickname Carlos had bestowed upon me the first time we hit the links and put two and two together.

All I could do now was wait. Tucking the new phone in my jacket pocket, I deposited my trash and headed out the door. I should have felt safe, but sitting steel made me feel antsy. Roxanne had taken an empty seat among a trio of college-aged girls, but when she saw me leaving she stood and transitioned to my side in a blur of speed. That was interesting—later, maybe we could experiment and see what sort of limits she had on her freedom of movement. *She might be more helpful than I thought.*

As I walked up on the bike, I considered the Arizona license plates with newly-paranoid eyes and winced. Like my driver's license, they linked to Kent and Jean's home address. If I got pulled over, hit a red-light camera, or even had the plate run on a routine check, that would surely throw up a red flag somewhere. I added 'swap license plate' to my to-do list, and wondered where I'd find an opportunity to do so. On the bright side, I could manage it while invisible if I was careful how I handled the swap.

What's the plan, now?

"Trying not to become more paranoid than I already am, to be honest," I joked. With a shrug, I added, "Holding pattern. If I can find out what happened to my friends, I—" The phone buzzed in my pocket.

I tried not to whoop as I read the text. There was a reason I liked to tease Carlos that his wife was the brains of the operation.

Been wondering how you were, Duff. Let me see if I have her number somewhere.

"Way to go, Karen," I said. "Tell me you've got a burner laying around, girl." There practically *had* to be one, the agency collected cell phones like some people collected stamps. Whether to loan out to contract workers or to manage less above-board endeavors, they were all over the place in the agency's office.

The wait was unbearable, though it was no more than a minute or two. My phone buzzed with a new notice, from a number I didn't recognize with a San Diego area code.

My hair's about to turn the same color as yours over here. What the hell is going on?

"That's not good," I muttered. The air near my cheek grew

colder, and I realized Roxanne was reading over my shoulder. Well, at least I was in good company.

You tell me—I was tied up for a few days and I can't find anyone. Have you heard from any of them?

They tied you up?

"Figure of speech. I don't think Division M will have this line tapped, but who knows."

Karen responded. **C told me K's house was on fire, that was the last I heard.**

"Damn," I said. **They were taking the RV back, but I hoped they didn't get caught up in the mess.**

It had been a desperate hope, but it was one that I'd clung to. The reality of my situation hit me. No tracking spell, no clues as to the whereabouts of my friends—I was back to square one. A wave of despair rolled over me, and I tried not to scream in frustration.

Karen—**We'll figure it out. I'll talk to some of Scope's friends.**

I debated how much to say. Surely they already had her under observation. Who knew how little, or how much, it would take for them to swoop in and move her to a secret prison as they'd done with me?

"Screw it," I said. **Ask them if they know what Division M is.**

CHAPTER NINETEEN

Valentine—Tuesday afternoon
Washington, DC

It didn't feel right to sit behind Director Newquist's desk, so Val set up shop in one of the conference rooms. If anyone had any problems with it, too bad.

He'd passed most of the director's day to day work off to his executive assistant Claudia. Val didn't want to get bogged down in the minutiae of expense approvals, incident reports, and memos. He had enough on his plate with the hunt for the Lockes and the investigation into the perpetrator behind the bombing of the Menagerie.

If there was a bright side to the near-total destruction of their primary base on the East Coast, it was that few of the prisoners in the underground facility had managed to escape. Falling debris crushed the majority of the detainees, but at least they weren't roaming through suburban Virginia wreaking havoc.

Val was of two minds on that. Their most dangerous prisoners merited a transfer to The Pit under Guantanamo Bay or summary execution under the Executive Order covering sapient non-human entities—NHEs—in place since the Coolidge administration. The creatures in the Menagerie were there for a reason. Not innocent, per se, but not definitively guilty, either. Certainly not deserving of being flattened by tumbling concrete. He was far angrier about the loss of experienced agents and *friends*.

Sorting through piles of paper, he collated Helen Locke's material into a stack and set it aside. As much as he loathed the thought, she needed to go on the back burner until she popped back on the radar. If Morgan's instincts were right—and in his experience they usually were—they had a temporary reprieve until she rejoined their timeline.

Morgan was on a plane to Europe first thing in the morning. Depending on how things went, Val hoped for some sort of lead there by the beginning of next week. The forensic crew hadn't found much of anything to work with at the actual site of the explosion, but they had found some *very* interesting traces in Kristin Hughes' townhouse. As soon as Eliot got out of the hospital, Val planned to let him take a look around. When it came to tracking cryptids or NHEs, his partner was even more effective than Morgan's spinning needle. If the suspected succubus was still in the States, she was a dead fiend walking.

Which left Paxton Locke as the current burr in his saddle. While Morgan's reasoning had allayed some of the suspicions he'd felt since first speaking to the kid in the hospital, the seeming ease with which the wizard had not only escaped but continued to evade capture annoyed and frustrated him. Nothing in any of their background information gave any indication that he possessed the skills needed to avoid capture.

"You can't mind control a surveillance camera, damn it," he muttered. "Where are you?" It was bad enough knowing that he might blown their best chance to stop Helen Locke. Not being able to find that chance to try and make amends was even worse.

Division M was limited in what active measures they could

use to track the younger Locke. He wanted to keep Morgan's tracking device keyed on Helen, and they didn't have another one to use for someone else. *Something we need to rectify at some point.*

Someone tapped on the door to the conference room, and he looked up. Claudia stood in the doorway. He'd known her long enough to read the expression on her face as one of worry. "What's up?" Val said.

"We just got a call from Senator Weeden's office. The oversight committee would like you to attend a meeting in an hour."

He groaned. "Of course they do. Just when I thought things couldn't get any worse. Do you still have them on the phone?"

"Yes, I do, Dir—Agent Valentine."

Val smiled, just a little. "He's going to pull through, Claudia. I'm just trying to keep the plates in the air until he gets back. Tell them I'll be there."

She returned the smile and said, "Will do, sir."

Left to himself once more, he rested his elbows on the conference table and massaged his temples. On the bright side, he didn't have to go to Capitol Hill. Those buildings had wards, but they weren't as dense as the secure meeting room in Division M's section of ATF.

The politicians were coming to him, but that didn't make the situation any better. Something told Val they were about to breathe down his neck, and hard.

Paxton—Tuesday afternoon
Phoenix, Arizona

I didn't know what to do while I waited for Karen to get back with me, so I just rode. Most of the roads in Phoenix were ruler-straight, and it would have been easy to zone out if not for the traffic. That, I supposed was the downside of such far-flung urban sprawl—*everyone* was on the roads. I'd rather have been out in the middle of nowhere, maybe a small town, but then again, those were the worst sorts of places to hide, weren't they?

Eventually, my surroundings struck a familiar note, and I took a turn as I realized I was nearing a dump site where Tlaloc's followers had left one of their victims. At this time of day, Desert Storm Park was empty save for an elderly dog walker doing a loop around the walking path. After parking the bike, I strolled through the grass to one of the tiered benches and sat down.

The place looked as though a giant ice cream scoop had taken a chunk out of the land and landscaped the rim. The benches lined one wall of the inverted dome, pointing toward the grassy bottom. I wasn't there to look at anything, particularly—I hadn't found much even when it had been a fresh crime scene, but it was a peaceful place to wait and think.

"I was here last week," I said to Roxanne as she walked by. Rather than sit, she pretended to tip-toe along the edge of the bench. I guessed she was amusing herself—I didn't think ghosts could fall. "Long story short, guy found an imprisoned Aztec demon and made a deal with it. Got a cult and a bunch of followers out of the deal. All it cost him was a few human sacrifices." *Not to mention his life.*

Roxanne turned around, looked at me, then looked out over the park. The light of the midday sun passed through her, ever-so-slightly, and lent her a more ethereal appearance than she'd had when I'd found her last night. *It's a little past the point where I can learn from my mistakes.*

"No lecture," I shrugged. "Just making conversation."

You seem worried.

"Well, yeah. Finding my friends was the quickest way to figure out what Mother had planned for Cassie and the grimoire. You still don't remember anything?"

I don't, no. Sorry.

"It is what it is." I thought for a moment. "Focus on what you can remember. Maybe you heard something, and just didn't think anything of it at the time. What did you do between busting Mother out of prison and coming here?"

She sat down now, crossing her legs with a thoughtful expression. *We spent the first the first couple days going to long-term storage facilities. She—Helen, umm...*

Amused, I said, "You can say her name. She's not Voldemort."

Roxanne cocked her head. *You like Harry Potter?*

"How old do you think I am? I'm only twenty-six." I waved a hand. "Go ahead."

Helen was pretty angry. She had stashed a lot of things—spells and magic items—for a day when she might need them, but Divi-

sion M found them. When Melanie first wrote her, we went to a few that weren't too far away and found one that wasn't broken into, but it didn't have much.

I thought about Melanie carrying the Edimmu under her skin like a messed-up talking tattoo, and her trio of cloned familiars. If that wasn't much, Mother must have managed to steal a lot more using her connections than I'd feared. "After that?"

She said we needed protection, so we went to the University of Iowa. I had a...friend who went there, and I visited him once. It seemed strange, but if I had to describe it I'd say Roxanne looked almost embarrassed. *It was kind of a two birds with one stone thing, you know? We needed protection, and I knew where we could get some big, strong jerky guys.*

I closed my eyes. "Familiars," I said. That explained the mess on the back of the RV. "How many?"

We each took two—well, not Helen.

I winced. Melanie had used a spell to literally divide her boyfriend into identical triplets. While the magic had replenished the lost body weight, it hadn't done the same to intellect. Uno, Dos, and Trace, as she'd called them, each had the mental acuity of a short-tempered Doberman with twice the loyalty. I didn't look forward to another fight with familiars like that without a shotgun or two. "So you had nine, plus the four of you?" Roxanne frowned, and I worried I'd gone too far. She had to have known about Melanie's demise during our encounter, but it probably wasn't very diplomatic to bring that up. Attempting to redirect the question, I added, "You said Mother didn't take one. Why?"

Roxanne shuddered. *She did something to one of the sorority girls at the party. Sucked out her youth, or her beauty, even. Helen called it a Bathory spell. When she finished, she looked twenty years younger, and stacked.* The ghost gave me a wary look, and continued, *She promised she'd teach it to me.*

Unsure how to respond, I said, "I see." Mother had always

been a master manipulator, alternately using charm or rage to take the easy route through life. As a child, the emotional ups and downs were confusing until I understood her act. I still wonder why my dad stuck around. He was smart enough to recognize her ways, and while we never discussed it, I felt before he died that we shared some silent understanding that we needed to walk on eggshells through a nitroglycerin plant when it came to Mother. Roxanne must have made for an easy mark—dangle the temptation of eternal beauty and watch her dance. Suddenly sick to my stomach, I shook my head and grimaced. "Damn it, Mother."

You must think we were pretty stupid.

I shrugged. "She's good at telling people what they want to hear. You're not the first. If I have anything to say about it, you'll be one of the last. What next?"

Roxanne told her story, and I listened, mostly silent. I asked a few questions here and there, but for the most part it was a linear progression. In a strange way, each stop Mother and her coven had made mirrored my own checklist. The thought of an illicit magic shop in San Francisco piqued my interest, but given Roxanne's description of the carnage they'd wrought, I doubted there'd be anything left.

The one thing I now knew was that Mother had refused to give the girls any details about her ultimate plan save for cryptic comments about 'saving the world.' As far-fetched as that seemed to me, Roxanne and the others had drunk enough of the Kool-Aid to go along for the ride. Until it cost them their lives.

"And here we are," I said.

Here we are, she agreed. *What now?*

I leaned my head back and looked to the sky. "I'm open to suggestions," I said. For a pregnant pause, I half-hoped that the entity that liked to wear my dad's face would pop in for a lecture, but no such luck.

My phone buzzed with an incoming text, and I dug it out.

Talked to Gordo. He says those guys are bad news.

"You don't say, Karen," I muttered. Gordo was a retired SEAL and part-time military contractor that worked the odd job here and there for the De La Rosas. **No kidding**, I replied.

I'm serious, Duffer. He didn't even want to talk about it. He looked SCARED.

That gave me pause. Gordo and I were about the same height, but he had biceps the size of my thighs. I'd worked a few cases with him back in the day before I went out on my own, and the dude could probably bench press a Volkswagen.

He, Scope, and a few others had kept some drug dealers at bay while a ghost led me to some kidnap victims the bangers were holding for ransom. Back before I'd figured out how to use my magic to defend myself, I'd appreciated rough and tumble types with machine guns watching my back.

I could use that sort of thing right about now. Stifling a laugh, I replied, **I get you. What does he think I should do?**

Karen must have had the reply queued up and ready to send: **Come home. We can figure out the next step from here.**

I tossed the idea around. I couldn't shake the feeling that I was running away, but at the same time, I was also running to something close to safety. Between Karen, Gordo, and everyone else who was out of Division M's hands, I'd have some backup.

Surrendering to the inevitable, I replied, **OK.**

CHAPTER TWENTY

Valentine—Tuesday afternoon
Washington, DC

The Mystical Affairs Oversight Committee didn't get much air time on C-SPAN, for obvious reasons.

Val walked into the warded conference room ten minutes early. He wasn't surprised to see that seven men awaited him, sitting in a row on the opposite side of the table from the door. *Great, they're playing games.*

The group was, by tradition, a mixture of senior Senators and Representatives—three of each—along with a Presidential appointee. In Val's experience, this was a good thing. The lack of publicity meant that the committee members couldn't grandstand in front of the cameras to raise public awareness for legislative efforts or future campaigns. For better or worse, anyone in this room—other than Val, of course—was here for reasons other than raising their public profile.

Deputy Attorney General Perez, the current Presidential appointee, sat in the center of the row, and he nodded to Val. "Have a seat, Agent Valentine."

"Sirs," he replied, taking the offered seat. He resisted the urge to doff his suit coat. He still carried his holstered sidearms, and he didn't want to make any of the men across the table antsy.

He studied their faces as he waited for someone to speak. Other than Representative Lucas of Indiana, there was a lot of gray hair and wrinkles trying to stare him down. Ironically enough, he was a hell of a lot older than every one of them, and in no way intimidated by such things as political power.

Senator Weeden, a balding, bespectacled fellow from Iowa, leaned forward. "First of all, how's the Director?"

"He's out of intensive care, but they're keeping him in a medically-induced coma. Still touch and go."

"Damn shame," Weeden said. "We called this—"

Representative Kovalchuk, a brash New Yorker, interjected. "Agent Valentine, under what authority did you assume command of Division M?"

Val fixed the other man with a hard stare before breaking into a smile, but this grin was far colder than the one he'd given Claudia downstairs. "Seniority."

Lucas shook his head and chuckled, but his counterpart wasn't dissuaded.

"This is hardly a laughing matter, Agent."

"I'm not laughing," Valentine agreed. "You're on oversight. You know my bona fides. What's your concern?"

"There are protocols to follow, a chain of command, which you have usurped, *sir*. I'd like to know why, and for what purpose."

"Our purpose?" Val let some of his annoyance at the dog and pony show creep into his voice. "Son, I was serving this country well before you were shitting in your Pampers. We're the rough men standing ready in the night so you can sip cocktails and screw interns instead of serving as a quick snack to entities that find things like protocol amusing. That's our purpose."

DAG Perez reached out and put his hand on Kovalchuk's arm.

CHAPTER 20

The other man's face was beet red, but the appointee spoke before the Rep could launch into a tirade. "Historically speaking, a political appointee holds the position. Director Newquist was a holdover from the prior administration and enthusiastically endorsed by this one, but, no offense intended, you're a political unknown, Agent Valentine."

"Translation," he replied. "You can't control me. Not that you have anything on Newquist, either, but he's a hell of a lot less blunt than I am."

"That's an understatement," Senator Hecke murmured under his breath. It surprised Valentine the old timer hadn't retired to Utah, yet. He'd been on the committee—and one of its more reasonable voices—since the late '80s. Val winked at him, not caring who else saw.

"Your reputation as a loose cannon notwithstanding," Perez said, "none of us can argue that you haven't had the interests of the greater good in mind, even when going against official directives. That, among other reasons, is why you're still here."

Kovalchuk had composed himself, and he snapped, "Insubordination from a field agent is one thing—it's untenable from a higher level."

Val shrugged. "Who do you work for, sir?"

Confused, the other man hesitated, then said, "The people of the 9th District of New York."

"And even with your position on this committee, I don't answer to you." He turned to Perez. "I don't answer to you, or your boss, or even the President. You want me gone? I'm gone. But that doesn't change my duty." He laughed. "Try to stop me from doing what needs to be done and you'll find out how far out of your jurisdiction I am." That was a bit of bluster. He hadn't gotten any calls for a while, but setting captives free was kind of how they rolled.

Senator Prince of Maine was the newest member of the committee and had remained silent up to this point. He leaned forward now. "What exactly are you trying to say, Agent Valentine?" His tone turned joking. "That you're on a mission from God?"

He stared silently at the Senator for a long moment. The other members of the committee held their tongues. A few had the good grace to look embarrassed for their counterpart; Representative Lucas covered his mouth with one hand to hide a smile. "Rough men and quick snacks, Senator," Val said. "If you ever have the need to know more than that, you'll be told, but not by me."

Prince's mouth opened and closed several times before he managed, "Ah. I see."

"I'm not here to make policy, gentlemen. I've handed off as much of the Director's day-to-day work to his staff as I can. I'm focusing on what I consider our top priorities—the attack on the Virginia facility and the hunt for Helen Locke. Period. If you have a problem with that, say the word. Lack of resources will make the job more difficult, but I'll still do it."

"That's acceptable," Perez said before anyone else could speak. "We simply want to ensure that the, ah, positive flow of communication established by Director Newquist continues, so we're not blind-sided by any developments."

"We'll keep you in the loop," Valentine agreed.

"Fair enough. That should suffice for now, unless anyone else has questions?" There were none, and Perez gave Valentine a tight nod. "Thank you, Agent."

He held back his sigh until he got out of the conference room and down the hall. From a logical standpoint, he understood the need for oversight. Over the years, he'd seen the sort of corruption that sprouted in its absence, but this was something else entirely. Unless he missed his guess, there was some sort of power struggle going on in the committee. He tried to pay as little attention to politics as was possible while living and working in the nation's capital, but he still picked up plenty.

CHAPTER 20

Mystical Affairs wasn't one of the big, publicly-important postings, but it was critical. Getting the post meant that the appointee was well-respected within their own party, and there was nothing politicians liked more than shiny badges to burnish their reputations.

Too much of that lost the entire point of the committee, of course, but someone apparently saw opportunity in the present crisis and wanted to throw their weight around. It would shock him if it wasn't that smarmy prick Kovalchuk. Val had seen him on the news more than once, crying crocodile tears over the crisis *du jour* and calling for 'something to be done.'

Perez, at least, seemed to get it. He would act as a buffer until the Director recovered. *If he recovers.* The elevator arrived with a ding, and Val winced at the thought as he stepped on and hit the button.

His mood soured even as he descended, and when his phone rang, he pulled it out with an annoyed snarl and snapped, "What?"

"Sir? Agent Valentine? This is Agent Anjewierden from the Phoenix office."

He forced himself to relax. "Sorry, kid. Bad day. What can I do for you?"

"I just got a strange call from a counterpart in the regional FBI office. We stored the vehicles from the Sikora crime scene there after we processed them because, well, to be honest, we don't have the room."

"Understood," Val said. Phoenix's Division M branch had an entire floor of an office tower downtown, but that was the extent of their resources. Except for a few small arms, they even stored most of their firepower off-site at a secured hangar inside Luke Air Force Base. Leaning on other agencies was part and parcel of how they did business. For the most part, the other branches didn't even complain. Long-running TV shows to the contrary, the FBI didn't have the expertise and personnel to deal with *chupacabra*, *culebron*, or other cryptids and gladly delegated the responsibility.

"Sometime between last night and this afternoon, the motorcycle on the back of Paxton Locke's RV went missing. They don't have surveillance cameras on the vehicle impound, but one of the FBI agents went in to check out another vehicle and noticed the discrepancy." The other agent's tone turned apologetic. "There was a mix-up, or they'd have called us sooner. I imagine there was a lot of second-guessing going on."

Val closed his eyes and thought. "The cameras on the rest of the area didn't see anything coming in or going out?"

"Nothing. Guards on duty didn't see anything, either."

He laughed. "I'm starting to like this kid. Somehow, he gets from DC to Phoenix, figures out where we stashed his stuff and steals some wheels right out from under our noses." Val thought furiously. "Get the word out. It's impossible to say if he's still in the area, but put some ears to the ground."

"That might be a little tricky. On the same hand, I think I've figured out what Locke was doing in Phoenix, to begin with."

"Lay it on me," Val said. He exited the elevator and headed back toward his place in the conference room.

"The local cops aren't giving us much, but it looks like there was some sort of cult operating in Phoenix. They kidnapped some kids, but someone busted in and took care of business. The surviving cultists, as well as a big chunk of the higher-ups in the police department, have all gone a little nuts. We didn't get an official request for assistance, which is strange in and of itself, but I did some checking, talked to a few of the former cultists. There are enough of them that they're spread out over pretty much every hospital in the Valley. The stories all line up—they woke up from what felt like a waking nightmare, and a young man with white hair brought them up from underground."

"Interesting. What about Locke's friends?"

CHAPTER 20

Anjewierden sighed. "They're still not talking."

"I may have burned that bridge," Val admitted. "Let me think on how to fix that. Worst case, we cut them loose."

"Sir?" the younger agent sounded surprised. "What are you saying, exactly?"

"I've come around on Locke," Val said. "I think we screwed up. He was on our side, and we need to figure out how to get him back there." He considered the stack of paper dedicated to Helen Locke. He thought about rituals and his comment about quick snacks. Breaking open a nexus would be more like an all-you-can-eat buffet. "Something tells me we're going to need his help."

CHAPTER TWENTY-ONE

Paxton—Tuesday night

Interstate 8, east of Yuma, Arizona

Out on the highway, I got the chance to zone out and just ride. Despite the lack of traffic, I forced myself to keep the Kawasaki a few miles an hour over the limit. Even with swapped plates, I wanted to limit the possibility of run-ins with the law. On the bright side, my helmet's visor eased any paranoia I held about facial recognition and traffic cameras. Cruising, I stuck to the right lane and passed only when necessary.

The most surreal part about the road trip, other than the fact that Roxanne sat on the raised passenger bump without any tangible sense of her holding on, was the fact that the rush of wind did nothing to silence her 'speaking.' That made perfect sense, of course, since I wasn't actually hearing her with my ears, but the first time she said something I still jumped in surprise.

Eventually, that oddness faded, and I grew accustomed to the sensation of the highway under me. It had been a long time since I'd ridden the bike anything but short distances on surface streets, but I was glad to have some mode of transportation that hadn't required the abuse of my powers. It was a bit over six hours to San Diego. If I could power through, I wouldn't have to worry about finding a place to sleep, either.

Roxanne left me alone with my thoughts for the most part. As I came up behind a lumbering semi and signaled to go around, she broke her silence and asked, *What's that? Do you feel that?*

I couldn't turn to look at her expression, but the strained tone of her ethereal voice almost sounded frightened. That made the hair on the back of my neck stand on end. There were things that could scare even ghosts, and they weren't much fun to deal with.

"I don't feel anything," I said. If the sound of the wind bothered her ability to understand me, she hadn't said so. That was a nice stroke of luck—I imagine my throat would end up raw sooner rather than later if I had to scream my responses back to her. "What are you talking about?"

The truck. It's not right.

I pulled back into the right lane and glanced in the mirror. The headlights made it difficult to make out specific details, but nothing struck me as particularly off about the semi's silhouette. "Not seeing it," I said.

I'm not imagining things. I know I'm not an expert at this whole being dead thing, but something about it gives me the creeps.

"Fair enough," I said. I accelerated to shy of eighty, quickly outdistancing the truck. Crossroads were few and far between in the desert, but after a few miles, we came across an overpass where a county road spanned the interstate. There hadn't been any exits in the interim, so unless the driver wrecked or made a U-turn, he was still heading our way.

Slowing, I came to a stop underneath the span and propped the bike on its kickstand. Keeping one ear to the east, I dug through one of my panniers as though looking for something. "Get another look," I said.

Lights appeared on the horizon, and I bowed my head while

keeping my eyes on the road. The driver must have seen me and the bike on the side of the road. He drifted over to the left, straddling the center line before he reached the overpass.

At highway speeds, I couldn't make out more than a man-shaped silhouette back-lit by the dashboard lights before he zoomed by in a rush of air. Other than indiscernible lettering on the doors that I didn't have time to study, there were no stand-out markings on the cab or the trailer. An owner-operator, I supposed, and not one of the bigger freight companies. With a shrug, I said, "Are you sure? I didn't feel anything."

I don't know what it is, but something in there isn't right.

Staring after the taillights, I tried to think of a way to check things out without alerting the driver. Holding the invisibility spell while on the bike wouldn't be too difficult, but that still didn't solve the problem of what to do once we caught up. I gave Roxanne a thoughtful look. "If I get you close to the trailer can you, I don't know, jump across, or something?"

What if I fall?

I tried not to laugh. "Seriously? Work with me here." I pointed to the road running above us. "Try jumping up there."

She looked dubious, but she crouched as though gathering herself, and in a silent blur, Roxanne disappeared. Out of sight, and I assumed, up on the deck, her voice sounded perfectly clear.

Okay, so I don't need to worry about falling.

"Interesting," I muttered. Depending on how far that stretched, that could be useful. In a way, it made her the perfect scout.

There was a blur from above, and she stood on the ground next to me. *What now?*

Straddling the bike, I put my helmet back on and said, "When I catch up, jump into the trailer and check it out. Once you've gone through there, check out the cab of the truck. If you see something, great. If not, we can chalk it down to ghostly indigestion."

If she had a snarky comeback, she didn't offer it up. I gunned the engine and got the Kawasaki back up to eighty, then doubled down and went for eighty-five. If there were any state troopers out shooting radar, I could always kill the engine and go invisible.

The next few minutes were nerve-racking, and I realized that the tight feeling in the pit of my stomach wasn't entirely due to unease at the road whizzing by beneath me. I might have denied it at first, but some instinct had come around to Roxanne's perspective. There was something *wrong* ahead.

And one way or another, I was going to take care of it.

Twin red lights, like the narrowed eyes of some deadly creature, appeared ahead, miles off yet. I considered the bike's headlight. The overcast sky lent no clearance for the moon, and I was reluctant to turn it off. Steeling myself, I went invisible, half-expecting the light to project out of the area of effect with no obvious source. Instead, the light itself stopped at the outer edge and the desert around us brightened ever-so-slightly.

Pondering the physics of that was liable to give me a headache, if not worse, so I went with it. The spell seemed to have some sort of built-in night vision function, and I'd never realized it. When it's pitch black outside, you don't have much call for invisibility.

Weird.

I laughed. "Right?"

As we edged closer, I pulled into the left lane and reduced speed. Slowly overtaking him, I didn't want to run the risk of splashing myself all over the back of the trailer if he happened to slam on the brakes.

Even with the back end of the trailer, I said, "Go!"

I half-expected some sort of inertia as Roxanne pushed off and blurred onto the back of the trailer, but reality was doing everything it could to stymie Newton.

Slowing, I let the truck move away, my eyes on Roxanne,

clinging to the back doors of the trailer. She gave me a nod, then pressed herself against the doors to pass through.

And remained there, hanging off the trailer. Cold blue light flared where she'd touched the metal, spreading in a growing outline of her form. The traces followed dense markings that bent back and around on each other. The longer I looked at them, the more they threatened to blur before my eyes.

Runes, or sigils—I'd seen something not so different inscribed in the outer walls of the cavern complex where a long-dead tribe of wizards had imprisoned the Aztec demon Tlaloc.

Question is, I wondered, *is this intended to keep something out, or something in?*

Out, I reasoned. The markings in the cavern under Upward Path's gymnasium pointed inside. While I couldn't understand the language of these symbols, somehow I intuitively knew these were meant to keep prying eyes away.

Either way, the spell on the trailer meant Roxanne was right. While that didn't change my need to take a look inside before taking more drastic steps, the fact that she couldn't scout it out mean that we had to try something different.

I pulled into the left lane and did my best to match the truck's speed. Staring at the spinning wheels, I tried to commit the image of the rear driver's side tire to memory. Easing off the gas, I drifted back behind the semi. Close enough that I hoped I was in the driver's blind spot, I dropped the visibility spell and envisioned a narrow blade of force jabbing into the sidewall.

At first, I wasn't sure it would work. A few weeks ago, it had taken every bit of my strength to pinch off a copper tube inside a water heater across the room, but in this case, the truck's own inertia helped. All I had to was envision the blade in a static position, and with a sharp crack of escaping air, the tread peeled off in a single continuous strip.

Braking, I switched back to invisibility and steered for the edge of the road. I'd seen the damage a flying 'gator' could wreak, and I had no desire to take one to the face. The tread flew past, flopping to the road along the centerline. A groaning noise sounded from ahead, and the trailer's brake lights brightened as the driver fought to bring his rig under control with a bare rim riding the pavement.

The Kawasaki shook under me as I steered it out of the breakdown and down the shallow ditch at the side of the road. Killing the engine, I stepped up onto the pavement and started jogging after the semi. It had come to a stop a quarter-mile down the road, hazard lights blinking.

Wow, what if he'd wrecked? Roxanne stayed at my side with annoying ease.

I considered the thought, then winced. I hadn't given my plan much thought—I'd just acted on instinct. "Back wheel like that, that's not going to happen. But that's one of the drive wheels, so it definitely stopped him where he might have been able to keep going a bit longer if I'd taken out one of the trailer tires. Front tire? Oh, yeah. He'd have flipped." As we came up on the back of the trailer, I lowered my voice and said, "Keep an eye on him for me, I'm going to try something."

The light had faded from the lines inscribed in the metal of the rear doors. Up close, I could make out the fine pattern of lines, though they still blurred the closer I looked at them. Some sort of 'nothing to see here' spell?

Padlocks secured the covers over the door latches. I glanced over at Roxanne. She looked back and said, *He's standing there staring at the wheel and talking on a phone.*

"Good." I took a deep breath, brought my hand close to the back of the trailer, and pushed forward slowly as I used the phase spell. Down in the cavern, I'd been unable to phase through the walls. Here and now, my hand sank through without a feeling of resistance. If everything else was the same, I wouldn't be able to come back out, but there was always the force blade option if I couldn't find an egress. "Moment of truth," I said, and stepped up on the trailer's bumper before pushing the rest of my body though.

It was cold inside, and a low, subtle hum filled the air. I hadn't realized the trailer had a refrigeration unit, but that was the only explanation for the atmosphere. I listened for a moment, straining to hear anything over the hum, but my shallow breaths were the only sound.

I pulled out my cell phone and turned on the flashlight function. Shrink-wrapped cardboard boxes stretched from floor to ceiling, held in place by yellow straps. Looking at either side of the stack, I tried to make out what lay beyond, if anything, but the boxes lined up with geometric precision. From the text printed on the containers, they held varieties of frozen vegetables. Shaking my head, I muttered, "I'm going to feel stupid if I wrecked the Jolly Green Giant delivery truck."

Phasing out, I moved forward through the boxes. I hit open air much sooner than I'd expected—there were no more than two layers of boxes between the back of the truck and the open space. The odd, coppery scent in the air gave a hint of what I was about to see, but I never could have anticipated the horrors revealed to me as I swept the flashlight beam around the hidden compartment.

Steel tubes ran along either side of the trailer, close to the roof. Every few feet, a large metal frame shaped somewhat like a hanger hung from the horizontal support. Rather than forming a bent triangle, the twin outer legs of each hanger sprouted a sharp metal hook. A naked human corpse dangled from each, the hooks punching through the calf above the ankle.

Most of the bodies were short enough that their outstretched fingers brushed the floor. A particularly tall corpse was without a head, the stump of his neck cut shy of brushing the floor. Vomit surged in the back of my throat, but I held it back. If I started now, I didn't think I'd be able to stop. The bodies bore few visible

CHAPTER 21

wounds, save for the decapitated corpse. I might have convinced myself they were sleeping if not for the light rime of frost coating each.

"Help me," whispered a weak voice. For a moment, I wondered if it wasn't another ghost, but just as quickly, I realized that I'd *heard* this voice. I stepped lightly down the center of the trailer, shying away from the dangling bodies. The hum of the refrigeration unit grew louder the closer I drew to the front. Past the last body, the steel support pipes bent and plunged toward the floor. The cage lay between the two, under the cooling duct.

The woman inside was clothed, though she shivered uncontrollably. The fine mesh of the cage was too tight for her desperate fingers to reach through, and the entire box was low and narrow enough to keep her in a semblance of a fetal position. "Help," she repeated.

I knelt. "Hang on," I said. "I'm going to get you out of here."

There was a thumping noise from outside, and I remembered the spare tires slung under the trailer. The driver didn't seem to be waiting for AAA—the clock was getting tight.

I kept the force blade short and made quick work of the side of the cage closest to me. If the blue light cutting through otherwise-solid steel impressed her, she didn't let on. *Close to shock*, I thought grimly. If she'd spent much longer in here, exposure would have killed her.

Her hand was small and cold in my own as I reached out for it. She sighed a tight sob but could muster no tears. "Oh, God, I thought I was dreaming. Please help me."

"That's the plan." I pulled her out and cradled in my arms. She couldn't have been more than a few inches over five feet, and I doubted she weighed more than a hundred pounds. Much larger, and the cage would have been too small. Turning away toward the passenger side, I phased the both of us and jumped out the side of the trailer, crossing my fingers that the spell would work.

We didn't flutter to the ground like leaves on the wind, but the impact on the scrub didn't hurt as much as it would have had we made the jump solid. I snapped back into phase, and the woman let out an abbreviated shriek of surprise. Outside of the trailer, the desert night was practically balmy, and the warmer air felt like fire on my skin.

I heard a scrape of boots on pavement and the hammer of weight landing on the roof of the trailer.

He just jumped! Roxanne blurted.

No kidding, I thought. Turning, I looked up at the silhouette of the truck driver.

He cocked his head far beyond the norm of a human range of motion, his ear brushing the shoulder of his flannel shirt. In a liquid voice, he said, "She is to feed the Void. This is not permitted."

I'd heard that kind of voice before, out of a traveling salesman with a dead body in his trunk. I didn't have backup or a shotgun this time, but it was actually kind of comforting to run into something familiar, as crazy as that seemed. "Not on my watch, asshole."

The thing on top of the trailer rocked back a step in surprise, then leaned in to study me. "*Magus*," it crooned. "I know your face. You, too, will feed the Void."

"So, quit talking and come get some, Doctor Octopus."

Arms outstretched, the thing jumped.

One thing no one's ever accused me of is being a slow learner. The last time I'd fought one of these things, it had gotten its hands on me and tossed me around like a rag doll. That made step one staying outside of its reach.

This was easier said than done. As I ducked to one side, its arms whipped toward me, stretching out from the cuffs of the shirt. Fingers and palm spread wide large enough to palm a basketball, it brushed my jacket.

I jerked a hand up, and with a sudden pop, the stench of burnt meat filled my nostrils. The driver landed on bent knees, pulling a tentacle arm back with a cauterized stump at the wrist.

The abandoned hand flopped around on the pavement like one of the face-huggers from the *Alien* movies, then dissolved into a tarry black goo that smelled about ten times as bad as the burnt flesh.

"No friends this time," the thing gurgled. A pair of tendrils pushed through the blackened flesh at the end of its wrist, twisting around as though searching for something to strangle. "I will taste your blood, wizard."

"Yeah, yeah," I said. Whipping out my left hand, I snared the thing's ankles with an invisible tendril of force and yanked. It stumbled and nearly toppled, but caught itself with its intact arm and used that leverage to propel itself at me.

Which is exactly what I wanted.

I went low and kept my hands clasped together, parallel to the ground. One arm brushed my shoulder, but I spun as I ducked. Our movements combined to push its chest through my paired force blades. Ichor hissed, and some ungodly foulness spilled to the pavement as the thing howled in obvious agony.

Completing the follow through, I planted and lunged for the thing. It stood hunched over, clutching at what I assumed were what it used for intestines to keep them from spilling out on the pavement. It had nowhere to run. Given the way it and its predecessor had recovered from dismemberment, I couldn't count on that disability to last. I hit it high, bowling it over and slamming it face-first to the pavement. This elicited another squeal of agony. Its shoulder joint rotated in ways a human body wasn't designed to move, lengthening fingers wrapping around my left arm and beginning to squeeze.

Grunting at the pain, I swept my other arm across and traced a burning line in the pavement that intersected with the beast's neck. The grip on my bicep eased, and a leprous-scalped head rolled down into the ditch. The stench of burning tar mixed with the scent of whatever it was, and I did throw up then, spewing my dinner into the weeds at the side of the road.

You okay?

I looked up at Roxanne and nodded. "How's the girl?"

Passed out.

"Thank God for small favors." I climbed to my feet and jogged to the cab. The passenger door was unlocked. Pulling it open, I waited, ready for something to rush out of hiding, but the driver was alone.

It was almost absurd how normal the interior of the semi looked. He'd left the radio tuned to a classic rock station. A fountain drink from a truck stop rested in the cup holder, and air fresheners plugged into the vents lent the inside the odor of clean linen.

Finding nothing of use up front, I stepped back into the sleeper. The small bed was made with military precision, the rest of the area clean enough to have come off the showroom floor. I didn't know what else I'd expected, given the steps the thing had taken to ensure its cargo remained secret and unnoticed.

The small refrigerator held bottles of water, and I helped myself to a couple. Back out on the pavement, I used the first to wash the foul taste out of my mouth and sipped the second more slowly.

The former hostage's breathing was slow and even, and she didn't stir when I picked her up again. I got her up into the passenger seat with some effort, and by the time I climbed over her and manhandled her into the sleeper, she was blinking at me with heavy eyes.

"You're safe now," I assured her. "Rest."

"Okay," she whispered, rolling onto her side. I untucked the blanket from its crisp military corners and threw it over her. She lapsed back into a deep sleep before I had her covered. The light buzz of her snores filled the cabin.

As of yet, no traffic had passed, but that wasn't going to last forever. I hopped back down to the ground and headed back to the headless corpse. If anything, the smell had gotten worse. A puddle of black goo slowly spread around the body, which almost seemed to be deflating. *Of course*, I thought. The dead one in Missouri had melted, too. Whatever these things were, a forensic study of their anatomy was out of the question.

Trying to keep my shoes out of the goop, I patted down the driver's pockets and extracted his wallet and cell phone. Pocketing the cash, I angled the driver's license so I could read the information on it. The license bore a Phoenix address, and the bland face the driver presented matched perfectly with the name 'Robert Page.'

After a moment of thought, I took a picture of the license with my own cell phone, wiped it down with my shirt, and stuffed it back in his pocket.

What the hell is that thing?

"I was hoping you could tell me," I admitted. "This is the second one I've run into. This one said something about 'the Void'—does that ring any bells?"

Your guess is as good as mine. Your mom wasn't big into information sharing.

"Figures." The driver's cell phone didn't have any contacts, and there was only one call in the history, outgoing to a 480 number—also Arizona. I hesitated, then hit the redial button. After three rings, the line beeped in my ear but remained otherwise silent. A voicemail box with no greeting? "Weird." I took a picture of the number, too, then wiped the phone down. I was about to pitch it onto the driver's body, but I wrapped my shirt around the keypad, dialed another number and hit send.

"911, what's the nature of your emergency?"

"There's a tractor-trailer rig broken down on I-8, west of mile marker 44," I said slowly and clearly. "There's a woman inside in need of help, I believe she's a kidnap victim. But you're going to want to check the trailer."

"Sir, can you repeat that?"

"No," I said. "You've got it on tape. I'm leaving this line open so you can trace the call, but I won't be here."

"Sir—" I missed anything else the dispatcher had to say as I gently placed the phone on the ground and walked back toward the Kawasaki.

Halfway between the semi and my own ride, I stopped and tried to calculate what the chances were that this was a random encounter. Yeah, Roxanne had tipped me off, sure, but I'd stopped believing in coincidences a long time ago. "You trying to tell me something?" I stared up into the sky but got no response.

Turning and looking back at the slowly-dissolving corpse at the side of the road, I realized that I'd been going about this the wrong way. I wasn't perfect by any stretch of the imagination, but I was the one out here taking care of the dirty work. Division M thought I was the bad guy? I didn't see them out on the road taking care of any half-squid serial killers. *You're a damn* hero. *Start acting like one.*

I pulled my own phone out and hit the call button. Karen picked up on the second ring, a worried note in her voice. "Are you all right? Where are you?"

"A little less then halfway," I said. "But I'm turning back."

"What? What are you talking about, Paxton?" At this point, I didn't even care that she'd used my name. Let them trace the call. This time, I was coming to *them*.

"I'm not leaving my friends behind." I swallowed and said, "Carlos wouldn't do that to me, and I'm not going to do that to him. Get me Gordo's number. I need to ask him a couple of questions."

CHAPTER TWENTY-TWO

P*AXTON—W*EDNESDAY MORNING
Phoenix, Arizona

I hadn't slept, but I was too wired to, anyway.

Gordo hadn't wanted to give me what I was looking for, but after ten minutes of back and forth, he seemed to realize that I wasn't going to take no for an answer.

Which is why, a few minutes after eight in the morning, I leaned back and stared up at the Bank of America Tower in downtown Phoenix. The former SEAL hadn't known much, but he'd heard enough scuttlebutt to fill me in. Division M was a top-secret subsidiary of the Bureau of Alcohol, Tobacco, Firearms, and Explosives—along with magic, I supposed—that took the lead on threats above and beyond the capabilities of more conventional agencies.

Considering what Mother had brought to bear at Kent's house, that made sense, and it added up with what Puck had told me back in Virginia. Leave it to me to run afoul of the real-life equivalent of the X-Files.

Roxanne blurred out the front of the office tower and took a seat next to me on the bus stop bench. "Well?"

I couldn't get very far past the reception desk—it was like the trailer. Which, I guess, answers the question, doesn't it?

"Yup," I said. Standing, I headed for the door.

Are you sure about this?

"No," I admitted. "But I've got a hunch that this is the right move."

Following your gut doesn't seem like a particularly sensible way to live your life, Roxanne pointed out. I stepped through the spinning door and headed for the elevator banks with a nod to the security guard. I'd kept the Bluetooth in so I could speak, but it had become a habit at this point.

"What have you got to worry about?" I said. "It's not like you can get hurt." As soon as the words were out of my mouth I winced at how mean I sounded, particularly considering it wasn't entirely the truth. I decided not to mention the Edimmu and its propensity for consuming the energy of ghosts. With luck, neither of us would run into one of those.

Yeah, well, if something happens to you, who am I supposed to talk to? No one else can even see me.

I didn't have much of a response to that observation, so I settled for, "Good point."

I rode the elevator in silence—a half-dozen men and women in business attire had joined us from the ground floor. Headset or not, the quarters were close enough to persuade me to keep my mouth shut. Some of the tension must have translated to my face because Roxanne didn't push things by making comments or funny expressions as she had in the past.

The ATF's floor was our first stop, and I squeezed my way out into the vestibule with murmured apologies. My fellow passengers were too engrossed in their phones or newspapers to pay much

CHAPTER 22

attention, and I took a moment to study my surroundings as they went on their way.

Another pair of elevators occupied the wall in front of me, while a blank door with an 'employees only' placard sat to the left. The glass doors to the right opened into a small waiting room with another 'employees only' door behind the broad reception desk.

"Here we go," I said, and pulled open the door.

The woman sitting behind the desk looked a bit older than me and wore a severe business suit. She cocked her head, an expression containing zero patience on her face as she sized me up. "Can I help you with something, sir?"

"I'm here to see someone," I explained. I leaned on the desk long enough to receive a frown and a raised eyebrow, then straightened.

"And that is whom, exactly?"

"Agent Valentine."

The hard cast to her expression slipped the smallest bit, revealing something close to worry or fear. She rolled away from the desk by the barest amount, and I had visions of her reaching for a hidden weapon with one hand. I put on my friendliest smile right as she spoke. "I see. And do you have an appointment, Mister ...?"

"Locke. Paxton Locke." It took everything I had not to put a little Connery-esque drawl in there, but from her demeanor, I didn't think the receptionist was much in the mood for jokes.

Her eyes went a little wide, and my sense that she was ready to draw down on me intensified. I forced myself to remain still, awaiting her response.

"I see. I don't believe he's in the office today. Is this something that another agent could help you with?"

"Very possibly. Is it all right if I sit and wait?" I turned with exaggerated slowness and pointed at one of the chairs in the corner, well within view from the reception desk. "Right there, maybe?"

She glanced at the chair but spent much more time in an appraisal of me. The receptionist relaxed minutely, then nodded. "That'll be fine."

I took a seat and folded my hands in my lap, right in view. Sitting down, I finally noticed the name placard resting on top of the desk, identifying the receptionist as 'Agent Carla Norman.' Interesting. When I'd dug a little digging online after Gordo filled me in, everything I'd seen had indicated that the Phoenix ATF branch was a smaller office—if they had actual agents covering the front desk, that seemed to indicate that they didn't get enough visitors to hire a full-time receptionist.

Although, I reasoned after a moment, *if you've got a bunch of people locked up in the office, you probably don't want admin staff around to ask questions about things like due process and habeas corpus.* Carla murmured quietly into the phone headset she wore. She kept her tone low enough that I was unable to make out most of what she said, but my own name was familiar enough.

She's got a pretty serious gun strapped under the desk there, in case you were wondering.

I pointedly didn't look at Roxanne but nodded all the same. I felt a vague vibration in the floor. The door behind Carla opened slowly. I might have laughed if the situation wasn't so grave.

It wasn't every day the boogieman walked in your door, after all.

The agent that emerged into the reception area wore black suit pants and loafers, though he'd shed his jacket and rolled the cuffs of his shirt up over forearms hard with muscle. I guessed that I'd have a few inches on him, standing up, but he could probably throw me to home plate without breaking a sweat. He had close-cropped black hair and a neatly-trimmed beard. The look of curiosity in his eyes was refreshing and did more than a little to ease the palpable tension in the air. "You're Paxton Locke?"

"That's me," I agreed. Hesitating for a second, I finally stood and extended a hand. The male agent flinched and I heard the click-click of metal on metal from under the reception desk. "Just a handshake," I added. "Scout's honor."

"Agent Jared Anjewierden," the agent said. He looked at my hand, back up at me, then shrugged and shook it. If anything, I'd underestimated the muscle he carried—my hand practically disappeared in his. "You were never a scout."

My laugh sounded a little nervous, but I felt entitled. "I guess you'd know that, wouldn't you?"

Anjewierden swallowed, then said, "Would you like to come inside? Sit down and talk?" Hurriedly, he added, "That's why you're here, yes?"

"Yeah," I agreed. "Let's talk."

Valentine—Wednesday Morning
Washington, DC

Everyone who could spare time from other ongoing work had crammed into the conference room. While looking for options to deal with Helen Locke in the present, they were nailing down the plan to deal with her when the time came.

"The center of the nexus is, approximately, right about here." Val tapped a point on the map tacked to the wall. "Northeast of the town proper. Not as far out in the boonies as I'd like, but somewhat isolated. This could be a problem." He traced a line running through the woods near the center of the nexus. "At one time, this was a narrow-gauge railroad. Now it's a hiking trail. If this were going down in the next few months, I'd say we had nothing to worry about, but in March, it's liable to be busy. Something we need to handle, we don't need any collateral damage."

Even over a transcontinental line, Morgan's voice was crystal clear, albeit piped through the phone in the center of the table. "Keep in mind, just because the center of the nexus is outside of the town proper, that doesn't mean Helen has to conduct her ritual there. If anything, I'd say she's liable not to. Anywhere inside its area of effect is sufficient, and that covers at least half of the town."

"Right," Val agreed. "So, rather than worry about blowing our cover or exposing the normals, we evacuate the town. It's a little unorthodox, but in this case, it's better to be safe than sorry."

"What's our cover story?" George wanted to know.

"Natural gas leak. The timing is going to be tight—we could shoot for the day before, but who knows how much prep time she'll need? We're going to have to get all the pieces in place, and as soon as we have a sighting, we move. If we don't see her by the day before, that's our kickoff. Either way, I want that town empty on March 15th."

"What kind of support will you need, sir?" Prather interjected. Rather than fold himself into a chair, the lanky agent had taken up a position leaning in one corner.

"We're keeping it small. Myself, Georgie, Morgan, and Eliot, if

CHAPTER 22

he's back on his feet by then. Anyone else will be on crowd control for the civilians." He gave the room a thin smile. "Not that I don't respect your skills, people, but we've got a limited number of anti-geas charms and no way to make more without Kevin and the Doc. Unless I can get Morgan to burn the midnight oil when she gets back."

"George's suit is my first priority, but you're not going to like the overtime." The gathered agents chuckled, and Val's smile turned more genuine.

"I'm good for it." Another agent raised his hand. Val recognized his face from around the local office but drew a blank on the name. "Go ahead, son."

"Say things go to hell. How do we support the four of you? Can we wear, I don't know, noise-canceling headphones, or something to keep from falling under her spell?"

"Morgan?"

"That should work, though we should look into straps or something to keep her from just pulling them off."

"Sure, that way she can pull off a head," George noted. The room broke up into a mix of amusement and disgust.

Val resisted the urge to give George a look. He was long-accustomed to the other man's gallows humor, but he was unsure how their subordinates would take it given the events of the past few days. With the rubble cleared, the final tally of the dead stood at 110, the lion's share upper management or other supervisory agents. If their mystery attacker had intended a decapitation strike, she'd pulled it off. Those left standing had guts, or they wouldn't be in the Division, but they lacked experience and were ill-equipped to go up against a witch of Helen's caliber.

Once everyone settled down, Val nodded to the agent who'd asked the question. "Good idea, you take lead on it."

A burly male agent called out. "Agent Valentine, all due respect—why not position snipers around the town and eliminate the subject before it becomes a problem?" He shrugged. "I'm still the FNG of Agent Andrews' tactical team, but for that matter—why not call in an air strike and wipe out the town? 'Oops, something sparked the gas.'"

"I have to admit that I like the first idea," Val agreed. "What's your name, Agent?"

"Tom Wallace. I was Airborne till about three months ago."

Val smiled. "I figured. For starters, there's a severe lack of high ground, which limits the potential shooting positions." He tapped a few sites on the map that he and Morgan had noted during their trip. "Note also that our subject *does* have a civilian hostage. Not to be harsh, but if it comes down to stopping Helen Locke but losing the hostage, I'll make that call every time." He surveyed the room, taking stock of the reaction of his fellow agents. "Wrap your heads around this, people. If we're right about what she intends to do, we're talking about the survival of the human race. As far as bombing—Morgan?"

She answered immediately. "They're not cleared for this, Val. Are you sure?"

"I'll smooth it over with Russ once he's back. Lay it on them."

"Fair enough. Ladies and gentlemen, there are places in the world where the fabric of reality is thin, as an analogy. We call this a nexus. Urban legend has grown up around many of them—the Bermuda Triangle, Area 51, Tunguska. For the most part, they aren't harmful to the average person, so we don't mess with them unless we have to. Sometimes things pass through from our side, and vice versa. It's not much of a problem. Randolph, though, is not so much worn thin as torn open. For hundreds of years, magic has stabilized the rip. If you know what to look for, there are older buildings and even survey markers in the area in and around the town inscribed with spells that keep things stable. Without them ... it's wide open, and what might come through makes your typical cryptid look like a cockroach."

"It's a Hellmouth," someone called out. "We get it."

"I'm not familiar with the term," Morgan said, "but yes, that's an apt description. Any damage to the stabilization spells could cause a cascade effect and bring the whole thing down."

"So, no air strikes," Val said. "We've got to do this the hard way."

"Correct."

"All right, people," he said. "We should have the benefit of time here, but keep this operation on your mental back burner while we try to put everything else back together. Questions, concerns, anything at all, come to me, George, or Morgan. Now? Get out of here." He waited until the conference room cleared before leaning closer to the phone. "How are things going over there, Morgan?"

"Nothing concrete, yet, but I'm getting some whispers. Our counterparts in Excalibur Corps have been surprisingly helpful."

Val raised an eyebrow at George. "That's interesting. Any idea why?" The relationship between the two groups had been cool for decades after working hand-in-hand during the Second World War. One would think the continuing survival of the human race would be enough for politicians to put their differences aside, but he was long past being disappointed by that sort of illogical behavior.

"They haven't come out and said anything, but my escorts have been downright twitchy. I'm starting to wonder if we haven't crossed paths with an ongoing investigation on their end."

George mouthed a silent 'wow.' Val gave him a thumbs up before he replied. "Well, I know how I'd handle that sort of thing, but I'm sure you'll approach it with far more diplomacy."

Morgan chuckled. "Depending on how things go over the next day or so, I'm going to brace them if they don't offer anything up. Something tells me I won't have to, though."

"We'll get out of your hair," he said. "Keep us posted."

"Will do."

He stabbed the disconnect button, ending the call. "How are things progressing with backup?"

"I've been working with the governor's office in Maine. In exchange for picking up the cost of deployment, Bravo company of the 3rd Battalion, 172nd Infantry Regiment will be on standby conducting," he hooked his fingers into air quotes, "training exercises and on call if we need them. They're a National Guard unit, but they're good troops by all accounts." George made an expression of distaste. "I'd prefer tanks, but even light infantry will have more firepower than even what we can bring to bear."

"We're not invading Sicily, George," Val shrugged. "And honestly, if we have to call these guys in, things will be desperate enough that we'll want something a bit faster than armor."

"You're a tad less cocky than normal. Everything all right?"

"What can I say, I'm enjoying the daily reminders that I've dodged command all these years for a reason."

"Well, take it from me—you're doing a fine job."

"Considering the source, I'll take it. We need—" Both men turned at the rap on the conference room door. The director's executive assistant had a strange look on her face. "What is it, Claudia?"

"I've got the Phoenix office on the line, Agent Valentine. You really need to talk to them."

CHAPTER TWENTY-THREE

P<small>AXTON</small>—W<small>EDNESDAY MORNING</small>
Phoenix, Arizona

"First things first," I said after Anjewierden led me into a small conference room and offered coffee. I tried to ignore the staring faces as we walked through the office, as well as the fact that everyone in sight had fallen into what a suspicious mind might call tactical positions. On the bright side, with the door open, Roxanne was able to slip in at my side. If I could filibuster long enough, she could do a quick recon of the office and tell me what I needed to know. "Where are my friends?" I concluded.

"They're safe," he said. "I assure you, no harm has come to them. A few of them suffered from smoke inhalation and burns. We've gotten them the best care."

Roxanne blurred into the room. *Holding cells are in the center of this floor, behind the elevator. Keeps them away from the windows, I guess.* I cocked my head to one side. She rolled her eyes, then lifted a finger and pointed. *Thataway.*

"Unless I miss my guess," I said to Agent Anjewierden, then

turned and imitated Roxanne's pointing finger. "They're right over there."

The other man went a little pale. "Well, uh ..."

"Look. I don't want to get off on the wrong foot. You say they're fine, I'll take your word for it, all right? I do want to see them at some point, but we can build some trust first."

"That seems fair." He stared at me in silence for a moment, then said, "What can I do for you, Mr. Locke?"

"Well, I came to see Agent Valentine ..."

"He's not here. We've got an issue back east."

I thought about the explosion and building collapse that had helped set me and Puck free and nodded. "I can imagine."

"I've got a call out, he should be getting with us soon. Until then, I guess it's two guys drinking coffee."

Trying not to laugh at the bemused expression on his face, I nodded. "You ever hear of anything called 'the Void?'"

He thought about it, then shook his head. "Not ringing any bells. Most of the things we deal with in the southwest are your garden-variety cryptids. What's the Void? That the cult you busted up last week?"

Now it was my turn for surprise. "You guys found about that, huh?" I'd thought they'd been following Mother and run across Kent's house that way, but it stood to reason that the mysterious agency would have its finger on the pulse of mystical weirdness with that high of a profile. "No, that was—different. I dealt with something last night that talked about the Void. Thought it might ring a bell since it was hauling fresh and frozen food through your territory. Let's just say his protein of choice walked on two legs."

He grimaced. "Where?"

"Over by Yuma on Interstate 8. I called the local cops, but—I don't know, do you guys assist on stuff like that?"

"I'll make some calls in a bit," Anjewierden said. "It's still early. My turn. Can I ask *you* something?"

"Sure," I replied.

"Why do you do it?"

I thought about being diplomatic, but the terrified woman in the cage and the bodies hanging from hooks popped into my head. The fury I'd felt on the side of the road had dissipated somewhat. I tried to keep it that way, answering in an even tone. "Someone has to. The only time I've run into you guys is after the fact." *Well, that probably won't help.* I took a sip of coffee. "I've spent the last few years roaming around the country, trying to help people. Maybe ghosts aren't a big enough deal for Division M, but what about Sumerian shadow demons? Wanna-be Aztec gods demanding human sacrifices? I didn't see anyone else stepping up to the plate. And I'm pretty sure my mom's little pep squad broke her out of prison under Division M's watchful eyes, no? If not me, who?" My hand was shaking as I set the cup down, and coffee sloshed onto the table.

Be nice.

I wasn't sure if Roxanne meant the comment as a defense of herself or to tell me to take it down a notch, but I didn't care. A white-hot rage had replaced the calm I'd forced myself to carry into the building. *These* were the bogeymen I'd been trying to keep away from? It was a damn miracle Mother hadn't gotten out of jail *sooner.*

Anjewierden gritted his teeth and took a few deep breaths before responding. "I'm going to be straight with you, man. You're not wrong. We're not out here combing through the weeds looking for clues. We're firefighters. More often than not, we come in when things have gone to hell, and we do everything we can to keep it from getting worse. That's the job. There are two dozen people in this office, and a bit less than a third of them are Division M cleared. The others know we're into something clandestine, but for whatever reason, they're not read in. Multiply that across the country, and we don't have the manpower. The big dogs can only be so many places at once."

"Big dogs like Valentine?"

"He's the biggest."

"He said he was—" I hesitated. The dream memory had become clearer as the drugs passed out of my system, but even after all I'd been through, I doubted my own recollection. "Something impossible," I said, finally. *Best not give him any reason to think you're off your rocker, Pax.*

Anjewierden composed his thoughts for a bit, then settled for, "I don't know how far up you need to be to get the full story, but I'm not it. There are rumors and stories, but who knows how much of that is true, if at all." He shrugged. "All I know is, I'm glad he's on our side." His phone chirped, and he glanced down. "And there he is. I'll put it on speaker." He shrugged. "Work on building that trust, right?"

I nodded.

The voice that filled the room when he answered the phone made the hair on the back of my neck stand on end. My memories might have been fuzzy from the drugs, but I remembered the voice.

"This is Valentine. Is the situation under control?"

"Everything is sweet as a peach," Anjewierden said. It seemed a strange comment, and to top it all off, it elicited an aggrieved sigh from the phone speaker.

"Of course, a duress code doesn't mean shit if he put a whammy on you and made you use it, isn't that right?"

"I don't do that sort of thing," I interjected. *Well, not much.* "If you didn't go off half-cocked and took the time to ask some actual questions, you might have figured that out."

"Paxton."

"What's up, Doc?"

CHAPTER 23

He sighed again. "I don't have time for this shit. What do you want?"

"My friends released, for one. They didn't do anything wrong."

"That depends on your perspective. I'd have to take off my socks to count the number of felonies they racked up just with the automatic weapons."

"Yeah, well," I responded lamely, "you need something with a little more kick when you go up against magic-using politicians and Aztec gods, what can I say? And last I checked, you're not exactly advertising your presence."

"Well, we can't all be on Craigslist."

"You should be."

His voice turned thoughtful. "Maybe so. What's in this for us?"

"I help you stop my Mother."

"What makes you think you can?"

"I did it once," I said. My voice sounded far more confident than I actually felt. "I can do it again."

Valentine fell silent, and I took a look at Anjewierden. His face was calm, but beads of perspiration were building on his temples. I got the sense that he'd rather be anywhere else than here.

You and me both, buddy.

"Here's the deal. I really am busy. I don't have the time to come to you and make a handshake deal. If you're serious, you come back to DC so I can look you in the eye."

"Anyone comes at me with a needle and all bets are off," I said. "I'll stop her myself," I bluffed. *Hell, I don't even know where she is or where she's going!* From the sound of things, though, Valentine had an idea.

"You've got it. Anjewierden? Cut the friends loose and get the young man on the next flight."

PAXTON—WEDNESDAY EVENING
Joint Base Andrews, Maryland

Between coughs, Kent told me I was a damn fool.

Division M had sequestered him, his wife Jean, and Father Rosado away from the rest of my friends in the base clinic at Luke Air Force Base. After I'd come to my agreement with Agent Valentine, Anjewierden arranged for us to meet in a small lunchroom used by the doctors. Between lectures, I wondered how they felt about being kicked out of their own space by secret agents.

My friends didn't like the deal, and they were happy to yell about it. That wasn't such a big deal for myself, but I felt bad for Anjewierden. The agent sat in one corner, a strange look on his face as he watched the proceedings.

"Look," I said, finally, cutting Esteban off before he could go into another spiel about *habeas corpus*. "I get it. I do. No offense, but you guys weren't shipped off to wizard Gitmo, either. This is bigger than me, and if I can get you guys free, I'm taking that deal. End of story."

"What if they change the terms on you?" Carlos said. He'd given me a bit less of a hard time than the others, but then, he'd also been texting like a mad man on his returned cell phone. I got the impression Karen, at least, was pretty ecstatic about how things had worked out.

I glanced at the agent in the corner. "That's not going to happen. Do I trust them completely? Of course not, they haven't earned that yet. But my eyes are open now. I'm not going to get blindsided again." Roxanne grinned at me from her position near Anjewierden. I hadn't told anyone about my new sidekick yet, and I planned on keeping her existence to myself as long as I could. If nothing else, she could be the eyes in the back of my head. "We'll stay in touch. If we don't hear from each other at least once a day, we get the lawyers and press involved."

Anjewierden grimaced at the mention of the media, but he didn't say anything. For all my talk of trust, everything that had happened since I'd spoken to Valentine boded well for their good intentions. I had my phone and wallet back, and another agent had brought my RV and the De La Rosa's van from the impound. Between the two vehicles, they'd all be able to get back to San Diego. Phoenix PD had fired Kent before Mother made her visit. It was up in the air whether the termination was official, given that the officers doing the firing had been under Tlaloc's influence, but losing his house had put my friend in a somber mood. I wouldn't have called him broken, per se, but he looked beaten down.

Their treatment hadn't been as bad as that of the De La Rosas, but I imagined being handcuffed to a hospital bed didn't help speed up healing times. I'd made my escape to San Diego and the ocean over a decade ago when dad died—I couldn't begrudge my friend for wanting to fight another day, himself.

In the end, Father Rosado was the peacemaker. "Kent, Jean— we know what Helen told us. She wants Paxton to come to her. The Lord only knows what horrors she has in mind, but it can't be good, no?"

I shuddered at the memory of the nightmare vision I'd received from the grimoire and nodded in silent agreement. Kent grumbled in annoyance, but he nodded, as well.

"You have to stop her, Paxton," the Father said. "If there's anyone I know who can do it, it's you. For us to try and keep you safe when this is what you're being called to do is purely selfish."

And that was that. My flight was waiting, and my friends were free to go. There were hugs and handshakes all around as I bid them farewell. Scope tried to talk me into bringing him along, but I pushed back on that as gently as I could. "I've got some tricks up my sleeve, man. They caught me by surprise the first time. That ain't happening again. But if I need backup, you'll the first one I call, I promise."

A few hours later, my third cross-country flight came to an end. It had been the most comfortable of the bunch. The Air Force personnel on the plane informed me that the C-21A was the military version of a Lear Jet, and the sumptuous interior confirmed that. After that initial exchange, the flight crew ignored me and went about their business. I should have slept, but my promise to Esteban and the others that I'd watch myself weighed heavily enough on my conscience that I forced myself to stay awake, watching the countryside roll by below us.

The landing was routine enough, and after we taxied to an open hangar, getting off the plane was a breeze—I was the lone passenger, and my only luggage was the backpack I'd carried on with me. *I could get used to traveling like this.*

The Division M agent waiting for me at the bottom of the stairs was alone, leaning casually against the side of a black Suburban that screamed government vehicle. Despite my earlier bravado, my stomach clenched a bit at the sight of Valentine. I swallowed my nerves and began my descent.

That's the glowing man, Roxanne said. She'd been quiet since

CHAPTER 23

I'd met with my crew, but we hadn't had much alone time to be able to speak. *The one who killed Kelsey.*

"He's dangerous, I get it," I mumbled. Throwing my shoulders back, I hit the bottom of the stairs, marched across the tarmac and stuck out my hand. "We meet again, Agent Valentine."

He shook my hand without hesitation. A hint of a smile crossed his face, but then he cocked his head to one side. "Who's your friend?"

"You can *see* her?"

"Not as such, but I know something was around. She?"

"Roxanne," I said. "From Kent's house."

"Ah," he said. "Miss Mills. I'm surprised she's still around."

I glanced at her—she didn't have anything to say, but she kept her face still as she stared at him. "She's a pretty good scout, actually. She had some interesting stories about the fight back in Phoenix. I was trying to figure out if the last time we met was a hallucination, and she threw another bucket of crazy on top." I looked around the hangar. We weren't alone, but the crew servicing the newly-arrived plane stayed well away. "Where's the robot and the werewolf?"

Valentine closed his eyes and shook his head. "He's not a werewolf," he said with a sigh. "And he just got out of the hospital."

I grinned, reveling in the fact that he seemed a little off balance. "What's your story, then? Roxanne called you the glowing man—do you prefer that, or something more vintage, 'Doc'?"

He frowned. "First of all, I'd appreciate it if you didn't blast my identity to the sky. I should have kept my mouth shut, but you've got a way of getting under people's skin, don't you?"

"It's a gift. It can't be shocking that I'm curious—you look pretty good for a senior citizen."

"Still spry enough to kick your ass, as I remember."

"Fair enough," I shrugged. "Seriously, what's your deal? Are you a vampire, or what?"

"Not exactly. Let's just say when a man with a burning sword makes you an offer you can't refuse, you accept it." He smirked. "I believe you two have met."

It was my turn for surprise. "I kind of wish he'd pop in right about now, actually."

He grunted and gave me the barest shadow of a smile. "He does have a way of leaving you to sort things on your own, doesn't he?"

"That he does."

"On the bright side, we seem to have the benefit of time, if we're right." He jerked a thumb at the Suburban. "Ready to go? We'll fill you in at headquarters."

Nerves or not, I didn't hesitate. "Let's do it."

CHAPTER TWENTY-FOUR

P<small>AXTON</small>—W<small>EDNESDAY EVENING</small>
Washington, DC

When Agent Valentine told me he was taking me to meet his team, I wasn't sure what to expect.

A bald guy in a wheelchair and a sloppy-looking agent in a rumpled suit sat on the opposite side of the long conference table. Hesitating in the doorway, I checked both sides of the room and immediately outside.

"Lose something?" Valentine said. He pulled out a chair and dropped into it with an annoyed grunt.

"No, I guess I expected more than three people."

Roxanne walked through and past me into the room and moved into the corner, as far away from Valentine and the others as she could get. *He's the werewolf,* she pointed at the scruffy guy. *Not sure about the bald one.*

Uninvited, I took a chair of my own. "Howdy, fellas." I stretched a hand across the table to the bald guy. "You must be the robot. Paxton Locke."

"George Patrick," he growled. "And it's an electro-thaumaturgical prosthesis. With machine guns."

"Nice." I shifted my hand over to the last man. "Hi."

Amused, he returned the gesture. "Nick Eliot. No wonder Val's in such a bad mood, he's finally met someone who's as big of a smart-ass as he is."

"One of these times, the doctors will cut out your sense of humor," Valentine muttered.

"You know me, that baby will grow right back," Agent Eliot grinned.

"Can I start, now?"

"By all means, lay it on us."

"Until the Revolutionary War, the British Excalibur Corps maintained the defense of the New World against otherworldly threats. Once the United States won their independence, that was obviously out of the question. When Congress passed the Judiciary Act of 1789, they authorized the creation of the first Federal law enforcement agency, the Marshals Service. James Madison urged President Washington to establish an organization similar to the Corps within the Marshals Service. Division M was born, and for the next hundred plus years, we held the line. We've never had an excess of personnel, but America has a way of attracting unique and talented individuals." Valentine smiled crookedly. "We made do. During Prohibition, organized crime became the primary trafficking source of illicit magic—along with alcohol—so Division M shifted from the Marshals Service to the Treasury's Alcohol Tax Unit. After 9/11, the Homeland Security Act moved us to the Department of Justice. In the end, the org chart doesn't mean a damn thing—we've held the line for over two hundred years. I've been here for over half that time. Welcome to America's bulwark against mystical threats."

I leaned back in the chair and considered that. Given Anjewierden's comment about firefighters, the lack of personnel

CHAPTER 24

explained their inability to do more than react to situations. Maybe that had worked in the old days, but things seemed to be escalating, of late. Cassie and I had discussed it during our trip to Kent's house—how there were more and more ghosts. Hell, just in the past few weeks I'd dealt with more 'otherworldly' stuff than I had in the last ten years.

An uptick like that certainly didn't signal a trend, but if things like the Edimmu, Tlaloc, and the Void were willing to move so brazenly in the open, these guys were outmatched. Worst of all, they didn't seem to realize it. Institutional blindness? Doing things the same way for what, *hundreds* of years? "You weren't joking, were you? You really *are* Doc Holliday."

"Not for a long time, son."

"Don't take this the wrong way, but you look nothing like Val Kilmer."

He frowned as Eliot started laughing. Annoyed, Valentine's Southern accent sharpened. "Don't take *this* the wrong way, but if you ask me to do the huckleberry line, you're getting two black eyes. And that's me being *nice*." He waited for a beat to make sure I understood, then shrugged. "I always liked Kirk Douglas more, myself."

I turned to Eliot. "Wyatt Earp?"

He shook his head as Valentine interjected, "This isn't secret identity day. Suffice to say 'there are more things in heaven and earth, Paxton, than are dreamt of in your philosophy.'"

"You're laying *Shakespeare* on me?"

"Whatever works. Here's the deal. Your friends told you that your mother wants you in Randolph, Maine, for the Ides of March?"

"Sure," I agreed, "but I don't understand why. She's got the book. Taking Cassie and baiting me doesn't make sense."

Valentine grimaced. "I'd conference in the fourth member of our crew, but she's overseas. I'm not sure she's available at the moment, but she has a theory. When Helen Locke killed your father, it was part of a ritual. You interrupted that and kept her from succeeding. We think she's going to try it again."

My heart sank. "With Cassie standing in for my dad."

"Theoretically. Without getting too far into the weeds, Randolph is a mystical linchpin—a dimensional nexus with enough magic securing it to make Hiroshima look like a firecracker. We think she's going to try and break the locks. Which, needless to say, opens our world up to all sorts of nasty things coming to visit."

My hands shook as I thought about the images of pestilence and apocalypse the grimoire showed me when I made the mistake of wondering what Mother had been trying to do. "If that's the case, why do the first ritual in our *house*? If she has to go to Maine now to complete it, why not go there the first time?"

Morgan made a face, as though my question had put a bad taste in her mouth. "In fact, that is an *excellent* question. Here's what you have to understand about ritual magic. It creates a battery of sorts, that the caster fills during the process of the spell." She shuddered though the room was a comfortable temperature. "Breaking one from the outside is a bad idea, as it can release stored energy in unpredictable ways."

I leaned back in my chair. "When I broke free of Mother's hold and *pushed* her to stop, I ended up in the hospital."

"Precisely. If you hadn't stopped her sooner, it might have turned your house into a crater. Whatever you did, you tapped into the collected energy and hyper-charged your own abilities. If it comes down to it, you putting yourself in the hospital again is an ideal outcome. If the feedback is bad enough in Randolph, she could blow the nexus wide open even if we *do* stop her."

I stared at the table, composing my thoughts. "It doesn't make sense. Don't get me wrong, I'm not trying to defend her, but I don't understand it."

CHAPTER 24

"What's to understand, she's crazy—" Val started, but Eliot raised a hand to silence him.

"Reason it out," the scruffy agent said. I met his eyes. Their burning intensity took me by surprise for a moment. If I'd underestimated him because of his rough appearance, that now seemed an ill-advised conclusion.

"Well," I temporized, "not to be simplistic, but what's in it for her? She lives in this world, same as us. If she opens up some dimensional gateway, is Gozer going to give her the keys to the Cayman Islands on the way through?"

"Who?" Eliot said.

Valentine sighed. "It's from a movie. What the hell do you *do* when we're not working?"

"I read, actually. And not comic books."

"They're like this most of the time," George informed me in a dry tone. "You get used to it."

"My apologies," Valentine said. "Continue."

"You have to understand something about the grimoire." I took a deep breath and tried to think how to say it without sounding insane. That was a challenge. "On the outside, it doesn't look like anything other than an antique. When you look at it, though, the pages change for you—for me, they turn into English, and the spell, most of the time, is something related to what I was thinking about."

The Division M agents frowned. "I've never seen anything like that," Valentine said. "A spell's a spell, it just looks a little odd if you stare at it long enough."

Ask him if they were loose or bound. Roxanne's silent voice normally had a hollow, emotionless sense to it, but now, it was almost forceful. I didn't hesitate to glance in her direction—Valentine likely knew she was in the room after all—but I still cocked my head and gave her a puzzled look. *Ask him!*

"Loose or bound?"

Eliot and George looked at each other, mystified, and Valentine's eyes flickered to the corner where Roxanne lurked. "Loose," he said, finally. "You can't exactly Xerox a spell, and transcribing them requires special materials, so the originals tend to stick around. The books fall apart, the pieces trickle out into the world. Handed down along family lines, sold in black markets. We've got significant chunks of several major editions, but the singletons far outweigh them. Over the years, we traced down most of the storage facilities where your mother cached the materials she was able to maintain. All of those documents we recovered were loose. There were rumors among the magical community that she'd found something whole, but we never turned anything up." Valentine frowned. "When she sent us a message using one of our agent's phones, we realized the rumor mill was right, for a change." He shrugged. "We checked your house a few times, but never found anything."

I nodded. For years, the book existed as a sack of ashes in a bag after I burned it. I'd hidden it, afraid that even the ashes might be dangerous, and I supposed that had made any search for it by someone who didn't know what to look for all the more difficult. Before Cassie and I set out toward Phoenix, I'd recovered it and discovered that the same magic that I used to heal myself made it whole once more. All things considered, that was looking more and more like one of my all-time bad decisions. I'd acquired my ability to phase and Cassie had learned her truth spell, but that had been the extent of the use we'd made of the book before Mother arrived and reclaimed it. "That's why you visited me in the hospital?"

"Not entirely—I wanted to take your measure. I needed to know if you were bent or not."

"If I had been?"

"Let's just say we wouldn't be talking, now." His smile was a little too cold to be comforting. "So, the book reads your mind. How does that play into your doubt?"

"The first few spells I learned were an accident. I happened upon the book, and it took my need to talk to my dad again and presented me the spell that allows me to talk to ghosts." I shook my head. "Of course, the stupid thing didn't tell me that the spell would turn me into a magnet. They just seem to find me." I'd used that to my benefit, in fighting the Edimmu, but that was a tale for another day. If it came down to scars and war stories, I had a feeling a seemingly-immortal former Wild West gunfighter had me beat. "And, you know, it was actually kind of cool at first. Then I happened to wonder what Mother had wanted to do with it..." I fell silent and shivered, though the room was a comfortable temperature.

"What did the spell say?" Eliot murmured.

"It wasn't so much what it said, exactly. This was different than anything I've ever seen. There were words, but to be honest, I was so scared by the other aspects of it that I slammed it shut before I saw more than a sentence or two. It showed me images. Horrific stuff—fire falling from the sky, cannibalism, smoke blocking out the sun. Even putting it into words doesn't do it justice—there was an emotional aspect to it. I felt like I was there suffering right along with everyone else, and I felt hopeless in the chaos." I closed my eyes and took a deep breath to compose myself. Even across the gulf of years, looking back on the memory made me feel panicky. "It was like a warning—sort of a mystical 'no trespassing' sign thrown up by the grimoire. I got the message. I slammed it shut and never looked for that ever again."

"How does that play into you disagreeing with the belief that your mother intends to open the nexus?"

"Believe me, this isn't me thinking that my mother isn't capable of horrible things. I *know* she is. The context isn't right." I fell silent. It was a hard thing to put into words. How did you sum up the totality of a person that you've known for your entire life into a few sentences? "Movies," I said, suddenly, and the other men around the table looked confused. "My dad and I loved to go to the movies, but we never took Mother. She turned her nose up at 'such plebeian entertainment.'"

"I'm confused," Eliot said. "What does this have to do with you seeing a vision of the end of the world?"

"It's unsophisticated. It's brute force—it's something out of a Hollywood blockbuster. If she wants to do something big, it'll be more refined."

"She burned down a frat house," Valentine said. "That's not exactly refined." He drummed his fingers on the table. "That said, though, she's had more than one opportunity to show off. Rather than fight me when she had the advantage of numbers, she ran. Blowing up a gas station was a little over the top, but again, she ran. She has the power to do whatever she wants. But instead of brute-forcing her way to her destination, she took the subtler approach. Why?"

I didn't have an answer. "I guess we have to catch her and find out, huh?"

"Easier said than done," Valentine said, his face grim. "I've got a tracking spell on her, but she's no longer in this plane of existence."

Replaying his words in my head to make sure I'd heard him right, I said, "Huh?"

"Dimensional nexuses are strange things. She hauled Cassie to one of the smaller ones and," He clapped his hands together. "Vanished. Our current working theory is that she's using it as a means to avoid capture, and she'll pop out at a time and place of her choosing."

"You're telling me she used magic to *time travel*?"

"Essentially."

I rubbed my forehead and closed my eyes. "Good grief. I

CHAPTER 24

should have studied more." A sudden chill went through. "What's to stop her from going back and doing the first ritual right this time?"

"I asked Morgan the same question—it's a one-way trip. The past is immutable."

That was at once comforting and depressing. Comforting because I knew the things I'd managed to achieve would stand, and depressing because it also meant that I couldn't go back and fix the multitude of errors I'd made along the way. Then again, dad always used to say that our losses defined us more than our victories. Without those clarifying moments, would I even be the same person? "Well, that's small comfort, at least."

Valentine checked his watch. "It's getting late. Let's wrap this up for the night. We'll get you a hotel room until we can arrange something more permanent, and start fresh in the morning. If you want a job, I'm going to take advantage of it. Maybe you can spot something in Leesburg our other folks missed."

"A job?" I echoed. "I thought I was just helping."

"Look, to be blunt—we need people in the worst way. And you've got more talent in your little finger than most everyone in Division M except for Morgan." He winked at Eliot and George. "It's not going to be easy on you. If you want in, we're going to run you through the wringer. No more getting your ass kicked all over the place by familiars."

"In my defense, there were three of them," I said, then chuckled. "I'm not saying no, I never thought about it as an option. It's not like I knew you guys even existed before a couple of weeks ago."

"Son, the government is a reflection of her people. In our case, that means clumsy, easily-distracted, but generally well-intentioned." Val cocked his head to one side and reconsidered. "Well, in the case of the IRS, pure evil, but that's a story for another day. I talked to Agent Anjewierden about this Void group. We've got zip on them, which is a problem. I'd like to compare notes—I'm guessing you've seen stuff that we've been too busy to notice. I don't like knowing that we missed things, because that usually happens right before something bites you in the ass."

Meeting his eyes, I hesitated for the barest of instants, then nodded. "I'm in."

CHAPTER TWENTY-FIVE

Paxton—Thursday morning
Washington, DC

The next few days got off to a weird start and somehow got stranger along the way.

Valentine offered to pick me up in the morning, but the hotel where I'd decided to stay was within walking distance of ATF headquarters. The Sofitel Washington was a hell of a lot fancier—and pricier—than your typical RV campground, but the return of my wallet and personal effects seemed as worthy a cause for celebration as any.

When I checked in the night before, I'd had a moment of panic when I unpacked my clothes and realized that none of the stuff was appropriate for a professional environment. After consulting with the front desk, I made the hike to a nearby Men's Wearhouse and laid down some cash on a plain black suit, a few shirts, black socks, and dress shoes. Unwilling to go full-on adult, I picked out a handful of ties with Star Wars and Marvel characters.

Dress code? What's that?

The most annoying aspect of the process was Roxanne. She

kept popping her head into the dressing room as I tried things on to make sarcastic comments. I'd left the Bluetooth earpiece back in the hotel room, so I had to settle for literally rolling my eyes and figuratively biting my tongue. The empty sidewalk on the way back to the hotel gave me the opportunity to return fire.

"If you're bored with the situation, say the word."

Oh, relax. I was just having a little fun.

"Sure, I get it. What was the deal with bound versus loose, earlier?"

Something Helen said, once. She said each page of the grimoire held layers of magic. The fragments we had lost most of that.

"That makes sense. I wonder, though..." I hummed thoughtfully.

What?

"Well, I was able to restore the grimoire. Could I do something similar if I had enough pieces of a larger whole? Something to look into."

For the record, I'm not bored. I'm a little perturbed that you're working with the guys that killed my friends, but it's a means to an end. If they help us stop Helen, it'll be worth it in the end.

I frowned. "In their defense, they may have pulled the trigger, but my mom is the one that put them in the line of fire. Don't lose sight of that. If she hadn't used and abused you all, they'd all be alive right now."

She considered that for half a block, then admitted, *You're right.*

"From the sounds of things, we're in for a wait." The fact that Mother had somehow gained the ability to *time travel* was disconcerting as hell. Presumably, she'd picked that up before breaking out of prison. I didn't think she'd had enough time between abducting Cassie and making her escape in Oklahoma. Then again, she did seem to have a bit more of an intuitive grasp of how to control the damn thing. For all I knew, she could use it as the magical equivalent of an Internet search engine.

But I had time. And I fully planned to take every advantage of it.

Eliot was waiting for me in the lobby and escorted me through security. My first steps were mundane enough—I officially became an employee of the Department of Justice after filling out enough paperwork to choke a horse. After spending a few days as a nonentity with no driver's license, it was surreal to see my name on a government identification card. The golden badge with blue lettering doubled down on that.

Eliot led me out of human resources on a brisk walk toward our basement offices. It was silent inside of the elevator until I broke it with a question I'd had since Gordo gave me the scoop on Division M. "Alcohol, Tobacco, Firearms, and Explosives. Why magic, too?"

Eliot smiled. "Institutional inertia, for the most part. But like I always say, there's not much more explosive than a pissed-off magic user."

"Fair point," I said. "What's on the agenda for today?"

"I need to grab something, then we're heading over the Leesburg annex so you can take a look through the damaged areas. Then we see what you can do."

I raised an eyebrow. "If you want me to show off some spells, let's order some extra pizzas."

He grunted, then said, "Noted. We might do some spell work, but it's best to hold off on that till Morgan gets back. She'll put you through your paces, there. I'm talking about more elementary stuff —shooting, unarmed combat, obstacle courses."

"Sounds like basic training," I said. On the bright side, Cassie had hounded me into running with her after I got out of the hospital, though the kidnapping thing had put a kink in our fitness regimen. I wasn't a slug by any stretch of the imagination, but I wasn't exactly ready to go all-out, either.

"Pretty much. You've got to understand, most of the agents we bring in come from the military or other law enforcement agencies. That prior experience gives us a known baseline to work with. Valentine greased the skids a bit, but we still need to make sure you're up to snuff. If you're not, we'll work on it until you are."

"I hope we have enough time."

The doors opened with a ding, and Eliot grinned. "Kid, if it comes down to you having to use a gun, things will have already gone to hell. All things considered, I'm most interested to see what kind of tricks you can learn from Morgan. She's ... pretty experienced."

"How about you?"

He gave me a wary look as we walked down the hall. "I'm up there," he allowed. "Valentine's got more than a few years on me, but Morgan's the senior agent by a good margin. Just—don't bring that up, you know?"

"She touchy on the subject?"

"No," he said, his tone a little confused. "It's good manners, isn't it?"

"Ah."

Once Eliot retrieved a duffel bag from his office, he led me to an underground parking garage and a waiting Suburban. Another dozen or so identical vehicles sat in neat rows, surrounded by more varied types that I assumed were personal vehicles. *They must get a bulk discount on the SUVs.*

Our return to the Leesburg facility brought me full circle. I seemed to be doing a lot of backtracking, these days. If I'd come in this way the last time, I couldn't recall. Eliot turned off the main highway and headed past a shopping center and a cluster of housing additions. I looked over toward the place I'd holed up in. He must have interpreted my study as curiosity, because he remarked, "I remember when this was all woods. Wish we'd have bought up the land around the campus before they started developing it, but bureaucrats would rather spend money on the flashy stuff that gets votes than operational security." He grinned, dispelling his morose tone. "Say it with me, kid. Institutional inertia."

"Is it safe? I saw some of the things down in the Menagerie." I thought it might be impolite to mention that I'd helped one of them escape, but that was a can of worms I wanted to put off talking about as long as I could.

"For the most part." He turned and gave me a look. "Up until recently, the Puck is the only thing that's ever escaped."

I shifted uncomfortably in my seat. "Yeah, about that—"

He waved a hand. "No worries. As I said, it's not the first time, and it's not likely to be the last."

"If I'd known it was dangerous, I'd have done more," I tried to explain. "For what it's worth, I *pushed* it not to eat any more people."

Eliot chuckled. "Trust me, if it were a major danger, we'd have killed it on sight. Although, after the last few times, I think Val's getting tired of chasing the damn thing. It's mostly a trickster, and harmless, albeit scary-looking. The guards blew the eating people a thing a little out of proportion."

"How exactly does that happen?"

He gave me another look. "The people in question were cooking meth out in the woods. No big loss." Eliot shrugged. "The Puck's people were here before the Pilgrims. As far as we know, he's the last of his kind. The way I figure it, he's got a right to live his life, same as us. As long as he behaves himself."

"That would seem to be a problem if you have to keep catching him."

"Well, you get old, you get set in your ways. We're here."

If I'd thought the building large from the rear, the front was all the more impressive. There were far more windows here than in the rear, showing me that there were two stories worth of rooms along the front—offices or classrooms, from what I could see from the car.

The parking lot itself was a broad, L-shaped affair, and filled almost to capacity. That, though, seemed due to the fact that someone had roped off half of the area to provide a parking area for an assortment of trailers, piles of materials, and heavy construction equipment. "Repairs?"

"The clean-up is complete. We've got most of the facility up and running, but the rest should be back in business by the first of the year." He led me into the front entrance and through security under the eyes of a pair of watchful guards. Normal behavior, or more alert after the attack? It was impossible to know for sure, but I couldn't imagine they'd been lackadaisical before, knowing what the building held under our feet. Whatever party had pulled off the attack had walked a narrow line of stealth and audacity. The timing had worked out for me, and that made me feel all the more guilty given the casualty numbers I'd heard.

The signs of the explosion were small but evident as I followed Eliot through the office. Here and there, light fixtures were dead. Cardboard covered the spaces left behind by shattered panes of glass in interior office walls. Sheetrock dust speckled some of the desks we passed, but intent men and women occupied many of the others.

"We do a lot of research and development here. The study of artifacts and cryptids isn't something you want to farm out to the private sector," Eliot explained. He led me through a set of double glass doors into a small waiting room. These had survived the blast, but the wall in front of us had not—it was mainly open, though a construction crew was inserting new panels into the divider that separated this room from the open space beyond.

The office complex seemed to surround a large gymnasium. I

CHAPTER 25

shot Eliot a questioning look, and he shrugged. "Some of our training methods, we can't exactly go out to Quantico or any of the open-air DOJ facilities. Keeps away the prying eyes." I gave him a questioning look, then glanced at the contractors. "No worries— retired CIA agent started his own construction business. His people are vetted. Come on," he said, leading me into the next room.

At a quick guess, I thought the spacious interior could have held at least three full-size basketball courts, but a series of walls, netting, and concrete tubes took up the center of the gym, stretching from end to end. "Obstacle course?"

"Got it in one."

Neat rows of stacked free weights and exercise machines lined the perimeter walls, and padded mats covered the floor in an open area to one side of the obstacle course. Some sort of sparring ring, I supposed.

Eliot walked me up to a whip-thin older man with piercing blue eyes and a paper coffee cup in one hand. "Paxton, this is Agent Andrews. Arlan, meet Paxton Locke." Andrews' position put him in a good place to observe the entirety of the gym, and I got the sense he'd been doing just that before we arrived.

Andrews' had a deep voice with a heavy Upper South accent. "Charmed, Agent Locke." His firm handshake wasn't too aggressive, but he put enough squeeze into it to tell me he was no wilting graybeard.

"Arlan's the head of the northeast region tactical response team. They're the ones that go out when Val's unit is otherwise occupied."

"We ain't the fearsome foursome, but we ain't the B-team, either. Call it the A-minus team." Both men chuckled, and I got the sense that the joke was an old one.

I scanned the gym. A half-dozen men and women in workout gear used the machines around the perimeter, but none of them seemed all that focused on their tasks. Several of them looked away when they caught me looking in their direction. Frowning, I turned back to Eliot and Andrews. "What's the occasion, Agent Andrews? You guys prepping for March already?"

The older man brought his coffee cup to his lips and spat a stream of tobacco juice inside. He winked at Eliot. "Got sort of a tradition we've developed, over the years. Anytime we bring a new agent on board, one of the available tac teams runs them through their paces. I got ex-Special Forces, big-city SWAT, a couple of former Airborne, and a sharpshooter good enough to swing for Marine Scout Sniper if she didn't use the wrong restroom."

"A little friendly hazing between coworkers, is that it?"

"All in good fun," Arlan assured me.

I eyed Eliot. He assumed an air of innocence. "Hey, I did say we were going to put you through your paces."

Trying not to laugh, I said, "Yeah, you did. I'd have dressed down if I knew this was what you had in mind."

"Locker room's over there," Arlan pointed helpfully. "Plenty of new stuff in common sizes."

Three steps toward the locker room I glanced down at my new shoes and tried not to wince. *Well, this should be interesting.*

"Paxton," Eliot called. I turned, and he pitched the duffel bag at me, underhand. "Size twelve, right?"

Laughter filled the gym as I unzipped the bag. I noted the new pair of sneakers inside with chagrin. "Cute."

Roxanne leaned against one of the lockers as I stepped inside. Neatly folded shirts and shorts occupied a set of shelves next to the sinks. As far as perks go, it was a unique one. I found an open locker and started shucking the suit.

Do you think they'll give you a wedgie? When I glanced over, my ghostly companion grinned from ear to ear.

"This has got to be a jock thing," I said. "But the joke's on them."

CHAPTER 25

I marched out of the locker room in a Department of Justice T-shirt and navy blue shorts. The sneakers were not only the right size, but they were also my usual brand. That might have been creepy if not for the time the Division M people had spent going through my RV. There was a probably an Excel spreadsheet somewhere listing the contents down to the last pair of socks.

Rejoining Eliot and Andrews, I spread my hands and asked, "All set. What's the drill, gentlemen?"

"Run the obstacle course, then step onto the sparring mat. Light strikes only—we're not out for bruises."

Reaching up to scratch my nose and hide my smile, I took a closer look at the obstacle course. The first task was a wall with several ropes hanging down it. The top wasn't all that far from the gymnasium's rafters. Foam chunks filled a depression in front of the floor. *Nice to know I won't break a leg if I fall from the top.*

Lowering my hand, I gave up and grinned. "So, uh, what's the course record?"

Agent Andrews squinted at me as though trying to decide if I was joking or not. "Solo? Fifteen minutes. No offense, son, but you look like a strong breeze might blow you over. No need for false bravado."

Shrugging, I replied, "Start the clock." Turning on one heel, I strolled toward the first obstacle, doing my best to ignore the expectant looks of the other agents. There was a narrow strip of solid floor between the safety foam and the climbing wall, and I side-stepped up to the first rope. I reached up, tugged on it a bit then let it drop.

The gasps as I phased through the climbing wall were audible, and I tried not to laugh. Jogging forward, I avoided the cargo nets in the same manner. Another, shorter climbing wall followed, then a broad concrete pipe sunk into the floor at an angle. I went in solid, flickering in and out of phase as I ran into pieces of rebar that would have forced me to squirm my up and around to get through. There were audible curses as I popped out the other end, and I did chuckle then, but the last thing in my way did give me pause.

Another foam-filled depression lay before me, but this one was longer and narrower than the one in front of the climbing wall. A pair of ropes hung over the pit, one about six feet above the other. Apparently, I was supposed to use it as a narrow bridge, holding onto the upper cable for support.

In all honesty, I was confident that I could do it, but a misstep now would shoot the entire production in the foot. Sure, I was showing off, but my demonstration had a purpose. I couldn't hope to physically compete with trained soldiers, but that wasn't why I was here. Valentine had brought me on board because of my more exotic skills. Thumbing my nose at Agent Andrews' course might piss him off, but it would also show the others that I was more than capable of pulling my own weight.

I took hold of the upper rope and got both sneakers on the lower. It pitched back and forth dangerously as my weight shifted, and I tried not to grimace. This wouldn't be bad at all if I could do something to stabilize the lower—ah.

My telekinesis spell had morphed into my magical Swiss Army Knife these past few weeks, and while it might have been too weak over distances, it was plenty strong enough to keep the lower rope steady as I crossed the span hand-over-hand on the top line. I shook a bit with fatigue when I hopped down, but I'd had worse.

Eliot and Andrews had followed alongside as I breezed through the course. When I turned to meet their eyes, the tac team leader had his jaw clenched with barely-suppressed anger.

"What's my time?" I called out. "Did I beat fifteen minutes?"

Eliot turned his head to hide a smile while the other man seethed. Finally, Agent Andrews called out, "All right, smart-ass. Care to show us what you've got in the sparring ring?"

CHAPTER 25

I didn't, as a matter of fact, but I couldn't exactly back down now. "I'll do my best, sir."

He did smile at that, but it wasn't a very friendly one. "Sharps," he barked. "Take our newest agent down a peg or three."

Unsure whether to leave my shoes on or take them off before stepping onto the mat, I waited on my side until the short Division M agent moved onto it in sneakers. He had an unlined face and black hair right on the cusp of shaggy. A few years older than me, I judged, but about the same mass even though I had a good six inches on him. "Agent Sharps," I said with a nod.

He grinned, then. "Call me Mike," he replied, then charged.

My opponent was muscular enough that I'd assumed he'd be slow, but his initial burst took me by surprise. As fast as he was, he *crawled* in comparison to the familiars that had accompanied Melanie.

Which was a good thing, since they'd beaten the holy hell out of me.

I dodged to one side, but Mike spread his arms wide, and I didn't think I'd get in clear before he pulled me into a tackle. Something Scope used to say popped into my head, then—if you ain't cheatin', you ain't tryin'. Going out of phase, I ignored the uncomfortable sensation of the other agent's arm passing through my incorporeal torso. I turned and snapped back in at his back. Reaching out, I planted a solid shove into his upper torso. Anticipating physical contact, he was already off balance, and my push took him over the edge. Arms waving, he slammed onto the mat face first.

As I raised my fists to wait for him to come back at me, a leg came out of nowhere, hooked around my ankles, and pulled my feet out from under me. I hit the floor on my side and tried to hop back up, but a steady weight pressed down on the back of my neck, pushing my face into the mat until I twisted my head to one side. I could go out of phase and escape the hold, but I grasped that move wasn't the point. If this were real, I wouldn't be in a hold. I'd be dead or unconscious because I'd succumbed to tunnel vision.

"First lesson," Agent Andrews said. "Always watch your back. Most of the bad guys we deal with think fair fights are for dummies."

The worst part was, that was a lesson I'd already learned once. The pressure on the back of my neck eased, and I pushed myself to my feet. "I hear you," I said. The agent who'd come in behind me was tall with a shaved head and a sandy blond goatee.

He stuck out a hand. "Frank Luke. Welcome to Division M, kid."

Shaking my head, I shook it. "Does this conclude the hazing portion of my first day?"

"Oh, yeah," Eliot chimed in. "It's all serious business from here on out." A few of the others laughed, and he looked around in mock confusion. "What? Did I say something funny?"

CHAPTER TWENTY-SIX

P*AXTON*—M*ONDAY MORNING*
Washington, DC

Once Agent Andrews' team got their fun out, things settled down over the next few days. Buzzing through the obstacle course might have gotten me a pass on running it again, but that gave the rest of the crew more time to spend training me in areas where I wasn't quite so capable.

Running, target shooting, more sparring—by Friday night, I was a mass of bruises, looking forward to a long soak in the hot tub. I hadn't had a chance to look for a more permanent place to stay yet, and part of me wondered if it was worth the bother. I'd spent so much time moving from place to place over the last decade that it had become a habit. Even staying in a hotel room was contrary to my preferences. On the bright side, the only ghost that seemed to haunt the Sofitel was Roxanne, and I was so tired that I had no problem sleeping while she lurked in the same room.

During my nightly check-ins, my current situation was a source of no small amusement to Kent, and he had to hand the phone off when his laughter spurred a coughing fit. I had to admit, the situation *was* a little funny. He'd been so worried about Division M throwing me back into a hole that he'd never considered they'd do something like run me through an impromptu boot camp.

My call to Mike Hatcher was the hardest thing of all. It might have been easier if he'd been furious with me, but he was anything but. When I completed my retelling of Cassie's abduction, he asked, "What about you? Are you all right?"

Shocked, I couldn't answer for a long moment. I stammered, "I'm fine, Mike. Did you hear what I just said?"

"I did. And it's taking everything I have not to run to Maine right this instant, but … I also know that I don't have what it takes to save my little girl. I have to trust that you'll do it." He stopped talking, and I pulled the phone away to see if we'd lost connection when he concluded, "Do you love her?"

It was a hell of a thing to have to say to my girlfriend's dad, especially when I hadn't had the opportunity to say the words to *her*, but … "We haven't even been on a date, yet, Mike. But—yeah, I do. Call it crazy. Call me crazy, but I do. I love your daughter."

Emotion strangled his laugh, but he said, "Then I trust you. Get her safe."

Sunday night I got a message to report to the basement headquarters for a morning meeting. This gave me a bit of extra time, as I wasn't beholden to Eliot's carpool service, and after a relaxing breakfast, I strolled over, wincing at the aches and pains of last week.

They'd fade, I knew, in time, and I told myself to take the pain as a good sign. It was the first step in preparing to stop Mother. If there was an advantage to her timing, it was this. After everything I'd been through in Wisconsin, Phoenix, and the holding facility in such a short period of time, I'd been riding the ragged edge.

My new badge got me through security with no issue, and

CHAPTER 26

when I stepped into the conference room, the usual trio and a new addition were waiting.

Valentine stood and pulled out a chair for me. "Paxton, this is Agent Morgan Laffer."

I extended a hand. Agent Laffer was petite, with dark red hair. She had one of those ageless faces that made it impossible to guess her age—she could have been anywhere from thirty to fifty. As she extended her own hand, the hairs on the back of my arms stood on end. It was, I realized, a sensation not all that different than the one I'd felt when I'd been my making my way through Dulles. It wasn't quite as powerful, but it was there nonetheless.

"Oh, my," she said with a warm smile. There was the faintest hint of a brogue to her voice, the trace elements of an accent almost entirely sanded away by the passage of time. "You're a strong one."

"What *is* that?"

"What, you didn't think witches and wizards go around wearing robes and pointy hats to identify themselves, did you? Once we reach a certain level of skill, we sort of ... vibrate, I suppose you could say. Helps to know when you're among equals—or when to be on guard."

That merited a frown. If one of Division M's most senior agents merited a mere tingle, what in the world had I passed in the airport? Before I could ask the question, Morgan headed toward the door to the conference room, pulling me along with her. Bemused, I shot a glance at Valentine and followed along. The other agent shrugged. This behavior, it seemed, wasn't out of the ordinary.

"I spent the last few days chasing dead leads across Europe. It'll be nice to get my hands on something more tangible."

"That, uh, sounds ominous, Agent Laffer."

She turned and grinned. "Call me Morgan. Needless formality tends to take up time when you need it the most, in my opinion. And no worries—I solemnly swear to leave everything intact." We ended up in front of an unmarked door in a section of the basement office I hadn't yet had occasion to visit. "Step into my office." Unlocking the door, she stepped aside and waved a dramatic hand.

If the rest of the space down here looked like your standard, off-the-shelf business decor, Morgan's office put that aesthetic on its ear. Floor-to-ceiling bookshelves lined the back wall, and the subdued glow of their cherry finish suggested that they were genuine wood. A matching desk, piled high with papers and—of all things—scrolls sat between the shelves and the door. As I stepped inside, I realized that the walls on either side were just as full, but these contained framed pictures and strange mementos mounted on what seemed to be trophy plaques.

Curious, I stepped closer. Before I could get a good look at what I thought was a misshapen metal coffee mug, Morgan grabbed my arm again and guided me to a well-padded chair sitting in front of her desk. Sliding around to her side, she settled into her own seat and raised an eyebrow. "What do you think? Valentine thinks I have too much stuff in here, but I hate electronic records. And I've got measures in place to ensure that nothing gets up and walks away."

I hesitated. It was easy to see how Agent Valentine could call the place cluttered, but I could sense a strange sort of organization in what first appeared as chaos. The office was homey. It reminded me more than a little of my dad's den at home, with its bookshelves sagging from the weight of old history books and the cherished paperback novels he'd read to near-rags. "It's awesome," I said. Taking in the yellowed pages on her desk, my hands itched to start looking through her archives. "Is this it? You guys aren't hiding a library anywhere, are you?"

"We don't have much of one. The Leesburg attack took out a

big chunk of our research materials. Artifacts are a different story, but we like to save those for special occasions."

I grimaced. "Ah. Well, isn't there like a White Council or a Men of Letters or something?"

Morgan laughed, then covered her hand with her mouth. "I'm sorry, that was rude of me. You have to understand. Most wizards aren't exactly social creatures. It's hard enough to get along with your contemporaries, much less run the world. Think of it as a collection of introverted bookworms and you'd come pretty close to the truth."

"That's kind of disappointing." I considered the implication of what she described, then grinned. "I'm guessing a wizard who advertises on the Internet wouldn't be well-regarded."

"If there were any sort of online message board where wizards gathered to argue and discuss things, that sort of person would be frowned upon, so to speak." I frowned and stared Morgan down, trying to decide if she was pulling my leg. "You're serious."

"Oh, absolutely. Remind me to give you the address later so you can get the old farts in a tizzy." She stifled her laugh, composed herself, then leaned forward. "Let's take a look at you." After a moment she said, "Been eating well? Plenty of rest?"

"I've worked with the tac team the last few days, I've never slept better."

"Good. Valentine mentioned you put yourself in the hospital overusing a healing spell." Morgan raised an eyebrow. "Using your own energy is dangerous, though I'm sure you understand that at this point."

"Well, not to be a smart ass, but what else should I use?"

"Emotion. Will. It takes practice, and honestly, it's why wizards don't grow on trees. It takes more than a little innate talent, and someone with the patience to teach you. Most of us are more interested in doing our own thing than looking out for the next generation. The fact that you've been able to do so much without formal training is more than a little unusual, and part of the reason why you're looked upon with such suspicion. Were, rather."

"Great," I replied, then raised my hands in air-fingers quotes. "I'm the chosen one. What about tapping other channels?"

Morgan went a little pale. "You don't want to mess with that sort of thing—where'd you even hear that mentioned?"

I glanced over, but for once, Roxanne was nowhere in sight. *Convenient.* "A little birdie, you know."

"You got the executive summary on nexuses, right?"

"Yeah."

"It's simpler to pass or draw energy through dimensions. You need a particular set of circumstances at a particular place to move, or be moved, outside of our reality." She made a face. "With a few exceptions, every major confrontation we've had with various witches and wizards over the years has involved power taps."

I frowned. "How could you tell?"

"Circle back around to using your own energy," Morgan pointed out. "Can you throw a boulder at someone?"

"No," I admitted. "But I can snag a beer at ten feet."

"Same logic goes for balls of fire, lightning, that sort of thing. Run into a spell caster that throws that kind of power around, it's a sure bet they're tapping if they don't collapse from exhaustion on the first few minutes."

"Well, that sucks," I said. "Sounds like going up against Godzilla with a pellet gun."

She smiled. "It simply means you have to be smarter about it."

"Is it a chicken thing or an egg thing?"

"How so?"

"Well, if the bad guys are tapping, are they doing so because they're bad guys, or are they bad guys because they're tapping?" I shrugged. "Is that why it's frowned upon?"

"To an extent," Morgan replied. "It's easy to think that they're being corrupted by some sort of dark force outside of our universe, but let's be honest—mankind is dark enough on our own. The type of person that's about power more than wisdom, that takes shortcuts to get there ... they're the exact sort of person you wouldn't trust with that power in the first place." She gave me a nod. "How many spells do you have?"

"Uh, well, six," I admitted. "I mean, I can use them in different ways, so they're more effective than that, but—"

She raised a hand to cut me off. "I get it. And that's a good sign. You had every opportunity to cram anything and everything into your head. Instead, you settled for what you had, took your gifts and used them for good. Think about that power in the hands of someone with less compunction about using it."

I didn't have to think all that hard—I'd only been a teenager when I got the *push*, and the anxiety over what I might do with it in mixed company had made me a hermit for most of the last decade. If I hadn't had that little voice in the back of my head, telling me that it was wrong to bend others to my will?

Why, I'd have been a monster.

"Not a happy thought," I admitted.

"Yes, well, that's water under the bridge, isn't it?" She stood and walked around her desk. "Speaking of, stay seated and relax."

"What are we doing?"

"Agent Valentine and I discussed the vision the grimoire gave you when you tried to study the ritual spell. I think with my help, we can get a better look at things."

Grimacing, I muttered, "I'm not sure how comfortable I am with that."

"Don't worry—I'll be there with you. I may not be able to turn invisible or walk through walls, but this is what I do." She stood behind me and pulled my head back until it rested on the padding of the chair back. "Close your eyes."

We'd just met, but for some crazy reason, I trusted her. I took a deep breath and closed my eyes. Morgan cupped my head in her hands and muttered under her breath. A slow warmth built, but it wasn't an uncomfortable one. The heat seemed to seep into me, and while I didn't feel drowsy, a great sense of relaxation fell over my body.

"That's right," she said in a more familiar language. "Show me that night. You're safe, I won't let anything happen to you."

At once, I saw a younger version of myself in the kitchen of my old house, bent over the open grimoire at the kitchen table. There were dark circles under my eyes. Part of me ached to comfort the grieving teenager I'd been even as I felt myself rush forward and assume that same position in my mind's eye. I looked out through my own eyes, and the bold text atop the page I'd summoned swam into focus.

I didn't *remember* reading any of the words on the page—the vision had overtaken me far too quickly for that, but the clicking of the wall clock slowed, then stopped. The page before froze in mid-translation, the ink rippling under the page to form English words out of the undecipherable ancient language it had been originally written in.

"Seeling the Night," we murmured in concert, reading the heading. The clock clicked as time returned to a normal speed, and scenes of terror and flame replaced the comforting sight of my home. The memory was crystal clear, but the warm sensation of Morgan's palms on my temples kept the terror away, somehow, and made the nightmare world easier to bear. For the first time since the grimoire tormented me with the imagery, I could look at them with unwavering eyes.

With that advantage, I got the sense that I was actually looking at two realities, laid over top of one another. The pressure on my head grew warmer, and the vision drifted apart. Separate, the imagery was so different that I might have thought one was significantly offset in time from the other, but some aspect of what we saw told me that the vision existed at the same moment in time. If I had any doubt that I was no longer bound by the constraints of my own physical form, I somehow focused on both images at once, realizing that they were of the same place and time—a telephone pole in one image sat in the same location in each, though it smoldered in the more terrifying alternative.

At once, it hit me, and I heard a sharp intake of air from Morgan. We weren't seeing any sort of time-lapse, before and after—these were two potential outcomes. The branching path of the future lay before us, and neither appealed.

In the first vision, I saw the main street of my hometown of Pleasant Prairie. Though I got the sense that it was midday, the sky free of clouds, it was dim as though overcast. Everything was still, but beyond that—the town was empty. Not only of people but of *anything* alive. The denuded, skeletal arms of trees stretched up to an empty steel sky.

This was a world at peace, but there was no *life*, either.

In the opposite realm, those that survived didn't seem to have much time left. Shadow-cloaked beasts stalked injured figures. A burning pile of bodies at the intersection sent ash aloft on plumes of black smoke while twisted figures danced and contorted around it. The sky here was black, but a band of red light shone on the eastern horizon.

I thought of the future I'd seen in Phoenix, of tortured subjects marching up the side of a rough-hewn pyramid to serve as sacrifices to an ancient Aztec demon. Was this the same world, the same potential outcome that I'd seen, then?

Something told me that it was.

The oppressive air of the vision fell away and I snapped back into my younger self, shoving the book across the table and away from me. Even that memory ended, and I found myself back in the chair, staring up into Morgan's face. She unclenched her eyes and met my own.

"Well, that was different," I managed.

"Not for me." Morgan made her way back around her desk. Sitting, she dug through stacks of paperwork. "Not the strangest thing I've ever had to interpret, but certainly one of the more frightening. Ah!" She pulled a thick book out from under a stack of paper-clipped documents.

"You have a grimoire, too?"

She smirked and lifted the book up so I could see the writing on the spine. "It's a dictionary, kid."

Webster's, to be exact, but I'd never seen one bound in cracked leather. "How old is *that*?"

"Not as old as me," she grinned, opening the book to about three-quarters and carefully turning individual pages.

"Right," I started, then realized she was serious. "Oh. Umm—speaking of, I have to ask …"

Morgan stopped flipping and raised a silent eyebrow.

"I couldn't help but wonder with the name and the accent, are you—" I drew up short. "Never mind."

"Val said he blew his cover to you. Are you wondering if I'm a celebrity, too?"

"It's just, my dad read me the Magic Tree House books when I was a kid, and, you know, Morgan, the accent—are you Morgan La Fey?"

She laughed and returned the dictionary. "Nope. I'm nobody special."

"Other than being a witch, of course."

"Sorceress, please. Witch has so many negative connotations."

"Ah—sorry."

Morgan hesitated and looked up to meet my eyes. "Don't worry about it. You're still in the head-spinning phase. Here's the thing you need to realize, though. Think back, oh, ten years ago. Look at that person you used to be. Are you the same?"

CHAPTER 26

"Not completely," I allowed. "You're saying that people change?"

"We grow, we learn. Think of the differences between the Paxton we saw sitting at the table and Paxton here and now, and extend that out a century or two. Yeah, Val was a bit of a scoundrel, even when I first met him. Now? He's someone entirely different." She gave me a melancholy smile. "Think about your friends and family growing old and dying while you ... keep on. I've been walking this Earth a long damn time, and unless something unexpected happens, I've got plenty of years left in me. As strong as your magic is? Your journey has only begun."

If she'd intended to give me something to stew over while she found what she was looking for, Morgan was successful. I considered a world without Kent, or Esteban, or Carlos, and tried not to grimace. So much of a person's means of defining themselves came from their relationships. Take those away, and what remained?

Will my teaching Cassie cause the same thing to happen to her? I opened my mouth to ask the question, but Morgan smacked an ecstatic hand on her desk.

"I found it," she crowed. "The title of the spell—you saw it, yes?"

"I did. Was it misspelled?"

"In any ordinary book, you'd think so, but that's not how magic works—typos in spells are *dangerous*. It's an old word. Seeling was a practice used in falconry. They would sew the eyes of the birds shut in order to train them. In more modern times, they simply hood the animals."

I frowned. "So, it's a spell to 'close the eyes of the night.' What does that mean exactly?"

"I'd wager it's metaphorical. Night, darkness—"

"The Void," I interjected. "I've run into a couple creatures recently. One of them said that was what they called themselves. Would that mean ...?"

"It's a spell to bring things of darkness to heel." Her eyes were wide, her tone hushed. "In falconry, the falconer uses the bird to hunt. If we're right, the ritual will let her control the things out there that we've been fighting for all these years."

"How does the vision tie into that?"

"It's a warning," Morgan said grimly. "It's not intended for the person using the ritual. It was a message to *you*—stop this, or there are two potential outcomes."

"It's a *book*!" I protested. "Is that even possible?"

"Very much so. Paxton, you have to understand something. We're able to hold the line partly because most of those things out there hate each other almost as much as they hate us. If someone assumed control, became their de facto general—they'd overrun us."

"A dead world," I whispered, staggered by the implication.

"Or one consumed in fire."

CHAPTER TWENTY-SEVEN

P AXTON—T UESDAY MORNING AND BEYOND
Washington, DC

November drifted into December, and my days blurred together. With few exceptions I spent my mornings in DC, working with Morgan, then traveled to the Leesburg facility in the afternoon to train with Agent Andrews and his team. I wasn't accustomed to a daily routine, but I found that I liked being able to switch my brain off and focus on the task at hand. If not for that, I'd have spent all my time worrying about Cassie when there was nothing I could do.

On the bright side, the ordinariness of the routine—or the company I now kept—didn't appeal to Roxanne, so rather than entertain herself with following me around and making sarcastic remarks, she spent her days doing whatever it was ghosts did when no one could see or hear them. Concerned that the sense of isolation might drive her closer to the level of ghostly insanity I'd seen more than a few times, I left the TV on throughout the day. It was a bit too much like looking after a pet for my taste, but it was the best I could do.

In her office, Morgan and I sifted through the debris of Division M's vault, hauled over by the cleanup crew. Some of the artifacts were within my ability to restore, but few were of any use. If anything, it was interesting to see how the wizards of old had used magic in their day-to-day lives. The clay pitcher that kept liquid stored in it fresh and right above freezing temperature was pretty neat, albeit of little utility after the advent of refrigeration.

Actual spells were few and far between. Even the grimoire hadn't been fireproof, and the explosive blast had reduced many of the loose sheets of paper in the research vault to ash. The sorceress wasn't eager to share much of what she had in her office with me, particularly after the lecture-slash-discussion about abuse of power. When I pointed out that it was likely that I'd be on the front lines with Valentine, Eliot, and George when the time came to stop Mother, she bent a little.

But, as it turned out, the grimoire had spoiled me. With few exceptions, the scrolls and parchments Morgan handed me to study might as well have been written in Klingon for all I could comprehend them. After the first time, I frowned at her and asked when it would translate for me.

"That's major league spellwork, boyo. You're certainly not going to find it on a loose-leaf fragment." She glanced at the parchment as she pulled it back and shrugged. "No real loss. It's intended to wean someone off of opium." She clicked her tongue. "We got it in—Hong Kong, I want to say? Among other things."

"That," I said, "seems pretty mundane for magic."

"You have to understand. Until the 20th Century, technology wasn't so widespread. Think of the pitcher—people used whatever they could to get by, and magic was simply another resource. It all comes down to the economics of scale—cheap electricity will beat rare wizardry all the time." She laughed. "For every dangerous spell we recover, we find a dozen spells to treat broken bones, tooth decay, crop blight—anything you can imagine."

CHAPTER 27

I chuckled, thinking of how my own healing spell had made teenage acne much easier to deal with. "Pimples. I get it."

Far more useful was the shield enchantment. The writing was Medieval English, but so long as I somewhat recognized the words, my gift for memorization kicked in and added it to the mental switchboard I envisioned to manage the mental focus required for casting. Phasing would still be a go-to, but the shield spell had a huge advantage—once it was in place, it powered itself from the kinetic energy of any impacts against it. In terms of my own abilities, that made it far more useful if I needed to defend anyone other than myself.

My work with Morgan rapidly brought me to the perspective that magic was only as powerful as its utility. Being able to cast one giant, apocalyptic spell might *look* impressive, but if it took you out of the fight, what was the point? Better to make use of something with endurance.

And in that regard, the shield spell was a major game-changer. I went from spending most of my time on my back in the sparring ring to very nearly holding my own. After I'd gotten the basics of self-defense down pat, Agent Andrews had given me the green light to use any spells I wanted—so long as there was no chance to injure anyone. More often than not, I could give as well as I got, or at least defend myself. In a real fight, Andrews pointed out, I wouldn't need all that time. I only needed to stay upright until I could phase out or throw up a shield.

The shift confused me until I realized that as much as the tac team was training me, at the same time I was giving them real-world experience in how to deal with an enemy spell-caster. For all her experience and knowledge, the lion's share of Morgan's abilities were mental or supportive. She'd done her time in the field, but when it came to fighting, she informed me, she was a far more conventional sort.

One day, I needed to ask about the black-and-white picture of

Valentine, Morgan, and Eliot in front of a Studebaker hanging up in her office. There was sure to be a good story behind it—the sorceress wore a victorious grin with the stock of a Thompson submachine gun resting on her bent knee.

A few of the Division M people got together for a meal before Thanksgiving, but I spent the actual day in my hotel room with Roxanne and room service, flipping between football games and cheesy movies. I briefly considered going out to people-watch amid the crush of holiday shopping, but I couldn't muster the energy to do it. I'd given so much of my focus over to preparation and training that even a short disruption in my schedule left me feeling adrift.

Agent Valentine was far too busy for much one-on-one time, but he pulled me aside a few weeks later, looked me up and down, then remarked, "When's the last time you took a break?"

Frowning, I said, "Had a long weekend on Thanksgiving, same as everyone else."

"Right—do much socializing, get your batteries recharged?"

"Sure," I said, but my voice fell flat in my own ears.

"Look, kid, this is a marathon, not a sprint. I appreciate your dedication, but if you burn yourself out before the mission kicks off, you're no good to me. Take a few weeks off and come back on ..." He turned and looked around for a calendar. "The 7th. That gives you Christmas and New Year's week. Check out of your hotel room, get some fresh air." He cocked his head to one side. "Visit your family."

I blinked at the suggestion, as it wasn't something that had honestly occurred to me was a possibility—but it was, wasn't it? There was nothing keeping me from getting on another plane, legally, this time, and doing just that. It hadn't started snowing in DC, yet, but the temperatures were dropping like a rock and the sun was an absentee friend.

Which was how, the next morning, I found myself walking up

CHAPTER 27

to the baggage claim at San Diego International Airport and trying to keep my feet while Carlos swept me up in a bear hug.

"Why the hell didn't you come sooner, *hermano*? We were starting to wonder if the men in black were holding you hostage again."

"Hostage to the job, maybe," I grinned. "And I've been asking myself the same question ever since I got on the plane. Everybody all right?"

"Ah, you know. You're looking fit, dude. Not quite as emaciated as the last time I saw you."

I grinned. "Regular meals and not getting kicked around by ghosts and monsters is a big help. And a couple of hours a day with the tac team doesn't hurt, either."

"Nice. Let's get out of here."

Even with a career, I'd still kept my minimalist ways, and everything I needed was in a single suitcase. As soon as we retrieved it, we headed out for the parking lot and got on the freeway toward the office.

"How's it working out with Kent?" The temporary stay in San Diego had turned permanent—I guess knowing that any number of the cops he'd worked with over the past few years had done so under the influence of a cult leader channeling ancient magic made it easier to pull the pin and walk away.

"He and Esteban spend all day busting each other's balls, it's awesome." Carlos laughed. "It's good, though, man. Felt weird, the feds cutting us loose like that, but it's been smooth, you know? They even gave us our stuff back." He glanced at me as he signaled for the exit. "Which isn't the weirdest part."

"What's that?"

"Ever since we got back, things have been strangely easy with law enforcement. Downright respectful, even."

I hadn't done much direct PI work with the guys before setting out on my own, but I did know that the cops basically regarded the guys as the equivalent of paparazzi with delusions of grandeur. And, to be fair, a good amount of what they did involved photography. Catching cheating spouses and disability fraud was the De La Rosa Agency's bread and butter. But every so often, the guys had a chance to right wrongs—tracking down missing persons that fell off the police radar, for whatever reason, or more off-the-books recoveries when the involvement of the police wasn't possible due to immigration status.

I'm generally a law and order guy, but if it came down to choosing a side between someone with a shaky green card and a kidnapper for a cartel, I go with the green card every time. And every now and then, the agency had run into something that, until recently, we didn't know law enforcement had the capacity to handle.

Grinning, I said, "Well, I may have mentioned something to my supervisor about you guys showing me the ropes, and helping to keep a lid on some of the little beasties that creep in from the desert."

"It's been quiet, lately. Everything has been fairly conventional. Which is how I like it. I got us a tee time tomorrow afternoon—you been staying loose?"

"I haven't played in months," I groaned.

"'S'all right. You know I'm going to win, anyway."

The best families—and friendships—don't suffer from separation. My return to Esteban's home was comfortable, lifting a weight from my shoulders that I hadn't even known was there. I laughed more in the first few hours than I had since the night Mother took Cassie.

With the thought of her, guilt crashed in on me, and I suddenly felt awful for enjoying myself. Who knew what she'd gone through and here I was—doing what? Waiting out the clock? I drifted away from the party and took a seat outside by the pool. The guilt and the shame turned into anger at Mother. Morgan was

CHAPTER 27

slowly teaching me how to use my emotions to fuel my magic. The way I felt at the moment, I could have phased a bulldozer through a wall and not broken a sweat.

I'd only thought that my absence had gone unnoticed. Father Rosado settled into the chair on the other side of the table from me with a contented sigh. We sat in silence for a bit, watching the sun go down over the ocean.

"You look good, Pax," he commented finally.

"Thanks," I said. "Recovered, I hope?"

"I get short of breath every now and then, but much better, yes."

"I'm glad—and I'm sorry. I should have been there to help."

He shook his head. "Nonsense. You were exactly where you needed to be." Father Rosado smiled. "What are an old man's lungs, weighed against the lives of two children?"

"Well, when you put it that way." I took a drink to give myself a moment to think. Division M wasn't so much top secret as it was 'don't talk about stuff that'll get you painted as crazy,' because the agency *would* shrug and allow other authorities to haul agents who talked too much off to treatment facilities. *Ghosts? Beats us, we're Alcohol, Tobacco, and Firearms—better get that guy some Haloperidol.* Very much a 'the Secretary will disavow any knowledge' situation. But if you couldn't talk to a priest, who else *could* you talk to?

"I hope that stays true. Because if I'm not in the right place at the right time this spring, it's going to be bad."

"Still no luck in the search for your mother and Cassie?"

"If the people I work with are right, Mother has taken her somewhere we literally cannot go. So, we wait."

"The ides of March," he said. "Randolph Forest, she said."

"That's the place and the time."

"And with the book, she will do what, exactly?"

I tried to decide how to frame it, exactly, and settled for, "Cause the end of the world."

At this, he laughed. "Nonsense."

"I'm not being dramatic—"

He cut me off. "I'm not laughing at you, son. Your Mother can't end the world, magic book or not. That's not in the cards."

"Well, the consequences of her plan seem pretty straightforward. Just saying."

"The world will end when it's supposed to end. No sooner, no later, and not changing for any of our desires. We've got a whole book about that, you know."

"That's the one where the dead are walking around?" I debated whether to tell him about Roxanne. She'd jumped at the chance to get out of DC, though she'd been scarce since I'd gotten to Esteban's. "Seems to fit."

"'The day of the Lord will come like a thief at night,'" he quoted. "It might be bad, but it won't be the end. And who's to say that you or something else won't stop her?" He shrugged. "Have faith."

"So far, faith's batting about .500." That came out more flip than I intended and I continued. "At least, I didn't get quite as much help the second time around. I'm kinda figuring this one's on me."

"And what will you do?"

"Stop her."

"How far are you willing to go with that, son?"

I frowned. "What are you asking? Am I ready to kill her?" I clenched my fists, digging fingernails into my palms. "Honestly, Father, I've been asking myself why I didn't do it sooner."

"No one can hurt us so badly as the ones we love, Paxton. They know all our weak spots, after all." He leaned closer, fixing me with a stare. "You can't keep hate in your heart—it might sound impossible, but you have to find it in yourself to forgive her."

"You can't be serious. You don't know what she's done! Killing my dad is just the tip of the iceberg. The stuff she's done since she broke out of jail? Calling it evil is an understatement."

He shook his head. "You're not listening to me. If you have to defend yourself, or one of your friends, and killing her is the only way? So be it. I know you're hurting inside, and if it's God's will to stop her, you will. This isn't about her—it's about you."

I resisted the urge to sigh. "Is this some Jedi thing? Hate leads to the Dark Side?"

He laughed. "Even better—it's a Bible thing. Forgive us, Lord, as we forgive those who trespass against us."

"I'll try—" I began. His face brightened, and as he opened his mouth, I interjected, "if you drop Yoda on me, you're going in the pool."

"Fair enough."

CHAPTER TWENTY-EIGHT

Paxton—Monday morning
Washington, DC

When I returned from the holidays, I had a new boss. For everyone else, it was a return to the status quo.

Deputy Director Newquist had the look of a bodybuilder who'd suddenly lost a good deal of weight. Considering he'd been in a medically-induced coma since the day I'd escaped, he had an excuse. His smile widened as I entered the room a few minutes after the scheduled start, and he pushed himself to his feet with a bit of an assist from the conference table.

"I'm glad we finally meet in person, Agent Locke."

"The same to you, sir," I said. "Sorry I'm late."

The director dropped back into his chair after we shook hands. "Only the four of you, then, Valentine?"

Val winked at me. "That's the plan, sir. Clear out the town, Eliot, Paxton, George and I go hunting. Morgan and Arlan's team are batting cleanup, with the National Guard providing perimeter security."

The director stared at the map pinned up on the wall and

CHAPTER 28

shook his head slowly. "Lot of moving parts. But I can't see any other way to do it. No worries, I'm not going to undercut you on this one. You've got my backing. Where are we on Krist—the bomber," he corrected himself.

Morgan chimed in. "My contacts overseas are still kicking the bushes, but I've got a few leads developing. We don't know who hired her, if anyone, but we should be able to track down the thing that impersonated Kristin."

"I look forward to having a discussion with it," Eliot growled.

"Be that as it may, Maine is our top priority at the moment," the director said. "Work it as it comes, but it's a secondary priority until we resolve this situation, understood?"

We all nodded agreement. No one pointed out that if we didn't stop Mother, we'd likely be too busy trying to stay alive to worry about catching the faux-Kristin.

"Morgan, I read your report on your findings on the ritual over the weekend. Good work, there." He turned and fixed me with an intense stare. "Agent Locke, can we count on you to do what needs to be done?"

The room shifted uncomfortably, but I remained stoic. If nothing else, my talk with Father Rosado had gotten the butterflies out on this particular topic. "Call me Pax. What's your preference, Director Newquist?"

That made him blink, and I thought I saw Valentine raise a hand to cover his mouth out of the corner of my eye. The director frowned. "Clarify, please."

"I'm still working my way through the processes and procedures manual, but as I understand it, the Coolidge Order only applies to non-human entities. Putting aside my personal preferences, are we bound to bring her in alive? Does she get a trial?" I shrugged. "If she does, can we at least agree that she does *not* need to be in minimum security?"

He stared at me for a moment, then said, "Lord, Valentine, it's like listening to a recording of you. What have you done to this boy?"

The others broke up in laughter, and after a minute, I joined in. "I'm trying to remain dispassionate about it, Director." I hesitated, unsure whether to explain further, then settled for, "I had a talk with my priest about keeping hate out of my heart. Which is tough, when I keep thinking that we could have avoided this entire situation had I gone further ten years ago."

I could tell he wanted to know how much I'd revealed to my priest, but he let it go. "Understood. And in a normal situation, yeah, we'd strive to bring her in alive. But can you honestly tell me that your mother wouldn't be a threat to others going forward?"

"No," I said, with zero hesitation. There was more than a little heat behind the statement, but the assessment was one of reason. Or so I hoped. *Baby steps, kid.* "I don't care how deep a hole we put her in, she'll never stop trying to get out so long as she lives. Based on what Morgan's told me, that might be a good long while."

"I'd say that answers that question. As always, the final decision is in the hands of the agents in the field, but you have my word that I'll back you, however it goes."

"Gosh, Russ, the way you're talking, it's like you don't expect me to be around to make the call," Valentine joked. "I'm not sure how I should feel about that."

"Well, depending on how things go, a geas could be faster than a bullet," the director said. "Who knows what sort of spells she's yet to use, or even picked up in the interim."

That was an unhappy thought that I'd had more than a few times, working with Morgan. Of course, what the director was polite enough not to mention was that based on our hypothesis, Mother didn't need the others for the ritual. There was no need for her to pull her punches, so if things went badly, it was very likely to come down to the two of us.

CHAPTER 28

This time, you won't pass out, I promised myself. *You're not that terrified kid, anymore. You've got this.*

Claudia, who I suspected had done the lion's share of work helping Valentine to keep the place afloat during the director's hospital stay, stepped into the conference room with a look of panic on her face. "Sir," she whispered. "Senator Prince from the Oversight Committee is here to see you."

Director Newquist frowned. He glanced around the table, then said, "We're about to wrap this up, Claudia. Go ahead and send him in." After she'd left, he murmured, "Scoot over a few chairs, Pax. Let him sit there."

I moved and Valentine grumbled, "I'm surprised the asshole knows how to find the place. He seems to enjoy summoning us to hearings too much to dirty his shoes up coming down here on his own."

"Oh, something's up," Newquist agreed. "Do maintain your calm, if you please."

Valentine snorted. I stifled a laugh—he'd been called into Oversight hearings a few times since I'd come on board, and he always came back in a sour mood. I didn't have to try to hard to imagine what it felt like to have your methods and activities called into question—but it couldn't have been fun, coming from a panel of seven.

Senator Prince was a tall, gray-haired man in a gray suit that probably cost more than my entire wardrobe. Every bit of him was long and lean, as though he'd been a man of normal build stretched out. That thought rose the hair on the back of my neck as I considered the Void, but he gave me only a passing glance as he swept into the room and took the seat I'd abandoned.

Before anyone could greet him, the Senator spoke. "Director Newquist, I'm happy to see you out of the hospital. What makes me less happy are the phone calls I've been receiving from people back home."

I frowned, confused by the 'home' reference until I remembered that Prince was the junior Senator from Maine. *Oh, shit.*

Director Newquist shifted to one side in his chair. "This is the first I'm hearing of it, Senator. I've gotten up to speed in the past week. If there are any concerns, we haven't heard them."

"You're hearing it now," the other man snapped. "Is it correct that a joint exercise between Division M and elements of the Maine National Guard is scheduled for mid-March?"

"Yes," Newquist said. "We anticipate Helen Locke's arrival to Randolph sometime around that time."

"Your Agent Valentine declared Ms. Locke to be one of the most dangerous threats to the security of the nation not all that long ago in a committee hearing. With no slight intended toward my fellow citizens, if she is indeed so dangerous, why are you only taking a single company of infantry to deal with her?"

"My apologies, Senator," the director said. "I believe you don't have the entire story."

"Please, enlighten me."

"The elements of the National Guard will be used to enforce a secure perimeter and to assist in the evacuation of civilians from the area. We don't intend for them to engage in direct combat. My team in this room is taking lead, there, with another tactical team in reserve."

Prince swept his eyes across the room. "Do you mean to tell me that this is your answer? Faced with what Agent Valentine glibly assured the committee was a potential 'extinction-level event', you're sending in a couple of agents, a cripple, a kid, and an old woman?"

"There's no need to be rude," Morgan murmured, but Valentine was less circumspect.

"You Yankee son-of-a—"

Newquist's arm on his shoulder silenced Val, but the director's own tone was even colder. "Senator, your position entitles you to

CHAPTER 28

certain information and historical documents. If you haven't reviewed those documents, I would contend that you're not fit to serve on the Oversight Committee and I'll be bringing it up to the chair."

Prince sniffed. "I've read them. I know all about your crew of misfit toys, Director."

"Then you should also know the danger of underestimating my people." Newquist leaned forward and pointed a forward at the senator to punctuate each point. "You send in a company of soldiers in to capture Helen Locke, you're giving her dozens of loyal servants that will *die* if she orders them to. Kamikaze slaves with firepower. Needless to say, we regard that as an outcome we'd prefer to avoid. Paxton's dealt with his mother in the past, on his own with no support. With backup, we should be able to contain the situation."

The senator turned to look at me now, and I wasn't sure that I liked the cold calculation in his eyes. I had no way of knowing what he searched for in his study, but when he turned away with a sneer, I knew he hadn't found it.

"What I don't understand is why myself or the Oversight Committee should give any credence to the supposed talents of a low-rent Harry Potter wannabe."

"Harry Potter wannabe?" I scoffed. "Kid was clueless. Newt Scamander for the win, Senator." His face darkened, but before he could snap back, I continued. "I worked solo for a decade before I even knew there was such a thing as Division M. I've tangled with things that would make you piss in your fancy suit with nothing more than a shotgun and a plucky attitude. When you take down one of the Void, you can judge me. Until then, kiss my ass."

"You little punk—"

"Senator, I think it's time for you to go," the director said quietly. "If you have issues with the plan, the next committee hearing is the proper place. Your position does not entitle you to barge into my office and berate my people. No," he snapped, as Prince opened his mouth to reply. "Out. Now."

"This isn't the last word you'll hear on this topic."

"I'm sure it's not, but unless you'd like to apologize for your behavior here today, you're no longer welcome in this office." Newquist waited for a beat. When Prince remained silent, he nodded. "Off you go, now."

Face red, he stood and rushed out of the conference room.

Valentine gave it thirty seconds, then mused, "What was the point of that?"

The director frowned but didn't respond for a long moment. Finally, he said, "I'm not sure, but he's on a wild goose chase. I've detailed the operational plan to the committee and at least four of the members are backing our play. He can't win a vote, and he has to know it." He turned to look at me and frowned. "Prince is no fool. He's up to something."

"What do we do?" George wanted to do.

"Keep working," Newquist said. "I'll take care of the politics. You take care of the fight."

CHAPTER TWENTY-NINE

P<small>AXTON</small>—F<small>RIDAY</small>, M<small>ARCH</small> 15
Augusta, Maine

The small warehouse was empty when we got there, so there was no telling what the prior tenants used it for. We didn't give the matter much thought, though, because soon enough we had it full of unloaded equipment and boxes. When we finished, dozens of crates surrounded a series of folding tables bearing a variety of electronics.

There'd been a bit of mid-morning chill in the air when we unloaded, but humming computers, displays, hot plates, and coffee machines quickly brought the temperature in the metal building past comfortable and to the edge of sweltering.

I wasn't wearing my body armor yet, which made it easier to strip down to my undershirt. "We should have packed some fans," I observed to George, who grunted. He stood bent over a piece of the massive suit of armor he wore into battle. The bald agent was the least talkative member of Val's team, but over the past few months I'd learned that he affectionately called the suit 'Beatrice.' For that matter, I'd also assisted Morgan as she went over the runes that Division M used to power the monstrosity. George had taken Beatrice into the first fight against Mother, and she'd somehow disabled it without damaging the surface. Much like the simple scratches I used to bind spell effects, the shape of the runes didn't signify anything other than the intent of the caster, but the heretofore unknown weakness required Morgan to go over each symbol and secure them with additional markings.

In this case, the marks sigils served as mystical batteries while also using the kinetic energy of any hits the suit took to top off the reserves. Here in the warehouse, George had plugged the machine into a 220-volt outlet as soon as we got it out if its shipping crate, and it had been happily drinking juice for a couple of hours now. The only sign of activity on the suit was the slowly brightening glow of the symbols on the massive machine's chest armor. The bright red incandescence was unnerving against Beatrice's otherwise pedestrian olive drab paint job.

"Paxton," Morgan beckoned me from her seat at the table. I moved over and took the seat next to her. She grinned and held up an empty ice chest. "If you think it's too hot, that sounds like a good practice opportunity."

In the past few months, Agent Andrews and his team had whipped my shooting skills into shape, but I was still this side of awful with a long gun. I'd made huge strides with pistols, but for whatever reason, I couldn't hit the broadside of a barn with a rifle no matter how good a scope I used. When Morgan heard of this difficulty, she'd relaxed her hold on Division M's spell archives and given me a little something to keep the playing field level if I had to fight outside the range of a pistol.

I still wondered if the spell wasn't Morgan's subtle attempt to balance the scales between myself and Mother. I'd never seen it, but per Valentine and Roxanne, Mother's preferred form of attack used a semi-liquid flame the agents called balefyr. It was next to impossible to use without tapping into other sources of energy. Ice, though—like the shield spell, it was pretty much self-sufficient. It didn't require me to push the cold away from me so much as it made me pull the very heat out of the air itself. I stretched out a hand and focused on the space inside of Morgan's cooler.

The interior of the warehouse was warm enough that the result was immediately apparent. Wisps of frigid air swirled inside of the cooler, and water crackled into small, frozen pebbles. The sudden temperature difference between the air outside helped in that regard—the natural condensation effect drew humidity, providing moisture for the ice. I could vary the effect of the spell, and draw water as well as heat energy, but that wasn't quite as heat neutral. This method left me with a slow-growing surplus that I could invest in other ways.

Switching gears, I threw the bonus power into my telekinesis spell and pulled the subzero air out of the cooler, throwing it out into the warehouse. The sudden breeze rustled loose paper, and there was a near-collective sigh from the gathered agents as the temperature inside of the building dropped thirty degrees in as many seconds.

It wouldn't last long, but we'd all appreciate it while it did.

"Nicely done," Morgan said. She rattled the cooler, and bits of ice rattled into a shallow layer along the bottom. "Saves me a trip to the convenience store."

"Thanks." I scanned the monitors lined up along the table. All but one displayed quiet city streets from a high angle. Over the past few weeks, we'd worked with the county road crews, adding cameras to several traffic lights under the guise of routine maintenance. Valentine and Director Newquist hadn't been happy about expanding the number of locals briefed in on the situation. The meetings at Governor's office and National Guard adjutant general had been tense, from what I understood—but there was no other way around it that didn't risk the population of Randolph catching on. "How's it looking?"

"It's a lovely spring day in Mayberry," she shrugged.

"Wasn't that down south somewhere? This looks more like the town from *Murder, She Wrote*." I waved a hand at the final monitor. The view there was far different. The director had pulled some strings and had a Predator drone sent up to provide overhead reconnaissance. The town was small enough that one in a constant orbit was enough to cover the gaps. If we missed Mother and Cassie on the street cams, the other perspective could be critical.

"Bit before your time, isn't it?"

"Mother didn't believe in cable TV. In the summers, the only channel I could pull in with an antenna showed reruns of *Perry Mason*, *Matlock*, and *Murder, She Wrote* all night." I scanned the rest of the displays for a few minutes, then wondered, "When they come out, is it something obvious?"

"Not sure," Morgan frowned. "None of the historical references I've found make mention of that. The displaced were usually found after the fact, wandering around in confusion."

I blinked. "That happens often enough that someone wrote about it?"

"A handful of times. The things that come out of nexuses aren't usually so benign. When it's a person, it's kind of like finding a gold nugget in a garbage dump."

"Interesting," I said. "Let me know if you need more ice, I guess." I wandered over to the corner of the warehouse with no windows. Not knowing how long we'd have to wait for Mother to make an appearance, we'd brought along plenty of folding chairs and cots. I pulled the backpack I'd brought along out of one of the seats and settled in. For a while, I tried to read a book, but my mind wouldn't slow down long enough for me to focus. Finally, I threw in the towel and took the same option as several members of the tac team—I settled into one of the cots and closed my eyes. My thoughts didn't settle, but the returning warmth made me drowsy, and I nodded off into a light sleep.

CHAPTER 29

Morning crawled into afternoon. Every so often some small noise would carry across the warehouse, and I'd lift my head and look around to see if it was time to get moving.

A little after twelve, a couple members of Andrews' team piled into a Suburban to go for pizza and drinks. When they returned, we ate in perturbed silence. No one seemed willing to speak up and ask the question, lest they incur Valentine's wrath. The senior agent sat well away from the rest of his, his eyes fixed on a steel rod that hovered a few inches over the table while it slowly rotated.

Eliot's phone rang. In the expectant silence, the sound was all the more startling. We turned to look at the other agent as he answered in a hushed voice and listened before cupping his hand over the mouthpiece and calling out to his partner. "Captain Gardiner wants to know what our status is, he's going to start rotating his men out of their vehicles for crew rest." The company of National Guard troops stood by at the August Armory, ready to deploy and assist in the evacuation as soon as we made the call.

"Tell him we're still in a holding pattern," Valentine said, his tone exhausted. "Do what he needs to do."

Eliot passed the message along, then ended the call. The reign of silence returned, and I tried to return to my book. It was a good thing I'd read it several times. More than once I found that I'd turned through several pages and couldn't quite remember where I was at in the story.

By four in the afternoon, Valentine was furious. He stood, throwing his folding chair to the concrete floor and walked back and forth in front of the row of screens with the demeanor of a caged animal. He wheeled on Morgan. "Why isn't she here, damn it?"

We technically still had eight hours left, but as our sorceress had explained it, ritual magic was time-consuming. It wasn't a simple matter of waving a hand or inscribing a rune, and if the spell was date-specific, the caster needed to complete it before midnight. Under those parameters, Mother and Cassie should have been in Randolph for hours already. Even if we missed them on the cameras, the tracking device would have alerted us to their return.

Morgan held up a finger. "Take a breath," she snapped, "And let me think." She followed her own suggestion, inhaling deeply as she closed her eyes. She remained in that position for several moments, then clenched a fist in frustration "Shit! The Romans used a lunar calendar. We thought it would be the 15th because of historical events, but they shifted based on the phases of the moon." She opened her eyes and shouted, "Someone check! When's the next full moon?"

Multiple people whipped out cell phones, and the race was on. I wasn't surprised in the least that Landry, the sniper on the tac team, was the first to hit on it. She called out, "March 20."

Valentine cursed under his breath. "We're early."

Eliot's phone rang again, but a moment later Valentine's did, as well. The two partners exchanged a look, then answered. The conversation was more intense in the case of the latter, and Eliot ended his call in short order.

"Yes, sir," Valentine said. "We have a new theory." He listened, then said, "March 20th. That's right." He made a face, as though holding in the urge to scream, then replied. "Understood."

He ended the call and glanced at Eliot. "Captain Gardiner," the other agent said. "The Governor's office called them and ordered them to secure Randolph using our cover story."

"Prince," Valentine hissed. "He got to them. That was Director Newquist—officially, we're benched. The Oversight Committee scrubbed the mission and handed it over to the National Guard."

"Unofficially?" Agent Andrews asked.

"We remain here on standby. When Helen shows up, we've got to snatch victory from the jaws of defeat."

I grimaced. No one came out and say it, but we all knew what was about to happen. One way or another, the short-sighted fools who'd ordered the National Guardsmen into the town had sentenced them to death. Whether that death would occur at the hands of my mother or at our hands when we had to fight our way in was a moot point.

"Let me go to the Captain," I said. "I can *push* him to stop his men. It won't keep them from sending someone else, but at least that'll give us a chance to make our case to Oversight."

Valentine made a face, and I could tell he was thinking about it. Finally, he sighed and said, "We can't. They're already suspicious of you, Paxton. If you do that, we'll be back to square one." He slammed a fist down on the table, shaking the monitors. "We have to let them finish screwing it up before we can swoop in and save the day."

Helpless, we could do little but stand and watch on the screens as truck after truck rolled into town. Guardsmen exited the vehicles and marched into residential neighborhoods, going house to house. We couldn't hear their words, but a steady stream of civilian cars and trucks, many loaded down with luggage, streamed out of town and headed for points unknown. If they'd stuck to the cover story, the faux gas leak had served us well, because by the time the sun went down, the only things moving on the streets of Randolph, Maine were Army green.

CASSIE—WEDNESDAY, MARCH 20
Randolph, Maine

HELEN MARCHED THROUGH THE FOREST WITH SUCH intensity of purpose that Cassie struggled to keep up. Pine boughs slapped her in the face as plunged headlong into a gap between two trees. They emerged into a long, narrow clearing.

Her captor paused, considered the area, then pivoted and began walking along the clearing. Glad for the clearance but already starting to sweat from the sudden increase in temperature, Cassie followed.

As they passed a metal sign that read 'Old Narrow Gauge Volunteer Trail,' Cassie called out. "How is this possible?"

"I'm more of an expert in Akkadian and Sumerian, but what I've found in the grimoire about the relationship between space and time would give the boys in the theoretical physics department heart attacks." She shrugged. "Let's say I put a girdle round the earth in a lot less than forty minutes."

She opened her mouth to proclaim the insanity of such a thing

CHAPTER 29

but realized the foolishness of that sentiment almost immediately. Helen had blown up a truck stop and had the ability to make anyone obey her with a mere word. Was time travel that far out of the question?

Their initial surroundings had led her to believe that they were deep in the middle of a forest. As they proceeded down the trail, the tree cover lightened and she realized that they were moving into part of a small town. Helen didn't stop to appreciate the scenery—she strolled out into the road and kept walking. Cassie hesitated as much as she could, given the order to follow, and when she looked both ways, the two-lane highway was empty.

And, now that she thought about it, there was a pervasive sense of emptiness. The two of them had been alone on the trail, but even the modest homes they'd passed before stepping out onto the road had a similar air.

Where is everyone? Cassie cocked her head to one side and tried to listen for the sounds of civilization. Save for the hiss of the wind through the trees and intermittent birdsong, the only thing she heard was the tapping of their shoes on the blacktop. "It's like a ghost town. What's going on?"

Helen paused in the center of the road and turned in a slow circle. Houses lined the road to their right, and the parking lot of a car repair business sat to the left. Other than that, they seemed to be alone. "I'm not sure," the other woman began, then stiffened. At the same moment, Cassie heard the whirring hum of off-road tires on the street behind them.

The men driving the pair of military trucks didn't seem concerned about oncoming traffic. The big vehicles rode side by side and took up both lanes of the highway. The sight of a camouflaged soldier standing behind the big gun mounted on top of each vehicle made Cassie's stomach tighten, and she'd have bolted for the ditch if she'd been in control of her own limbs.

Helen stepped up beside her and waited with stone-faced

patience as the big trucks stopped less than twenty feet away. They were called Humvees, Cassie remembered, and the passenger door on the left one opened up as a soldier with steel-gray hair under his helmet headed toward them. "Ladies, this is a restricted area," he barked. "What are you doing here?"

Before Cassie could even consider saying anything, Helen said, "Oh, my—we were hiking the trail, I'm sorry—we didn't know."

The soldier stepped a little closer, and Cassie read the name GARDINER on his chest. "The trail starts by the IGA," he said, scowling. "That's inside the restricted area, too. Hands in the air!"

"Do whatever they say," Helen said, raising her hands. Cassie couldn't help but notice the satisfied smile on her face, and her stomach clenched in a tight, nervous

What's going on? At first, she'd thought that these soldiers represented her rescue, but Helen acted as though this wasn't even a bump in the road. Thunder crackled in the distance, and a cool wind ruffled her hair.

Gardiner grabbed Cassie's arm with one hand and Helen with the other. He steered them between the idling trucks. He pushed Helen into the truck on the right, then gestured for the men in the other truck to open op. Her limbs were still a little lethargic, but a frustrated bark of, "Move your ass, blondie!" unlocked Helen's prior commands and she found herself able to climb inside of the vehicle.

The Humvee's engine roared, heading down the road as fat raindrops splashed on the hood and windshield. She craned her neck, trying to get a look at the gathering storm. When they'd emerged into the forest, there hadn't been a cloud in the sky, but the coming darkness over the horizon made that seem a distant memory.

The pattering raindrops turned into sheeting rain, and the driver cursed. The soldier beside her was too busy flipping through a small notebook. When he found the page he'd been looking for, he held it up so that he could study it and Cassie at the same time.

He shouted over the roar of the storm. "Cassandra Hatcher?"

Helen's command to 'do whatever they say' seemed to have overridden everything else because she found herself able to speak and react normally. "Yes, that's me." The soldier nodded, then hit a radio control attached to his vest.

"Captain Gardiner, confirm that we've got subject two. Ma'am, can you identify your companion?"

The ma'am threw her for a moment. When she realized that the soldier was speaking to her, Cassie stammered. "Yes, she's Helen Locke, you need to be careful, she's dangerous—"

"Yes, yes, we've got it under control."

She wanted to shout at the idiot, to tell him how wrong he was, but she was too shocked to do so. Before she could muster the will to speak, the driver of the Humvee pulled into the parking lot of a brick building with tan siding. Large letters affixed to the side read 'Randolph Town Office.'

More Humvees flanked a large tent. Dozens of men and women in camouflage uniforms ran through the parking lot, moving equipment and seeking shelter from the sudden downpour.

Someone opened Cassie's door from the outside, and the bedraggled officer who'd met them out on the road pulled her out into the lot. He gave Cassie a shove, and she turned sideways as she staggered forward, catching the look of serene pleasure on Helen's face. Her hair hung in sodden strands, and the rain had turned her blouse scandalously transparent. Which was a problem, Cassie realized, because most of the men around them were more intent on the wet t-shirt contest than the fact that the witch in their midst had plucked the leather-bound book from her satchel and cradled it in one hand.

Gardiner must have seen Cassie's horrified look because he turned and saw what the others had missed. "Drop the book!" He pulled a pistol out of a holster and aimed it at Helen. "Drop it now!"

Too late, she thought, as Helen stabbed her free arm into the air, fingers spread wide. Above them, the black storm clouds roiled, thickening and swirling in a spiral centered above the witch's outstretched hand.

White-hot lightning crashed down into the parking lot, and the ensuing thunder drowned out Cassie's screams of terror—but not the screams of agony from the soldiers as lines of fire descended from heavens and into the gathered National Guardsmen.

CHAPTER THIRTY

P<small>AXTON</small>—W<small>EDNESDAY AFTERNOON</small>
Outside of Randolph, Maine
Flying in airplanes didn't faze me.

Riding in the jump seat of a helicopter, treetops whizzing by beneath our feet, right outside the open doors? My knuckles were white on the grab handle mounted above the row of seats.

Across the way, Valentine gave me a confident wink. Beside him, Eliot had his eyes closed, his head leaned back against the bulkhead. How he could sleep at a time like this was beyond me, but I tried to tell myself to try and relax.

It wasn't like I could get hurt in a crash—all I had to was phase out and drift to the ground.

That was the logic, but it didn't help much—particularly given the dark blot of storm clouds in front of the helicopter.

"Crosswinds are getting to be a bitch," one of the pilots complained. I heard him, clear as day, through the headphones Valentine had passed out as we boarded the helicopter. After the engines started up, I'd figured them for mere ear protection, but they at least gave us the means to communicate with one another without exaggerated hand signals.

"Get us as close as you can," Valentine ordered. "We'll go in on foot the rest of the way."

When Prince and the rest of the Oversight Committee forced us to stand down, they'd pulled the drone—but forgotten about the other cameras we'd wired in place. It had been a boring few days, but as soon as Cassie showed up on the screen, things got exciting.

We'd lost visuals in the torrential rain and ensuing lightning storm, but we'd seen enough. Captain Gardiner and his troops had captured Cassie and a woman that Roxanne confirmed was my Mother. Not long after, the entire Guard contingent stopped responding via radio and telephone, and the video feed from the cameras and drone went out in a flash of static.

We'd assumed as much would happen, and we were ready. As soon as I shouted out at the sight of Cassie, Valentine ordered the team into vehicles and headed toward the airport. Gardiner's unit had brought a quartet of Black Hawk helicopters along for support.

They weren't all that interested in helping us out at first. I was ready to offer to *push* them into it when Morgan stepped forward and handed the senior warrant officer her cell phone. From the "Yes, sirs," and "No, sirs," that followed, she had someone high up on her speed dial, ready to dance, but when I gave her a questioning look, she shrugged and smiled enigmatically.

The pilots maintained a standoffish demeanor, but they'd allowed the team to load up, at least. The man sitting in the copilot's seat turned around and waved wildly.

With a nonchalant air I couldn't imagine taking, Valentine hit the release on his restraints and moved closer to the front of the chopper. I couldn't see what had the men up front so concerned, but we all heard their conversation on the headset intercom.

"Got what looks like a chewed-up police blockade on one side

CHAPTER 30

of the ME-27 bridge and our boys on the other—why the hell would Guardsmen open up on cops?"

Valentine's tone was grim. "Someone told them to, I'd imagine." The helicopter jerked to one side, and he reached out to seize the bulkhead to stabilize himself. Roxanne didn't have any such concerns, but she did roll her eyes at me as his hand plunged through her torso. *Wonder if she actually feels that.* My ghostly companion hadn't been as chatty over the last few months, but she was more than ready to head to Randolph when the time came.

The other pilot screamed, "Ground fire! Evasive!"

The repetitive sparking of impacts drew my eyes to the helicopter flying in formation on our right side. The other aircraft seemed to freeze in midair before smoke boiled out of the upper half. Wobbling, it sagged out of view.

"Mason's going down hard! We're out of here!"

Valentine stole a glance over his shoulder. George and Beatrice took up a helicopter of their own, and the other thirteen of us had spread out across the remaining three. I wasn't sure who'd been on the downed craft, but it looked like we'd just lost a big chunk of the tac team.

"Morgan," Valentine called. "You're with Eliot."

Before I could open my mouth to ask what was happening, the senior agent crossed the passenger compartment of the helicopter, pausing long enough to hit the release button on my safety harness.

I knew Valentine was fast, but when he grabbed me by my body armor, yanked me out of the seat, and pulled me out of the helicopter after him in an awkward swan dive, I saw little more than a blur of blue sky, green trees, and the lazy murk of the Kennebec River below us.

We were low, but it wasn't like we'd been flying nape of the Earth—I had a few seconds to contemplate my sudden change of circumstance.

A few months ago, I might have panicked. But the delay had given Valentine and the other agents of Division M the opportunity to sharpen my instincts. Agent Andrews was particularly fond of sneaking around the office with an Airsoft gun. I'd taken more than a few painful welts before magical muscle memory kicked in.

Which was the point, of course.

Valentine had a fierce hold on my right arm. I curled my left into a protective position in front of my chest and envisioned a bowl-shaped shield, large enough to catch both of us. A split-second after it snapped into place, we—on top of the shield—slammed into the surface of the water.

I grunted at the sensation of the impact, but water sprayed up around us, and I felt the shield strengthen as it siphoned the kinetic energy of our fall to power itself. We floated, but the effect didn't last long—as the juice from the impact faded, I had to choose between dropping the spell or powering it myself.

With a pop of displaced air, we dropped into the water. I kicked my legs, trying to keep my head up, then my feet found the bottom. We'd landed close to the bank, in the shallows.

Beside me, Valentine stood, soaked and bedraggled. "Really?" he growled. "You couldn't, you know, float us out of here?"

I need to hang out with these guys more often, Roxanne laughed. She'd drifted down and settled onto the bank.

Score one for being incorporeal, I guess. Ignoring her, I snapped at Valentine, "Maybe if I'd had more than two seconds notice!"

He started to reply but the booming sound of machine gun fire cut him off. "Fair point," he conceded after they fell silent. "Let's go."

We climbed up on the bank and headed for the bridge. Intentionally or not, we'd ended on the opposite side of the river from the town, and by the time we made it to the State Police roadblock, Morgan and Eliot had found us. The other two agents were dry as a bone, and I gave the sorceress a suspicious look.

CHAPTER 30

"You have a clothesline spell you didn't tell me about?"

"It helps not to land *in* the water," Eliot said dryly.

Morgan actually giggled. "When we get out of this, we need to practice free falling."

"I can't wait."

The police had fallen back, leaving the burning ruins of two patrol cars in the center of the bridge. The National Guard Humvees on the other side had stopped firing, but the half-dozen cops seemed content to huddle behind their own armored vehicles. A burly black cop in body armor much like our own looked us up and down with a scowl as we approached.

"Who the hell are you supposed to be?"

"Homeland Security," Valentine said absently. He had his eyes on the opposite side of the bridge. "You got this covered?"

"Hey, man, at this point I'm just trying to keep those nut-jobs from turning any civilians into hamburger. What the hell's got into those boys?"

"Classified," Eliot and Valentine said, simultaneously. The latter smirked, then tapped on his radio.

"These things are waterproof, right? Radio check, anyone out there? Arlan? Georgie?"

I fished my own earpiece out of my vest and hooked it into my ear. I gave Roxanne a look and jerked my thumb to the opposite side of the bridge.

She sighed theatrically. *Aye aye, Captain.*

Static hissed in my ear. "This is Agent Andrews. We managed to set down north of the bridge on the Randolph side. What's the plan?"

"Who's with you?" Valentine wanted to know.

"Wallace, Hopper, Landry, and Sharps. Did you see what happened to the other choppers?"

"Frank's went down." That must have been the one that I'd seen hit—Agent Luke, the former Chicago SWAT member who'd helped welcome to me Division M and his team had been aboard. The loss hit me, and I grimaced. I'd only known them for a few months, but once we'd gotten the initial strutting out of the way, every member of Andrews' team had accepted me as one of their own. Much like the De La Rosas, they'd become the equivalent of older brothers—sisters in the case of Landry—almost overnight, and even more quickly, some of them were gone.

Damn it, Mother. No more.

Valentine's shoulders sagged. Composing himself, he said, "Understood. Georgie? Come in, Georgie." Silence.

"There's another fire between us and the bridge," Andrews said. "I'm thinking it might be the last helicopter."

Valentine spat a curse. "Move forward and check for survivors. Hold position when you get there, I'll let you know when we're ready to link up."

Andrews didn't reply for a long time, then came back with, "Understood."

Turning to look at the three of us, Valentine said, "You ready? Let's do this little thing."

The local cop stepped forward and inserted himself into the conversation. "I don't care what agency you're from, you're not getting any support from us. And if you go out on that bridge with some sort of armored vehicle, it's your funeral."

Morgan patted him on the shoulder. "Thanks for your concern, officer. We'll be fine. You're doing a marvelous job." She glanced at me. "You and I are leading the way, Pax."

The cops had left a narrow opening between their angled SWAT vehicles. Long range or not, I felt more than a little exposed as we passed through and stepped out onto the bridge deck. "Shields up?"

"Indeed," she said. "Pitch it, like a roof—it will send the ricochets to either side. Just like we practiced."

"Got it," I said. Unlike the invisibility spell, the shield was quite noticeable. It appeared as a slight blur in front of me, though it remained clear enough to see through.

"Excellent," Morgan proclaimed. "We're taking this slow. It's a walk in the park."

Sure. It'll be fun.

Eliot and Valentine filtered through and took up positions behind us—the senior agent behind me, and the other behind Morgan. Valentine put his hand on my shoulder, hesitated, then said, "Game face, Eliot."

"That bad?"

"Gut feeling."

Eliot winced. "You get stomach trouble, wars tend to break out." He took a deep breath. "All right."

I'd long stopped wondering why Agent Eliot tended to wear baggy clothing. And, frankly, there was enough mind-blowing stuff going on at Division M that one agent being a slob was a minor curiosity.

As his shoulders broadened with repetitive clicking pops and new muscle swelled along his extremities, I got it.

It was more than mere muscle. Eliot seemed to almost take a step back along the evolutionary ladder. His forehead jutted forward as his brow thickened with heavy bone, and the hair on his forearms and the back of his hands thickened and turned ink black.

I'd have called Eliot a steroid-jacked Neanderthal Arnold Schwarzenegger, but I could see why Roxanne had described him as a werewolf. It was hard to make out in the daylight, but I thought I detected a faint green glow to his eyes.

Eliot growled, his lower jaw something more like a steam shovel than anything typically found on the human body, and clenched his massive fists. "Oh, yeah, I can smell the ozone."

Valentine winced. *"Blitz soldat?"*

"Yeah."

"What's that?" I interjected. "Sounds like a fancy pastry." The attempted joke fell flat.

"Lightning soldier," Morgan said, quietly. "The bodies of the recent dead, reanimated with elemental spirits. Cruel and cunning."

Zombies, Roxanne said, appearing at my side in a blur. *There are zombies with guns over there and*—she noticed Eliot and jumped. *Holy shit!*

"Yeah, he's been working out," I said to her. "How do we fight them? Shoot them in the head?"

Valentine had a pistol in his hand. He confirmed the magazine was full and slammed it back into place. "Sure, if you want a headless corpse to disembowel you. Ice, fire, or explosion. Wreck the body bad enough, the elemental will get frustrated and head home. Until that point, watch your ass. They're nasty little fuckers." He looked at me. "How many?"

I raised an eyebrow at Roxanne.

Twenty? Should I go count?

"That'd be nice," I said. She blurred away. "Twenty, maybe more. She's working on an exact count."

"Start walking," Valentine ordered.

The patrol cars in the middle of the bridge still smoldered, but the smoke had cleared enough to get a good look at the other side of the bridge. I could make out flashes of camouflaged fabric behind the pair of Humvees parked on the road, but I didn't see anything close to twenty people if I could still them that. Cunning, as Morgan had said—and smart enough to hide out of sight until they could spring their trap on us. It might have been easier to spray us with the heavy machine guns mounted on each truck, but something told me that wasn't quite as fun for them. Wasn't *that* a happy thought?

Of more concern was the sight beyond the roadblock. I'd have found the black clot of storm clouds unnatural even without the

CHAPTER 30

blood-red streaks of lightning crackling through them. The pulsing mass seemed only to be a few miles across. While wisps of gray surrounded it, for the most part, the sky surrounding it was clear and blue.

We reached the patrol cars, and Valentine murmured, "Hold here. Let's see if they get antsy." He plucked his cell phone from a pocket in his body armor and pointed the camera over my shoulder in the direction of the unnatural clouds wheeling over the center of town.

"What are you doing?" Eliot said. The transformation lent a gravelly bass to his voice and made it hard to determine his mood, but he sounded irritated.

"Sending Senator Prince a text," Valentine said. His fingers flew over the touchscreen. "Nice ... job ... asshole. Send."

I laughed, but there was a little hint of hysteria there. If the others picked up on it, no one said anything.

Roxanne returned, and I flinched.

Twenty-three. I counted twice.

Valentine grinned when I reported the number. "That's six for us and five for you, kid. Here we go."

We resumed our slow march, and I couldn't help but wonder what the cops behind us made of it.

If they found this impressive, they hadn't seen anything yet.

"Roxanne," I murmured, eyes intent on the Humvees. "There's nothing more you can do here—check the rest of the town. See if you can find us a clear path to my Mother."

She didn't take the time for any snark, but she blurred out of sight.

"Too bad she can't carry a radio," Valentine murmured. "Heads up."

We were three-quarters of the way across the bridge when two of the lightning soldiers popped up in the machine gun turrets and opened fire.

Each impact on my shield translated into a solid thump to my arm, but it didn't hurt, exactly. It was certainly better than the alternative. With each shock, blue sparks cascaded through the spell. Half-inch bullets flattened into disks and rattled to the pavement.

"Keep going," Valentine urged. "They won't be able to hold their bloodlust down much longer—when they rush us, it's on. Pax, Morgan— cover the sides. I've got the center. Eliot, take out the machine guns."

"My pleasure," the other agent growled.

The gun on the left went silent, and the lightning soldier flipped open a cover and fiddled with something for a few seconds before pulling itself out of the turret and onto the hood of the Humvee. It moved with a strange, crustacean grace, as though its transformation had broken or replaced the joints of its human shell. My knees and elbows sure didn't bend that way. The thing let out an unearthly howl and hit the ground on all fours, heading toward us at a terrifying rate of speed.

As though the howl had flipped a switch, a swarm of camouflaged figures appeared, rushing toward us. Some moved on all hands and knees like the machine gunner, but others ran upright. Their screams filled the air, and the hair on the back of my neck stood on end.

Valentine waited for what felt like an eternity. Once all the lightning soldiers had rushed the bridge, he barked, "Now!"

None of the attackers had retained their weapons, so I dropped the shield as I stepped closer to the north side of the bridge. Valentine took two steps forward to fill the gap, a blazing pistol in each fist. The spray of fire ended almost as soon as it had begun. I blinked in amazement as his hands blurred to his waist. He released the slide locks on his pistols before the empty magazines hit the pavement, chambering fresh rounds. If nothing else, such a demonstration soothed any remnant of the wounded pride I held at his ease in taking me down.

Morgan shouted something I didn't understand. Her shield rushed away from her and slammed into the leading edge of the swarm on her side, bowling them over as the spell dissipated in an ethereal flash. Eliot sprinted forward, leaning into the run as he headed for the momentary opening.

I hadn't learned the shield-throwing trick, so I went with something I *had* mastered. Dropping the defensive spell, I thrust both hands out and focused on two of the closest runners. In my mind's eye, a cylinder-shaped space from my palms to the inside of each soldier's chest formed, and I pulled the heat out with everything I had.

It was the cooler on a far larger scale. The water in the air crackled into ice, tracing a line between me and the running figures. With no support, the crystals cracked and rained down on the bridge, but inside of each reanimated soldier's chest, the remaining moisture reacted instantly and violently. Flesh solidified and cracked, staggering them in place as their upper bodies froze solid. Even so, the things kept trying to move, heads swiveling to look at me.

Valentine finished them off, emptying his pistols once more into frozen torsos. The ice shattered and exploded, and I tried not to look at the resultant mess on the ground. The bits of flesh wiggled for a few seconds, then fell still as a subtle flash of light flickered out of each.

"Reloading," Valentine called. His hands blurred again—before the word was out of his mouth, he had both pistols tucked back into their holsters, swinging his arms back around with a replacement pair. "Look out!"

I shook my head and turned back to the fight. *Pay attention, damn it!*

The warning turned out to be moot, because a trio of running soldiers turned on a dime and rushed past me toward Valentine. I blinked in surprise, wondering if they hadn't seen me, and then it hit me.

Mother needs me alive.

Valentine had a split-second to react. I expected surprise as the trio bypassed me and headed for him, but the look on his face was more annoyed than shocked. They bowled him over, and he disappeared in the dogpile.

The ice spell was too risky with Valentine in the mix. I grabbed one of the lightning soldiers by his equipment harness and tried to pull him away. The thing growled, snapping its head around. Blood smeared the gnashing teeth—while I knew Valentine was inhumanly tough, I doubted he could survive being eaten alive.

The thing in my grip struggled, and I almost lost hold of it. Just having a hand on it made my skin tingle. *It's a man-eating Van der Graaf generator.* Trying not to laugh, I heaved with all my strength, toppling us both. It tried to pull away, and I thought I heard Valentine's angry scream over the sudden boom of close-range gunfire.

The monster gave up trying to get away and wheeled on me. "She wants you alive—that doesn't mean you need your legs, human!"

I tried not to grin as the force blades formed at the end of my outstretched hands. "Funny. I could say the same for you." The beast screamed as I whipped cerulean fire through its knees and hips. It tumbled to the ground in a pile of noisome pieces, flesh sizzling. The intact trunk tried to hand-over-hand toward me, but I'd learned my lesson the first time I'd faced one of the Void. I speared it through the head with one blade to hold it steady and proceeded to reduce the rest into fist-sized chunks. The same light as before flickered away, and I dropped the blades.

The bodies on top of Valentine had fallen still, and he pulled himself out from underneath them. Viscera coated him from head to toe. He started to holster his pistols, then grimaced at the blood and unidentifiable chunks coating them. "I hate those damn things," he sighed.

All of the lightning soldiers were down, a few still moving with mixed results. I'd missed Morgan's technique after she'd thrown the shield, but she seemed to have held her own. Eliot had done the lion's share—he held one of the machine guns from the Humvees by the barrel, the battered and blood-stained receiver resting on his shoulder like an olive-drab baseball bat.

I took a breath and looked around. "Is that it?"

Morgan wrinkled her noise at Valentine's appearance. She waved a hand, and the blood and offal dried and flaked off of his clothing and equipment. Raising an eyebrow, I said, "So you can do that, but you leave me soaking wet?"

Smiling, she said sweetly, "It doesn't work on water, alas."

On the other end of the bridge, Eliot found a lightning soldier that wasn't completely dead, and he brought the square end of his gun-club down with a liquid squelch. "I guess he's next, anyway," I said.

Ignoring the interplay, Valentine keyed his radio. "Andrews, move up to the bridge, we're advancing in force as soon as you arrive."

"Roger that, Valentine. You'll be happy to hear that we're bringing help. Agent Patrick knocked himself silly in the crash. He's got a few dents and some scorched paint but he insists he's good to go."

It occurred to me as Valentine closed his eyes and pumped his fist that I'd never seen the man elated. His emotion typically ran a narrow gamut between bored and pissed off. Something so far out of the ordinary was actually a nice morale boost—*we've got this*.

Of course, then he had to go and bring it back to Earth. "We're going to need him. There are another hundred of those things, if not more."

"That's not the most important thing," Morgan murmured. "They didn't attack Paxton."

Valentine stared at me then, his face blank. "Okay," he said. "How do we use that?"

Morgan smiled.

CHAPTER THIRTY-ONE

C<small>ASSIE</small>—W<small>EDNESDAY AFTERNOON</small>
Randolph, Maine

T<small>HE CIRCLE</small> H<small>ELEN DREW WAS FAR SMALLER THIS TIME, AND</small> given that her medium was city hall's parking lot, she had to make do with chalk rather than a simple stick.

At least the rain stopped. The black clouds overhead persisted, and intermittent flashes of lightning rippled through them, lending crimson illumination on the early twilight. Ordered to sit on the curb, Cassie shivered and hunched over. The day had turned even colder than it had been in Oklahoma. She didn't feel nostalgic, exactly, but a slow death by frostbite sounded more appealing than the current horror show of red lightning and zombie soldiers.

Learn some magic, become an amateur exorcist, what could go wrong? She planted her chin on her knees to hide her grimace. Four of the risen soldiers surrounded Helen, stabilizing a collapsible awning against the intermittent gusts of wind. Another pair loitered not far from Cassie, but she wasn't sure why her captor had bothered—it wasn't like she could get away.

Under the tent, Helen was on her hands and knees now, scribbling with growing frenzy. Every so often she paused to consult the grimoire, and as she did so, Cassie realized for the first time that the pages didn't so much as stir in the wind.

Be honest, are you surprised? Sighing, Cassie stretched out her legs to ease the ache in her butt, but that was as far as she could move—sitting meant just that, and her ass stuck to the ground as though cemented in place.

Cassie.

She flinched, looking to either side. It had been a woman's voice, but none of the remaining soldiers were female. *Am I losing it?*

You're not losing it.

"Holy shit," she said, flinching again at the sound of her voice. Helen didn't seem to notice, but the soldier standing to her left turned and looked at her with dead eyes that glittered with a malevolent intelligence. She forced herself to stare back defiantly until the thing turned away with a shrug.

Don't talk. I can hear you.

She licked her lips and tried to keep her face calm. *Who are you? What are you?*

A moment of silence, then, *I'm Roxanne. I'm here, with Paxton.*

Her heart leaped in her chest. *He's coming?* She frowned, then: *You didn't answer my question.*

We've met before, you and I. Back in Phoenix, when Helen forced me to kill myself.

Cassie blinked as she remembered the redheaded witch, choking under the pressure of her own hands. *How are we talking? Pax is the one who can do that sort of thing.*

I guess you could say I'm cheating—I'm in your head.

She blanched, thinking about the shadows running under the skin of the girl in Paxton's basement. *Some sort of possession thing? Great, as if my week wasn't bad enough.*

You know the truth. Do it.

Inhaling, Cassie activated her truth spell. Up to this point it had proved to be more than useless—she might as well try and get something out of it. *Why are you in my head?*

Because I can help you, and you can help me. And I can't make you do anything you don't want to.

A smile spread across her face. Truth, truth, and truth. All of it. *What do I do?*

Relax, and share.

Her butt ached and her fingertips were numb with cold, but Cassie tried to relax. After a few moments, pins and needles danced up and down her legs, and the ghost in the back of her head giggled.

Oh, I'd forgotten what it feels like to be cold. Her tone turned wistful. *I didn't even realize what I was missing.*

What now? Cassie demanded. The sensation wasn't uncomfortable, exactly. It felt like her arms and legs had gone to sleep a bit ago and she was still in the process of shaking the feeling back into them.

She leaned over to one side, lifting her butt off of the curb for a moment before leaning back the other way. It was still uncomfortable, but shifting positions scratched the itch in the back of her head and eased some of the panic she'd felt with her body not being entirely under her control.

Of course, it still wasn't, but this felt more symbiotic than authoritarian. It was, she realized, the mystical equivalent of a loophole. Helen had forbidden Cassie to move on her own, but no such orders pinned Roxanne down. She didn't know how long that might last if Helen realized she'd found a way out, but it gave her a chance she hadn't had a few moments ago. *What now?* She repeated.

Now, we wait. Just for a little while. Cassie shivered at the sensation of invisible fingers flipping through her memories, like a massive card catalog. *And see if I can teach you a few tricks in the meantime.*

Paxton—Wednesday afternoon

Randolph, Maine

Men shouted, guns crackled, and the air thumped with the sound of explosives.

Meanwhile, I ran.

The cacophony of the battle behind me brought with it no small share of guilt, but at least I wasn't alone. Val and Eliot flanked me to either side, though the latter drew ahead as we moved—scouting the way. Twice, he signaled for us to stop our mad scramble, and we huddled together under the cloak of my

CHAPTER 31

invisibility spell while lightning soldiers sprinted toward the fight at the bridgehead.

Which was the idea, of course, but that didn't mean I had to like it.

The soldiers faded into the distance, and we stood and resumed our own run. We cut through residential streets and lawns, only slowing when forced to pick our way through trees or other foliage. Navigation wasn't an issue—the center of the swirling cloud bank was evident, and except when forced to by the terrain, we maintained a path toward it.

"Getting close," Valentine said. Pausing at the edge of a road, he checked both directions before leading us out and into the trees on the opposite side. As we picked our way through the copse, my skin tingled uncomfortably. Licking my lips, I slowed, choosing my steps with more care. Valentine and Eliot's positions didn't vary much. Though they remained silent, something told me that they felt it, too, and slowed to keep pace.

Eye of the storm, I guessed.

Valentine hissed under his breath and crouched behind a squat, overgrown bush. He reached out and gave a tug on one branch, revealing the sight beyond.

Military equipment filled the parking lot. A female figure crouched on the pavement underneath a square tent, with a soldier holding position at each of the four legs supporting the assembly. I kept looking, and my heart leaped in my chest as I caught sight of Cassie, flanked by two soldiers of her own. *Hang in there,* I wished I could say.

"Two to one," Eliot growled. "I like those odds."

"Three," Valentine corrected. "We take the soldiers, the kid takes his mom." He gave me a squint-eyed look, as though trying to determine whether I was worthy of the trust he was laying on my shoulders. "You got it?"

Taking a deep breath, I nodded. "I'll do my best. What's the plan?"

"Times like this, I find a plan's more of a distraction than anything else." He pointed. "The bad guys are that way. Let's go kick their asses."

We pushed through the tree cover behind the town hall. A grassy field lay behind the main building and parking lot. Its only major feature was a towering radio relay station, and I winced with every crack in the sky, ready for the tower to turn into a lightning rod.

Eliot bent over in an awkward, broken run that still managed to outpace us. Thunder rumbled, and the sudden red light gave Valentine's smile a wicked cast. "Well, don't stand there and watch him, kid—run!"

We sprinted across the grass. At some point, Mother's security detail noticed the attack coming from the rear, and they peeled away from the tent to greet us. By then, Eliot had crossed the distance, and he took one down in a leaping tackle. Thrusting my hands forward, I considered the trace heat in the air, and two of the soldiers staggered as my frost lances pierced their chests and turned them solid. As on the bridge, Valentine's guns roared, the frozen things shattering. Eliot had the advantage on his first target, and with a roar, he spun and heaved it against a parked Humvee. The impact rocked the vehicle up onto two wheels. The noticeable crater in the side as it settled back down and the boneless way the lightning soldier flopped out told me we weren't going to have to dismember *that* one.

Valentine and I wheeled onto the final member of the guards, but Eliot twisted and bounced across our line of sight before we could execute our one-two punch. As though it had some inkling about what was coming, the lightning soldier actually turned and fled until Eliot slammed his knees into its back. On the way down,

CHAPTER 31

he tore both arms from its shoulder sockets and proceeded to use them like macabre drumsticks.

I had to avert my eyes. Throwing up in the middle of a fight was hardly the bad-ass thing to do, and even Valentine sounded a little perturbed.

"Dial it back, old son—think green thoughts."

Eliot screamed again, bellowing to the sky in pained triumph. I had to hope that Valentine could get him back under control—at the moment, I had bigger fish to fry.

Standing, Mother turned to face me. She discarded the nub of her chalk and brushed the dust from her fingers. If Roxanne hadn't told me about the spell she'd used, I'd have thought the figure before me another person entirely. They say everyone has a twin, somewhere in the world, but sometimes I think it's more common than that. The first few years after my dad died, I saw him more than once out in public until the conscious reminder that he *couldn't* be there hit me. At that point, I'd realize that the person really didn't look all that much like my dad; it was a trick of the light or a similar mannerism.

The woman under the tent resembled Mother more than the fathers I'd seen in those ephemeral moments. She might have been a cousin or younger sister, but the smooth voice was the same as she studied the three of us and smirked.

"Paxton, you naughty boy—you weren't supposed to bring any friends!"

I resisted the urge to duck my shoulders or grit my teeth. "I must have missed that stipulation. You should call more often."

Her smile widened and she shrugged. "That's all right—I can make sure we're left to our own devices." She turned and stared Valentine down. "Leave us."

I couldn't feel it, but the subtle vibration of her voice told me she was using the *push*. I'd learned the hard way that it didn't work on him. Her widened eyes and obvious alarm were more than a little enjoyable.

Valentine leveled one of his pistols at her head and muttered, "Sorry, darlin'. Your sweet little voice doesn't work on me."

"It's a long story," I added. "You wouldn't believe me if I told you."

She sniffed in disdain and waved a hand. Valentine had time for a grunt of surprise as an invisible fist knocked him off his feet, but it was more than enough for him to pull the trigger. He flew back across the field and into the woods. The ricochet of his shot off the invisible shield surrounding Mother made for an odd accompaniment to the sound of cracking wood.

I winced. *That's a new trick.*

"You got this, kid?" Eliot growled. He edged onto the parking lot. His voice was edging back toward normal—green?—though he'd maintained the physical aspects of his transformation.

So help me God, I didn't hesitate.

I snapped both palms toward Mother. Frost lances poured out to take her in the chest, but the ice shattered on an invisible barrier outside of the tent.

Shit. Before I could open my mouth to use the *push* myself, Mother's face darkened, and she snapped, "Stand down, or the boys will start pulling parts off of your sweetheart."

The three of them shuffled out from behind one of the Humvees, and it took everything I had not to move. The lightning soldiers stood on either side of Cassie. Each had hold of an arm, gripping it by the bicep and wrist. Mother wasn't the bluffing type, and so far as I knew she didn't even have to speak to direct the reanimated bodyguards.

Mother rolled her eyes and shook her head. "All the years in prison—what do you think I was doing? Quilting? Even if it was in my head, I planned for this moment day and night. There's

CHAPTER 31

nothing you, your pet monsters, or Cassie can do to stop what I've put in motion."

Behind Mother, a strange smile crossed Cassie's face. The confusion must have shown on my expression because Mother turned to stare at her hostage.

"There's just one problem," Cassie informed her.

I frowned—something about her voice was off, though the timbre was familiar. *Where have I heard that voice before?*

"I'm not Cassie."

CHAPTER THIRTY-TWO

C<small>ASSIE</small>—W<small>EDNESDAY AFTERNOON</small>
Randolph, Maine

When Cassie learned the truth spell, the sensation had been something like bubbles in her head—like a drink of champagne that tickled your palate.

Whatever Roxanne was doing *burned*.

You need *this, girlfriend. If you don't learn to tap, the first time you use the balefyr you'll pass out and be no good to anyone, and we're running out of time!*

Tears welled in her eyes as she gritted her teeth.

The abrupt chaos that had led her pair of bodyguards to pull her around the back of one of the military trucks trailed off into silence, and she heard Helen's voice.

"Paxton, you naughty boy—you weren't supposed to bring any friends!"

Cassie resisted the urge to cry out in joy—the burning sensation of power coursing through died down to a more manageable trickle as she got a grasp on the spell. Compared to the truth spell and the fire spell Roxanne had passed onto her, the tap felt like

CHAPTER 32

trying to handle a fire hose solo, and something told her she wouldn't like the answer if she asked just where all that juice was coming from. But the reply from the other side of the parking lot pushed that concern away for another day.

"I must have missed that stipulation. You should call more often."

"Oh, hell, yes," she whispered under her breath. Roxanne crowed victory in her head, distracting her from hearing the rest of the conversation until Helen cried out.

"Stand down, or the boys will start pulling parts off of your sweetheart."

Jerking out of their patient stillness, her guards tightened their grip on her arms and dragged her around to take in the scene. Paxton was there, strangely clothed in black clothes similar to the ones the National Guardsmen wore, only without any insignia or name tape. Another figure, hulking and movie monster ugly stood nearby, wearing the same uniform. That, she supposed, meant that he was on the good guy side, even if he didn't look the part.

If she'd had any lingering doubts about the truth of Helen's time travel claims, Pax's appearance laid them to rest. When she'd last seen him, he'd shown the aftereffects of his mystical overexertion when he'd healed her. Now, he looked as though he'd put on a good thirty pounds, most of it muscle.

In front of her, Helen shook her head. "All the years in prison —what do you think I was doing? Quilting? Even if it was in my head, I planned for this moment day and night. There's nothing you, your pet monsters, or Cassie can do to stop what I've put in motion."

Inside, Roxanne giggled, and Cassie let herself smile.

Let me break it to her?

Go for it.

Roxanne took control of her mouth, and if the sensation of the ghost girl controlling her limbs had been an odd one, this put that to shame. "There's just one problem. I'm not Cassie."

Now, Cassie—let's do it.

Power surged inside of her. Helen's command to stay still extended to being able to look down, but she got the vague impression of a sudden glow down by her hands. Roxanne twisted her forearms around and grabbed hold of the reanimated soldier standing on either side of them.

Do you like Five Finger Death Punch, Cassie?

I'm more of a Breaking Benjamin gal.

Well, as the song goes—

Roxanne opened their lips and screamed, "Burn, motherfucker!"

The glow of her hands turned blinding in the cloud-shrouded darkness. The guards tried to pull away, but they couldn't outrun what Roxanne had taught her.

Under control now, she had the vague sensation of the fire hose pouring power into her stomach, proceeding up through her chest and down along her arms. The pain was gone, the fire inside warming her against the unearthly chill. She bared her teeth, the expression a hybrid of a smile and snarl, unsure which expression belonged to her and which her guest.

White-hot fire poured from her palms, flowing more like a viscous fluid than fire, sinking into the bodies of her guards at the point where she'd grabbed hold. They screamed in stereo, smoke pouring out of their mouths as molten death coursed through them.

Cassie cringed at the stench of scorched flesh. Roxanne took two steps forward, leaving a pile of still-smoldering remains behind, and raised her hands to aim them in the other witch's direction.

"You were saying, *Helen?*"

CHAPTER 32

P*axton*—W*ednesday afternoon*
Randolph, Maine

What do you say when you haven't seen your girlfriend in months, and she's turned into a bit of a bad-ass in the meantime?

"Hey, Cass."

She kept her hands pointing at Mother, but she flashed a smile and replied, "Hey, Pax."

Thunder rumbled in the sky, and when I looked, the clouds seemed closer, somehow. Eliot followed my eyes and cursed.

"We're getting closer to culmination."

I glanced at Mother, but she just smiled at me, serene.

"I'm a little out of ideas on how to crack that open," I admitted. From what Morgan had said earlier, I didn't know if I *should*. "What do you think?"

Eliot pressed a hand to his ear. "The others are coming. We'll see what Morgan thinks." He cocked his head, then turned to look back the way we'd come in. Valentine limped out of the woods, cradling his left arm to his chest. He'd zip-tied his wrist to one of the straps, and even at this distance, I could see the unnatural bend in his forearm. "About time you woke up!" Eliot called out.

Another peal of thunder drowned out the reply, but I could guess as to the content. Behind us, Mother gave an exaggerated sigh.

"Your friends won't arrive in time, Paxton. Time runs short. We need to complete the ritual."

"Not happening," I scoffed. "You're insane. And short a sacrifice, it looks like." I shrugged. "Sorry to ruin your plans for world domination."

The few times in my life I'd mustered up the courage to lay sarcasm on Mother, she'd reacted in one way—anger. The last thing I expected now was the obvious shock on her face.

"What? What are you talking about?"

I hesitated, then said, "The grimoire showed me, Mother. It showed me what you'd make of the world. You can't seriously think—"

"You don't get it!" she shrieked, cutting me off. "It's not about me. Earth is a happy little paradise in a sea of torment. There are *things* outside of our existence that would consume our universe for a snack. That's what the grimoire showed me. Things like the Edimmu slip through the cracks and keep a low profile. If something like the Void ever held sway here, it would be catastrophic. That's what I have to *stop*, you damn fool."

"The Void," I repeated. "They're already here."

"Scouts," she scoffed. "Slipping through the cracks in reality. I can't keep them out, but I can 'seel the night'—I can blind the darkness to our presence." She shrugged. "What they can't find, they can't invade."

Valentine stepped forward, opening his mouth to interject, but Mother waved a hand. The air pulsed around her circle, thickening. It felt as though she'd plunged me in mud up to my neck, and the sound around me turned garbled and muffled.

"You can't trust the word of an ancient Sumerian demon, Mother. Why would it help you?"

CHAPTER 32

"The enemy of my enemy," she said, her voice clear as day. "It sustained itself on ghosts. No people, no ghosts, no food. Why *wouldn't* it want humanity to survive?"

God help me, I understood.

The vision the book showed me wasn't an event or result Mother wanted to bring about. It was something, absent intervention, that could happen.

What could drive a woman to kill her own husband and countless others without the barest hint of shame? A sincerely-held belief that it was all to fulfill a greater good. If that vision came to pass, every person she killed was dead already.

That wasn't to say she was right. Your average—sane—person would fight against that sort of reasoning with everything they had. Most of us aren't logical when it comes to life and death. We react with stubborn emotion to the cold logic of the grave.

Mother always had been the sort to sneer at that quaint rejection of reality.

Which made sense—for her to take the path she had, she needed to be a few degrees out of true. The magic served only to push her over the edge after showing her and I visions of apocalyptic nightmares.

The mistake that myself and the others had fallen into was to believe that stereotypical motivations were what moved Mother. There was nothing personal in the ritual murder of my father, no malice in her kidnapping of Cassie and luring of me to this place and time. We were all mere tools, things to be used for a particular purpose. Cold, logical—and, if she was telling the truth, for the greater good.

To be honest, I didn't know if that was better or worse than the alternative.

"The cost is betrayal?" I called out.

"Not to me," she replied. "Otherwise, I might have had to sacrifice a department chair." Her laugh was out of place, but I couldn't help but shake my head and smile darkly. Yeah, things would have been quite a bit different had that been the case.

"I'll be your sacrifice," I said. Cassie gasped, and I thought I heard Valentine or Eliot try to scream something, but Mother's spell hadn't weakened one whit. "Cassie means nothing to you. And yeah, killing someone your son loves qualifies, but it pales in comparison to killing my dad, doesn't it?" Pity swelled in me as I considered that she was broken on such a fundamental level that she couldn't measure the relative morality of her own actions. "Filicide is pretty heinous. Betrayals don't get much worse than that, wouldn't you say?"

"I suppose not," she said. For a moment, it seemed like she wanted to say more, but she settled for waving her hand. The pressure around me eased, and I stepped forward. The circle protecting her from bullets and magic turned out to be no obstacle at all, though the space beneath the tent seemed suddenly confining.

We stared at each other in silence, the entire situation as strange as it was awkward. What did you say, at a time like this? She'd never been much of a hugger—that was all dad. Mother was more the omnipresent sword of Damocles looming over our household than she was the June Cleaver type.

I settled for, "What now?"

The weapon she drew from a sheath at her waistband wasn't the same one that she killed dad with. It didn't compare at all, really—ten years ago, she'd used one of our kitchen knives. This had a cruel, military look to it, and I wondered if she'd brought it with or taken it from one of the soldiers. The former meant that she'd indeed planned this out whereas the latter meant—what, exactly?

It's not like it matters. Dead is dead. What am I doing?

There was a catch in her throat, but she pushed past it. "Turn around," she said. "On your knees."

Following her instructions, I was both relieved and disappointed that the resulting position put Cassie to my back. I didn't want her to see this. I would have given anything to see her face one more time. "Don't watch, Cass," I said. Considering, I added, "Don't let her watch, Roxanne."

We weren't to be entirely without an audience, though. Eliot and Valentine remained, stuck in the mystical morass, and past its border, I saw the survivors of Agent Andrews' strike team. The runes on Georgie's massive combat suit shone bright red, the system nearing its energy capacity. Between the helicopter crash and the rest of the lightning soldiers, he must have taken a hell of a beating. Morgan stood beside him, a trio of faint scratches running down one cheek, but I didn't think that was the reason why her face went pale.

It would have been a good time for a farewell speech, but I didn't think Mother would spare the time for that. For some reason, that didn't bother me as much as I thought it should have. Blinking slowly, I took note of the strange lethargy that taken over my limbs. I've faced death more than once, and terror has always been the common thread.

Death had kindly stopped for me, and this time, the most I could muster was a mild curiosity. Through thick lips, I mumbled, "What comes next, Mother? Once you save the world, what happens then?"

"Oh," she said, her tone breathy. "I hadn't thought much about that. I suppose—well, I'll be in a position to provide *guidance*, won't I? And it's not like anyone will be able to turn me down. They'll be better off, and isn't that a good thing?"

I closed my eyes and tried not to sigh.

Two visions, both horrific in their own way—an empty world at peace, and one burning in flames. *Some say the world will end in fire, some say in ice.*

Either way, it was the same outcome. The only difference was the architect of each apocalypse. I leaned my head back, focused on the clouds above through unexpected tears, and said, "I forgive you, mom." The glint of the blade broke through my line of sight.

Her hand froze on its descent, the knife stopping inches from my chest. "What—what did you say?"

"It's okay," I said. She shrieked then, the cry wordless and full of despair.

Above, the clouds boiled, and the intermittent flashes of lightning turned staccato. I could barely hear the screams of my friends through the peals of thunder. Asphalt and chunks of sod burst into the air as the red lightning hammered the ground around us.

The strange sensation departed, and I pivoted as Mother staggered back. The knife and grimoire tumbled from her hands. I reached out by sheer reflex and snagged the book before it hit the ground. The motion drew her attention, and she lunged toward me with outstretched hands.

The bolt of lightning speared her through the chest, hanging in the air for so long that I almost thought it something solid. Her mouth opened and closed wordlessly as she herself fell—and kept falling. The pavement under her feet had turned molten, and her scream turned into one of agony.

Another figure rushed through the circle and tackled me. The impact carried me out of the circle, and as I hit the ground, I realized that the interior of the area Mother had shielded was a good thirty degrees hotter than the outside.

"Move your ass, Pax!" Cassie screamed in my ear. It wasn't the time for it, but I had a big, stupid grin on my face as I scrambled to my feet and rushed away. More and more lightning slammed into the ground behind us. When I looked back, I saw that it had all hit within Mother's shielded area. The tent was no more, the aluminum legs drooping in the heat and leaning toward what looked, for all the world, like a pool of lava in the middle of a parking lot in suburban Maine.

CHAPTER 32

A final bolt struck, and the ground shook. I hit the ground again, alongside Cassie. By the time I looked up, the dark clouds in the sky were fading away, cut through by traces of actual sunlight.

In the parking lot, blackened, twisted bone and metal stood as a monument to Mother's hubris in the center of a cooling circle of molten asphalt. I stared at it and eventually decided that I couldn't tell where the tent ended and her remains began. I forced myself to look away.

Cassie's smiling face was a far more pleasant sight.

I hesitated, then said, "Is Roxanne still in there?"

"No, why?"

"Good." I reached out, cradled her face with both hands, and drew her in for a long-delayed kiss. I'd screwed up our first and done a little better on the second.

Our third was this side of perfect.

Coming up for air, I realized we had an audience around us. Morgan had her arms crossed with a stern look on her face. Valentine, in something close to a miracle, seemed to be holding back laughter. Eliot had shifted back to normal, and he looked more tired than usual.

"Hey, guys," I said. "Go us. We won, right?"

Valentine coughed and Morgan's frown deepened. "It would seem so—but I'd like to know just what in hell you were thinking."

"Well," I temporized. "Are we good? Are the shields on the nexus intact?"

She gritted her teeth. "Yes."

"That's good. I was hoping the world wouldn't end. I'm really looking forward to the new Avengers movie." Morgan made a face, and something told me she'd be tapping her foot if we weren't on grass. Quickly, I continued, "A wise lady once told me that a person who prefers power over wisdom is the kind of person you shouldn't trust with that power in the first place," I shrugged. "So, I put her to the test." That was only half the story, though, and I wasn't sure how to explain the strange relaxation I'd felt through the entire process. "Another person, who is also far wiser than I, informed me that I needed to forgive Mo—my mom. Not going to lie, I struggled with that. But I guess when you forgive someone, that kind of takes the wind out of their, well, betrayal sails."

Morgan closed her eyes and rubbed her temples with her index fingers. "We talked about this. Breaking the spell creates a feedback loop for the accumulated energy—oof."

"Sure," I said. "But I didn't break it. Mother did. Something told me that would keep things in house, so to speak."

She leaned over and jabbed a finger into my chest to emphasize every word. "Do *not* do that, ever again! We're lucky this town isn't in orbit right now."

Valentine touched her shoulder. "Not luck," he murmured. He nodded toward the woods.

We turned to follow his look. Predictably, my dad—well, something that looked like him, anyway—leaned against a fallen pine tree. "About time he showed up," I muttered. Pushing myself to my feet, I looked around. "You guys coming?"

"He's here for you," Eliot said. The agent had a strange little smile on his face. "He'd look different for any of us."

I stared, waiting for him to continue, but the other man had nothing else to say. "Okay."

Lightning strikes had left the field blackened and brittle in intermittent spots. For some reason, I wove through them, sticking to the fresh green grass and reveled in the sound of it whisking against my shoes. It was a nice reminder of what we'd almost lost, and despite all the pain she'd brought to me, a lump thickened my throat at the thought of my mother. *If only*—but that was a pointless road. She'd taken the steps on this journey on her very own, and while the effects on my own life had been at times horrific, would I change it if I had the opportunity?

I had every right to be fatalistic, but instead, my experiences had left me with the powerful conviction that no matter how bad things got, they usually turned out all right. Not perfect—but okay.

Someday, something might happen to change that sentiment, but for now, I was going with it.

Stopping a few feet from the figure, I nodded my head in greeting.

"Let me guess, you're here to angelsplain, again."

Even knowing it was an affectation, the familiar smirk of amusement put a subtle pain in my heart. I don't know if he realized the effect it was having on me or not, but he stilled his features and said, "That does seem to be the way these things work, doesn't it?"

"Well, in this case, I get it." I thought back to Father Rosado's talk on forgiveness and shrugged. "Rumors to the contrary, I'm not a complete imbecile. I do have one question, though. Why not stop her in her tracks months ago? All the people that she killed between here and there, all the chaos she caused—why not just zap her like Melanie?"

"You make the mistake of assuming this was all about your mother."

That stopped me in my tracks for a moment, until I managed, "Who, then?"

"Why, you, of course. A man stands at a crossroads. He's lost everything—he's at the end of his rope. But he's not helpless. This man is blessed, though some might call it a curse. In spite of that blessing, he still has free will. What will he do with it?"

"It was never about stopping her?" I cocked my head and looked at the entity wearing my father's face. If he was still pissed off about how I'd acted the last time we spoke, he didn't show it. That was more like my dad than even the visage he'd borrowed.

"Her success or failure wouldn't have changed much, from our perspective. The end will come when it comes, and no mortal can say when. A soul teetering on the edge of darkness is another story entirely. I'm Michael, by the way." He touched his cheek warily. "I hope your father's face doesn't bring you discomfort."

"Well," I said. "I guess knowing your real name helps a bit. What do I do now?"

He looked surprised. "I'm surprised you have to ask. I'm not here to give you orders, boy. Just encouragement."

"Encouragement, huh?"

"Well, you weren't granted these talents to scam fools out of their money by banishing imaginary ghosts from their homes."

"In my defense, they could afford it." I glanced over at Cassie and the surviving Division M agents. At my team. "And I think I'm past that, at this point."

Michael smiled, but the suddenly intense cast of his eyes belied what might have otherwise been an expression of mirth. "For today, a great victory is won. And yet, evil persists. What are you going to do about it?"

"Hope for the best, I suppose. But I'm guessing I don't get that luxury." I made a face and shrugged. "Hey, how bad can it be?"

"I've got bad news, kid. To whom much is given, much is expected. You ain't seen nothing yet. Still interested?"

I thought about Tlaloc, running free somewhere. I thought about an organization of faceless beasts that called itself the Void. The mystery of the crew who bombed the Leesburg annex. All the people out there, waiting for the firefighters of Division M, who more often than not didn't make it before the metaphorical house burned down. Up until this point, I'd been doing this on my own, but I sensed in the hanging question something more official. Call it a job offer. If I survived, I was liable to be at it for a long time. But if magic was to curse me to live for centuries, at least I wouldn't stand alone. "Bring it," I said.

He grinned fiercely. I'd given the desired answer. Light flared suddenly, and through a squint, I could just barely make out the fire-tinged outline of an enormous blade.

CHAPTER 32

Man with a flaming sword makes you an offer you can't refuse, you accept it. With a sonorous voice, the being wearing my dad's face intoned, "Kneel, Paxton Locke."

My knees hit the grass. An intense, comforting warmth tapped me on one shoulder, and then the other. Michael lifted the blade, then lowered it and rested the flat on my upturned forehead.

"The charge is accepted. Rise, Paxton. Rise, paladin."

I stood blinking, suddenly alone. I turned back to my companions and took in expressions ranging from pride to awe. Valentine gave me a knowing nod. A grin exploded across my face, and I strode across the scorched field. Shoulders back, head high—full of purpose.

It was time to get to work.

CHAPTER THIRTY-THREE

Liliana—Saturday night
Ft. Lauderdale, Florida

They called it a gentleman's club, but it was nothing of the sort. Of course, the work was a lot less dangerous than serving Knight—to say nothing of the lack of strings attached to the money.

Sure, there was the occasional customer who thought they could get more than a peek at the goods. Inside, that's what the bouncers were for. At least one creep had waited for her in the parking lot after her shift, but that was all right. She'd been hungry anyway, which solved the problem of disposing of the body.

As ever, she found it ironic that the human woman didn't care much for her. They had better survival instincts than their male counterparts, and even if they didn't realize it consciously, something told most of them that a predator walked in their midst. Her fellow dancers kept their distance, and that was fine by her.

CHAPTER 33

Except for all the damn glitter, it'd be a perfect job. I should have been doing this all along.

Garter overflowing with bills, she swept off the stage and strutted toward the locker room to raucous catcalls and the booming voice of the club's DJ. "Let's hear it for Eve, everybody!"

It was an ironic appellation that only she could appreciate, but that was fine, as well. She was starting to see the appeal of a low profile these days.

She ignored the cocky nods and waved hands of the customers demanding her private attention. She was due for a break, and—she stumbled, just a bit, on the absurdly high heels as she noticed the redhead standing next to one of the secondary stages, staring at her.

It wasn't that she was a woman. A surprising percentage of the club's clientele were female, but there was something about her that raised the hackles on the back of Liliana's neck. She watched her out of the corner of her eye, trying to ignore the stare.

Halfway to the to the exit, it hit her. One of the other dancers, a brunette with the unlikely stage name of Chyna Rose, walked *through* the redhead and plopped herself down onto the lap of an intoxicated college student.

Liliana kept her head straight, turning her eyes toward the exit. The club was shy of three-quarters full, but she had no difficulty picking the pair of suited men out of the crowd. They flanked the main doors with their backs to the wall. She inhaled, trying to ignore the scents of perfume and lotion, and swallowed as she got a scent of cordite and ozone from the hard-faced man on the right side of the door. She'd never seen him before, but that scent was legendary in certain circles.

The gunfighter—and if he's here, it's time for me to head for the hills.

She swept into the locker room, heading toward her belongings. There were a few other dancers inside, but they pointedly ignored her. Which was good, because it gave her the opening to tear the shank off the combination lock securing her things. An over-sized shoulder bag held sneakers, sweats, and her wallet. She shoved the money into the bag and threw on her street clothes, thankful to kick off the ridiculous shoes. It might have been easier to manifest her work clothes, but she'd adopted the human garb as part of her disguise.

Liliana's sudden departure did arouse questioning looks from a few of the dancers, but she ignored them and hit the safety bar for the rear exit. A narrow alley ran along the side of the club. To the left, a block wall separated it from the front parking lot—the dancers who smoked used the resulting nook to get their cigarette breaks in.

She turned right, heading toward the fenced-in employee parking lot. Her sneakers scraped on the pavement as she broke into a run. *I'm going to make it—*

Her ankles slammed into what felt like a steel cable, and she ended up sprawled flat on her face. The impact knocked the wind out of her, and she rolled onto her back, groaning.

Metal scraped on stone, and something massive hit the ground in the smoker's nook. She raised her head and blinked as something that looked like a massive suit of armor straightened, glowing eyes fixed on her.

She cursed a guttural snippet of the old tongue and climbed to her feet. As she turned to run from the armor, a pair of figures blocked her path to freedom.

The man was tall, slim but muscular with close-cropped hair the white of dry bone. The glowing cerulean blade stretching out from his clenched fist told her all she needed to know. *Wizard.*

His companion was blond and female. Though not much shorter than her companion, the short pixie cut and her athletic curves made her seem much younger. *Not as much of a threat*, she judged, tensing to jump toward her before she realized the other woman cradled a brutally-short shotgun in her arms.

"It's the old tricks that work best," the wizard said. "Remind me to teach you that one, Cass." He stepped forward and grinned at Liliana. "Mystical tripwire—just needed to get you running where wanted you to, eh?" The expression made her realize how young he truly was—the white hair must have been bleach.

"I don't know what you're talking about." She snuck a little Valley Girl into her voice, hoping to put them off guard. "What's going on?"

"Drop the act, Boobs McGee," the girl said. "We know what you are."

"Been to Virginia, recently?" The wizard's grin faded. "Let's talk about the bomb you planted."

She froze, debating whether to keep up the act or switch gears. Liliana did the math, didn't like what she came up with, and stammered, "He'll kill me if he finds out I talked to you."

"True," the blond said. "Interesting."

"It won't be if we take care of him first," the wizard said with a grin.

She stuck her chin out in defiance. "Good luck with that," Liliana sneered. "I'll never talk."

"Now that," the wizard's companion said. "*That* is a lie."

AN EXCERPT FROM HELL SPAWN

While you're waiting for the next Paxton Locke book, try reading HELL SPAWN by Declan Finn!

Chapter 1: Odd Saint

My name is Detective Thomas Nolan, and I am a saint.

This is neither boasting nor an exaggeration.

I only had an inkling on the morning I chased Anthony Young, purse snatcher...again. Kid was your years older than my son. Young Anthony (see what I did there?), a 20th time offender, had upgraded to double duty, on this day both snatching the purse as well as the iPhone of Malinda Jones. Malinda was one of many careless New Yorkers who are so deep into their phones that they barely registered oncoming traffic, to heck with noticing a thief running up on them.

My radar was already up after Anthony bumped against me as he brushed past. I didn't bother checking for theft. I had nothing in the pockets of my tan overcoat, and my pants pockets were out of the reach of even a skilled thief. I merely continued my morning offering as the Opus Dei had taught me and was about to go into the Our Father.

Then Anthony charged forward, sweeping Malinda's purse from her shoulder, and plucking the iPhone from her hand. It was the latest model, over a thousand dollars' worth of technology in one easy-to-steal package.

Obviously, Anthony didn't see the all-caps NYPD emblazoned in gold letters on the front AND back of my policeman-blue baseball cap.

To make matters worse—for him—was that he did this in front of the mental health court for Queens, heralded by the black wrought-iron fence about ten feet high, which was serviced by the NYPD as their security. Further down the block was a housing community with its own private security.

In short, there was no real way that Anthony was going to get to the end of the (admittedly very long) block.

I was still under an obligation to chase the idiot. "Freeze! Police!" I barked before I took off after him. As expected, it made him run faster, but he obviously heard me, so he had his fair warning.

I pounded along the pavement behind Anthony, who was built for speed over anything else. He was short and slight, but he could run. I was bigger, a bit over six foot, and broad in the shoulders. Every big man will tell you one thing—running was just a great way to destroy your ankles and your knees if you do it right. I was a lumbering truck chasing after a motorcycle, but the moment Anthony ran out of gas, the impact would be similar.

As I ran, I mentally recited the Our Father and was on the Hail Mary when the strangeness happened. Suddenly, I could see myself ahead of Anthony... while at the same time, standing in front of him, I saw myself chase behind Anthony. It was a strange, vivid experience, with each view of Anthony as clear as the highest definition television—with almost more clarity than real life.

It was odd, but I was also too busy to ponder it. I held out an arm, leaned into it, and Anthony just ran into my arm. He clotheslined himself so hard, his feet left the ground. I swept back under him as fast as I could, catching him just before his head hit the concrete. It wouldn't do for him to have brain damage over a stolen purse—it wasn't like he had little gray cells he could afford to lose.

I smiled into his face. "Hi Anthony. Would you like to tell me your rights? We've done this dance too often."

He merely smiled widely and shrugged, even as I hauled him to his feet. "Eh, you win some, you lose some. Still ain't gonna serve any jail time."

Anthony was a poster boy for juvenile recidivism and a great example for anyone who agitates for prosecuting all criminals as adults. He wasn't necessarily a bad kid, but he could use an extended stay in Boys Town—or an overnight in Rikers Island to scare him straight.

"It would help if you won any," I suggested.

"Can I cuff myself this time?" he asked as I took his wrists behind his back and cuffed them. "Guess not."

I rolled my eyes. "Anthony, have you considered that if you want money, you get a real job?"

He laughed. "You mean work for a living? Hey, that's racist, yo."

I shook my head and sighed. This kid was going to give me a headache. "Meet me halfway, find a crime you're at least good at?"

Malinda caught up to us at long last. She was 48, 4'9", and 180 pounds, so it took her a while. She looked at the perpetrator and frowned. "Anthony Young! I should have known. Just wait until I tell your gramma! Wait until I tell Father Pawson!"

Anthony finally looked concerned. "Aw, come on, Missus Jones, do you have to? I didn't know it was you."

Malinda wound up for a smack to the back of his head, and I twisted him around to put myself between them. "Mrs. Jones, you can't do that. I've got him cuffed already."

Malinda glowered. "Fine. But you take him right to the station. I'm going to meet you there. Taking my stuff. How dare you, Anthony!"

She stormed off ahead of us, not even waiting for me to hand her stuff back. I pocketed her phone and slung the purse over my shoulder—it was big enough to be a satchel, if worse came to worse.

"How'd you get in front of me, anyway?" he asked. "I don't remember you being that fast."

I blinked. That was a good question, to which I didn't have a good answer. I had heard that deja vu was simply a matter of slow communication between two halves of the brain. Perhaps it was serious brain lag?

No, that explanation didn't even work for me at the time, but since I didn't have a good answer for him, I merely told him the truth: "I haven't the foggiest notion."

"Ugh. Do you gotta use all the big words, Tommy?"

Argh.

As we walked down Winchester boulevard, we had a brief conversation in which Anthony read me his rights, and we confirmed that he wouldn't be getting a lawyer but a phone call to his mother.

Anthony was sulking by the time we got to 222nd street, and we passed in front of his public school on the way to my precinct. The school and the precinct were diagonally across the street from each other. An outside observer could tell that it wasn't a typical precinct, since the patch of grass to the right of our walkway had a full-color statue of Our Lady of Lourdes about two feet high, and the left had a statue of Jesus. Did our Catholicism show any? Just don't tell the ACLU.

This was the 105th precinct, otherwise known as the "French Bread" precinct. Since it was on the border of Queens and Nassau, Long Island, the boundaries of the Precinct followed the border. You could almost see that it was the last precinct established as the population went East—the 105 got whatever was left over. It went from Queens Village, Cambria Heights, Laurelton, Rosedale, Springfield Gardens, Bellerose, Glen Oaks, New Hyde Park, and Floral Park. If you're looking on a map, that means it stops at Rockaway Boulevard at the south end, Francis Lewis Boulevard at the west, and the Grand Central parkway to the

North. Since the boarder on the East was uneven, so was our boundary. And, since the western boundary followed Francis Lewis, it came down at an angle. (Manhattan has the famous grid pattern layout to their streets. In Queens, they followed former cow paths that wandered all over the place.)

We entered the station, and I waved to the black woman at the front desk, Sgt. Mary Russell. She was 5'8", stocky, with short cornrows that didn't travel too far down the neck. As far as fashionable hairstyles for women cops went, it was probably the closest equivalent to a crew cut.

"Hey, Tommy," she called. "You brought us a repeat customer, and you didn't even sign in yet? You bucking for another promotion?"

I nodded at her as I tugged on Anthony's cuffs, bringing him to a stop. "Mary, I found this wayward son on the way to the office this morning."

Sgt. Russell rolled her eyes. "I don't think community policing works like that."

I smiled. "It is when you live and work in the parish." I patted Anthony on the shoulder. "If you could call his mother? I think she's number nine in the speed dial by now. I—"

At that moment, I was hit by the smell. It was so repulsive that when it hit me, I gagged, and nearly vomited. It was horrific, and ungodly, and those were adjectives I used before I knew the source. If you've ever found a rotted human corpse, perhaps one dredged up from a body of water, you have an idea of what the stench was like. Then add in rotten eggs, fecal matter, sit and stew on a hot summer day for six hours.

This was worse.

I spun around for the nearest waste basket, expecting to vomit. I gathered myself together, and slowly composed myself, struggling to keep my breakfast down.

"Hey, Nolan, you okay?" Russell asked me.

I stayed there a moment longer, then straightened and turned back towards her. Even Anthony looked concerned.

Hand over my nose, I asked, "Don't you smell that? Smells like something died in the vents and cooked there."

Russell and Anthony shared a glance and a shrug. "Nope."

I took a slow, controlled breath, then scanned over the station. There wasn't anyone there who appeared that dank, dirty and unwashed. For someone to smell that bad, the only presumption was that he, she, or it looked like they had slept in garbage. But everyone there looked relatively tidy. Even one or two of the obvious drunks (red noses, half asleep, barely responsive to the officers with them) looked cleaner than I expected for such a repulsive odor.

I cautiously moved forward, taking small sniffs every few steps, just to keep tabs on the smell. Even that little was unbearable. Anthony stayed with Russell, and I worked my way through the station methodically. Whatever it was had to be toxic—and if only I could smell it, that didn't bode well in the long run for everyone else. If I were going insane, all well and good, but if it was real, things like a generally odorless, colorless gas, unleashed in a police station, could have all sorts of implications, and could end badly all around.

The source was what most civilians would picture as a "typical" junkie—the type who has obviously hit bottom, He was anemic, malnourished, scrawny, and painfully underweight. At 5'8", he may have weighed all of one hundred pounds. His hair was black, stringy, and greasy, and his eyes were a pale, watery blue. I couldn't tell if he was about to cry or bite someone's nose off ... or just curl up into a ball and die, since he looked close enough anyway. Sunken cheeks, protruding cheekbones, and he hurt to look at. His hands were cuffed behind his back, but the elbows were so bony, I was concerned he could stab someone with those alone. lol

And he smelled like death, decay, and made the stench of garbage trucks smell sweet in comparison.

"Okay, Hayes," one of the officers told him, "you're almost done. You can be in your cell in a bit."

As I approached Hayes, he started, his back becoming ramrod straight. He turned to look at me. His face went from being passive and wishy-washy to a mask of rage. He roared loud enough to hurt my ears and make the cops around him flinch.

With a loud crack, his arms shot forward. He'd dislocated his left thumb to get out of the cuffs. He grabbed the nearest policeman, hurling him across the room with maniacal strength. The cop slammed into a desk, then smashed through a window.

The cop behind him grabbed on, and the perp whirled, smacking him aside. He grabbed the cop's nightstick, and cut the leg out from under the officer.

Hayes whirled on me, bellowing, "Era uoy tahw wonk I!"

Then he lunged.

Keep Reading Hell Spawn now!

My name is Officer Thomas Nolan, and I am a saint.

Tommy Nolan lives a quiet life. He walks his beat – showing mercy to the desperate. Locking away the dangerous. Going to church, sharing dinner with his wife and son. Everyone likes Tommy, even the men he puts behind bars.

Then one day a demon shows up and he can *smell* it. Tommy can smell evil – *real evil*. Now he's New York City's only hope against a horrifying serial killer that preys on the young and defenseless.

But smell alone isn't enough to get a warrant. Can Tommy track down the killer and prove his guilt?

Dragon Award Nominated Author Declan Finn returns with his typical action-packed, Catholic influenced style, in this ground-breaking horror series about an honest, religious man given the powers of a saint to fight demons in the Big Apple.

How do you do forensics on a killer possessed by a demon?

Can Tommy catch the killer before he becomes a martyr? Or will the demon bring darkness beyond imagination to the whole of New York? Read Hell Spawn today and find out!

PAXTON LOCKE AND DIVISION M
WILL RETURN

IN

The Sacred Radiance

REVIEW REQUEST

Did you enjoy the book?

Why not tell others about it? The best way to help an author and to spread word about books you love is to leave a review.

If you enjoyed reading COME SEELING NIGHT, can you please leave a review on Amazon for it? Good, bad, or mediocre, we want to hear from *you*. Dan and all of us at Silver Empire would greatly appreciate it.

Thank you!

ABOUT DANIEL HUMPHREYS

Daniel Humphreys is the author of the Z-Day series of post-apocalyptic sci-fi thrillers and the Paxton Locke urban fantasy series. His first novel, "A Place Outside the Wild", was a 2017 Dragon Award finalist for Best Apocalyptic novel.

Dan enjoys sci-fi movies, target shooting, and tinkering with computers. He has spent his entire career in corporate IT and suffers from elevated blood pressure due to a lifelong love of the Arizona Cardinals. Daniel lives in Indiana with his wife and family.

 facebook.com/DanielHumphreysAuthor

 twitter.com/NerdKing52

bookbub.com/authors/daniel-humphreys

JOIN THE EMPIRE

Silver Empire

Keep up with all the new releases, sneak peeks, appearances and more with the empire. Sign up for our Newsletter today!

Or join fellow readers in our Facebook Fan Group, the Silver Empire Legionnaires. Enjoy memes, fan discussions and more.

COME SEELING NIGHT

PAXTON LOCKE BOOK III

By Daniel Humphreys

Published by Silver Empire

https://silverempire.org/

All rights reserved. No part of this publication may be reproduced, distributed, or transmitted in any form or by any means, including photocopying, recording, or other electronic or mechanical methods,

without the prior written permission of the publisher, except in the case of brief quotations embodied in critical reviews and certain other noncommercial uses permitted by copyright law.

This is a work of fiction. Names, characters, businesses, places, events and incidents are either the products of the author's imagination or used in a fictitious manner. Any resemblance to actual persons, living or dead, or actual events is purely coincidental.

Cover by Christian Bentulan

Copyright © 2019, Daniel Humphreys

All rights reserved.

CPSIA information can be obtained
at www.ICGtesting.com
Printed in the USA
BVHW082309151020
591039BV00003B/119